Soldades

A Silent Enemy

A Silent Enemy

Sheila Closs

Copyright © 2014 by Sheila Closs.

Library of Congress Control Number:		2014917143
ISBN:	Hardcover	978-1-4990-7669-1
	Softcover	978-1-4990-7670-7
	eBook	978-1-4990-7668-4

All rights reserved. No part of this book may be reproduced or transmitted in any form or by any means, electronic or mechanical, including photocopying, recording, or by any information storage and retrieval system, without permission in writing from the copyright owner.

This is a work of fiction. Names, characters, places and incidents either are the product of the author's imagination or are used fictitiously, and any resemblance to any actual persons, living or dead, events, or locales is entirely coincidental.

Any people depicted in stock imagery provided by Thinkstock are models, and such images are being used for illustrative purposes only.
Certain stock imagery © Thinkstock.

This book was printed in the United States of America.

Rev. date:09/23/2014

To order additional copies of this book, contact:
Xlibris LLC
1-888-795-4274
www.Xlibris.com
Orders@Xlibris.com

ACKNOWLEDGEMENTS

I would like to thank the following people for their encouragement and support throughout the creative process for this book. Without their help, this book may have taken much longer to finish.

First, I would like to thank my two editors, Cheryl Rotenburger and Keith Balkwill; each of them contributed so much to the story by correcting the mistakes that would have made it very hard to keep up with my fertile mind.

Elaine Wall, Ethel Atkinson, Mar Fedyk, and Elsie Monk are all special supporters who cheered me on my way when I found myself second guessing motives and strategies. They are all good sounding boards who gave me excellent advice.

Terry Maydonik for all her home grown wisdom and excellent attitude towards life. May you always be Blessed, Terry.

Most importantly, my publishers who helped me to realize a dream come true and the support needed to make it happen.

There are many others out there who are too numerous to mention; their tips and answers to my questions have ignited a wonderful fire in my life. May it last long and never go out.

PROLOGUE

The air conditioning in his office made Ryan more comfortable than his co-workers in the outer offices. It had been a struggle making it to Senior Supervisor over the others; but the struggle had been worth it. After years of scraping by until the end of the month, the last two years in his present position had afforded Ryan and his wife of ten years a new house large enough to raise their three children, and put a little aside into a savings account. The work itself was satisfying as well. He supervised twelve co-workers at the clerk's office in the city hall.

Ryan was well liked in his role as supervisor and he knew it. The day had been a long one with several people coming in to pay taxes under protest. Old man Johnston did this every year at the same time and raised such a ruckus with the clerk that Ryan felt moved to take over every time. Today was no different. After listening to everything old man Johnston had to gripe about, Ryan just smiled and told him he was right and he would look into trying to get his taxes lowered, and a different MLA, and a different Mayor, etc. Johnston took it well. He paid and then waggled his forefinger at Ryan as a cautionary gesture.

"Don't forget, young man, if the city tells me my land is no good to annex, then they shouldn't charge me like it was worth ten million." Johnston wobbled away with his cane and Ryan wasn't sure if Mr. Johnston would make it another year. But then, he was probably stubborn enough to prove Ryan wrong. Ryan smiled and waved goodbye as Mr. Johnston tottered out the door.

Back in his office, Ryan heaved a sigh of relief. In five minutes he could turn his lights off, lock his desk, and go home to Denise. The two year old was running a fever and needed more medication which he planned to pick up on the way home. Ryan reached for the phone when it started ringing. Startled, he automatically picked it up and answered before his secretary could.

"Ryan here. Is that you, Denise?" He asked as he smiled into the phone. Sometimes she could be a little impatient.

"No it isn't Denise." A very familiar male voice said. The smile froze on Ryan's face and he began to get a sick feeling in his stomach. "Well?" Came the voice. "Aren't you going to say hello to your old buddy?" A chuckle sounded through the receiver.

Ryan paused to try and swallow the lump in his throat and closed his eyes.

"Hello. What do you want this time?" Ryan's voice was timid with dread. Any request this man made to him was never a good one. He knew this from experience. Cold clammy sweat formed on his upper lip and forehead.

"Now is that anyway to talk to a friend? I'm disappointed in you Ryan." The man's voice had that false note Ryan knew could change from nice to cruel in the flash of a second. The grip Ryan had on his receiver turned his knuckles white.

"You are no friend of mine. You never were. You are a bully with no consideration for others." Ryan said and then took a deep breath to continue.

"No consideration?" The voice had icy steel to it now and Ryan could picture the smooth features turning cruel in his mind. "Who was it that found the discrepancy in the accounts and covered it up so you could keep your precious job?" Ryan's fear began to be replaced by anger.

"How dare you insinuate the missing funds were my fault? I told you, I have no idea what happened to them, and I won't tell you again. Now leave me and my family alone. Whatever it is you want me to do for you, I won't be a party to it."

"It would be a shame if you were to hang up on me Ryan. I'm not sure you could handle what your refusal would mean to your family." The line was deadly quiet as Ryan tried to suck in a badly needed breath.

"What are you talking about? You leave my family alone!" Ryan almost shouted into the phone and his hand holding the phone began to shake.

"Be quiet you fool! You don't want anyone to hear this conversation, do you?" Ryan tried to loosen the knot in his tie as his face became red.

"Don't you ever threaten my family again." Ryan's voice held more of a warble than it did a command. The voice on the phone changed again.

"Now that depends on you, doesn't it, Ryan?"

Glancing out the window at the setting sun, he realized the man had him in a corner. One he couldn't get out of unless he came clean and lost everything. "What do you want?" The chuckle came through and irritated Ryan's already frazzled nerves.

"That's more like it." The caller cleared his throat and Ryan could picture his gloating face in his mind. "Now, that Bed and Breakfast I wanted you to stop, why is it opening?"

"I couldn't hold it back any longer without it seeming odd. I put it back as long as I could. I can't stall it any longer. The Mayor himself pushed it through council." Ryan tried to ignore the panic that was replacing the anger.

"So then lose it." Came the voice.

"What do you mean?"

"I mean lose the damn permit, or the Inspector's report, or both, something to cause it not to open." The voice sounded as if he were talking to an imbecile instead of Ryan.

"How the hell am I going to do that? She already has the permit in her possession." Ryan's voice came out in a rush.

"What about her Inspector's Certificates? You know, from the Board of Health?"

"I suppose I could lose that document. But only for a short time. If I withhold anything else from her, my job could be on the line because of incompetence." Ryan shook his head at his own compliance. He also knew that if he lost this job, Denise and the girls would leave and he would have nothing.

"Ryan, haven't you learned how to protect yourself yet?" The voice oozed the oiliness. "You don't just delegate responsibility; you delegate the blame onto someone else." Ryan paused as he realized that might just work. Maybe there was a way out of this yet.

"You know, Ryan, if you can do that for me, I will forget about the missing funds."

"*Yeah, right.*" Ryan thought to himself. "If you do, I would appreciate it very much." Ryan tried to make his voice sound sincere. The voice began to chuckle again.

"There you go, my boy. You can do it after all! And just to sweeten the pot, I will tell payroll you have just received a huge raise in pay."

"I don't need anything to sweeten the pot. Just leave me alone after this."

"Too late buddy. It's already done. If anything goes wrong, I can always say you blackmailed me into giving you the raise and you will be seen as an accomplice." The voice warned him. "So remember, spend the money wisely." A dial tone sounded in Ryan's ear. Breathless, he replaced the receiver and sat wondering what he was going to do. The quiet hum of the building's air conditioning clicked off and the silence of the nearly empty building seemed to press down on Ryan's shoulders as he tried to think of his options.

If he did what he was told to do, he would probably end up in jail. Unless he could do what the other man suggested and delegate the blame on someone else. He summoned up a list of coworkers in his mind and went over all their character traits and focused in on the new guy. He had only been there a month and had made several horrible mistakes. If he could keep the guy on long enough, he could maybe blame all the missing documents on him. Ryan's cold clammy sweat started to dry on his body and he started to smile. That was it. He would blame the missing documents on the new guy. All he would have to do is change his own signature to the new guy's signature and put the original documents in the garbage.

Ryan stood up and snapped his fingers. If it worked for those documents, maybe it could work for the missing funds as well. It would take a few late nights but Denise would understand. Ryan reached for his sports jacket and moved for his office door. He had to get home with the two-year-old's medication. Besides, he also wanted to sit in his home office and form a plan of action. Turning out the light, Ryan closed the door and smiled a goodbye to his secretary.

CHAPTER ONE

Ethan slowly drew in a deep breath as a trickle of sweat slowly made its way down his forehead. The foliage overhead allowed a brief respite from the heat until Ethan's hair on the back of his neck prickled with what Ethan called his "Spidey Sense". Careful not to make a sound, Ethan went down on his bended knee and tried to spot the thing that made him so uneasy. It would be impossible for Ethan to not hear a skilled huntsman come up behind him with all the dead leaves from last fall carpeting the mossy ground. He felt the unseen opponents' eyes upon him and knew he was in trouble. He was going to have to change his strategy for capture and bring his team in a little closer to distract the gunman that was now stocking him and his team. Ethan's team was behind him and taking cover behind trees and stumps and fallen logs.

There was only one more gunman to find. They had captured the other two in this close knit little group but this last one had evaded them and Ethan could see why. Ethan's raised fist suddenly opened and he flattened it as he brought it down for his team to see. Immediately, Detective Phil Harmon and the new hot shot recruit on the force went face down in the leaves. There were no sounds of the forest around them as they waited to see if their quarry would make themselves known.

Ethan felt the withdrawal of their opponent and he made a motion for his team to regroup behind a deadfall log. Slowly they all melded to the side of the downfall like ghosts in a mist.

"Phil, what do you think?" Ethan asked in a whisper that was barely audible.

"She's gone." Came his terse reply.

"Tony, did you see which way she went?" Ethan asked the new recruit.

"She's probably running back to the clubhouse as fast as her sweet little butt can move." Tony snickered out loud. Ethan glanced back at his new recruit with distaste for the man's attitude. Ethan looked into Phil's eyes with a silent question and saw a glint of laughter in Phil's eyes.

"You're wrong there." Phil chortled. "You obviously don't know our quarry."

"What's that supposed to mean?" Tony demanded with a churlish look at Phil. Ethan was ready to let Tony's attitude lead him into trouble, if only to teach him a lesson about taking a quarry's abilities for granted, just because she's a woman. Especially this woman.

Off in the distance a magpie took flight from the top of a tall evergreen a few yards down the cutline. Phil put a cautionary hand on Tony's arm to prevent him from rising and giving off their position. Tony shrugged it off and stood.

"She's gone, I said." Tony crouched and began to move forward past Ethan with an awkwardness that showed he had never been hunting before. "Come on you two. She's probably sitting back at base shaking like a leaf and drinking one of the beers in the cooler. Besides, she's a girl. She'll never capture us." Tony's grin of confidence went from ear to ear.

Ethan's eyes narrowed in silence at the misplaced barb directed towards Dorothy Adam's hunting ability. Anger sparked in his eyes. Phil started to rise from his crouch to follow Tony. The bugs and the heat had made him eager to follow. Sunlight glinted from something near the tree where the magpie had taken flight. Ethan grabbed Phil's arm.

"She isn't the type to get careless this way, letting a buckle shine in the sunlight." Ethan whispered so only Phil could hear. "I think she's up at the tree and is daring us to come and get her." Ethan thought out loud and looked at Phil for confirmation. Phil began to smile.

Dorothy Adams was leading the second team of all female paint ballers, and from his experience with her, Phil Harmon knew that Ethan was right. When Dorothy first came from Toronto to join her family, Phil had done some background research on her. She had spent several years in the military, two tours of duty in Kandahar, and had been sent home on a medical discharge for some shrapnel in her abdomen. The 6 months in counselling while she set up one of the most prosperous security businesses in Toronto had enabled Dorothy to come to terms with a past that she had not been proud of. A car accident with two deaths and two injuries, had almost devastated Dorothy but she had finally taken responsibility for her part in their deaths when she returned to Redwood to be with her family again. Her father's subsequent death, and rumors that said she was responsible for that as well were quickly dispelled when Dorothy had helped his boss, Chief of Police, Ethan Barns, find the killer. The training she had received in the military had also helped Dorothy come to terms with her family as well. Now she was happily building her own Bed and Breakfast so she could remain independent of her family, and that told Detective Phil Harmon that Dorothy did not give up easily.

"Shall we let Tony find her?" Phil grinned in a quiet whisper to Ethan. Ethan grinned back and nodded.

"Why are you guys being so cautious?" Tony sounded like he was tired of swatting mosquitoes and was ready to quit. "That woman hunter has gone back. She's no more a hunter than my sainted Grandmother. Come on!" Tony stood tall in his arrogance and began walking forward. Brazen to the core, he opened his water canteen and slurped noisily until it was gone. "The only thing a woman is good for is cooking and cleaning." Tony said out loud.

Ethan just about cleared the deadfall before Phil pinned him to the ground.

"Shush! If we could hear him, Dorothy could certainly hear him. And revenge is good!" Phil whispered into Ethan's ear. Slowly he let Ethan up to peer over the top of the deadfall.

"Guys?" Tony turned to see if Ethan and Phil were following behind. Their absence on the trail behind him made Tony nervous and he heard a noise in the bushes not far in front of him. He turned back towards the deadfall where Ethan and Phil were hiding, intending to run and dive over it when he dropped his rifle. Bending down in his haste he didn't realize his butt was sticking out like a red flag.

Phil and Ethan were now peering from beneath the deadfall and trying to stop laughing. Ethan's anger at Tony's misspoken words had evaporated when he realized what was going to happen next. Sure enough there came a 'pfft' and a 'whap'! A paint ball had hit him in the butt and Tony started bouncing around, howling in pain, while he reached behind to hold himself.

"That's not fair! She broke the rules! She's eliminated!" Tony screamed. At that moment he tripped over his rifle and he went down face-first into a pile of leaves with his butt still sticking up in the air.

There was another 'pfft' and a 'whap'! The paint ball hit Tony on the other cheek.

Ethan and Phil were trying desperately not to laugh out loud but they finally exploded when the second paint ball hit. Both of the men were laughing so hard, they were draped over the deadfall unable to pick up their rifles. Phil slipped to the ground and began holding his stomach and Ethan finally managed to stand upright.

"Tony, quit squirming like a little kid and take it like a man." Ethan gasped out as he crawled over the deadfall. Missing the first step, Ethan fell down on his knees in helpless mirth. Tony was still howling and rolling around in the leaves when Dorothy Adams emerged from the bushes almost directly in front of Tony. Farther up the cutline, under the evergreen where the magpie had taken flight, another figure emerged, waving her arms in the air. Elva appeared to be using binoculars to view the situation.

Tony was still crawling around on the ground when he came face to face with Dorothy's boots. Looking up he had tears in his eyes when they connected to Dorothy's face.

"You cheated!" He said out loud in a sulky little boy's voice. Tony tried to rise to his feet and finally made it. Dorothy lowered her rifle with a little smirk on her face.

"And you insulted every woman you have ever known by that one statement you made." Dorothy quietly informed Tony.

"What statement?" Tony couldn't seem to look away as Dorothy carefully took off her helmet. Ethan stopped laughing and became still as he recognized Dorothy's serious face. Afraid that if Tony didn't keep his mouth quiet he might goad Dorothy into doing something stupid, he took a step forward. Instead, it was Tony who did the stupid thing, he gripped his rifle by the barrel and swung it like a bat at Dorothy's head.

"Dorothy, look out!" Dorothy simply leaned back, deflected the blow with her own rifle, and kicked Tony soundly in the sternum with her right foot. Tony went flying backwards, landing on the bare ground of the cut line and feeling slightly dazed. Coughing, he slowly sat up while Ethan scrambled to reach him. Phil was close behind.

"Tony, you stupid son of a b---"Ethan began when Dorothy cut him off.

"He'll be all right. I didn't kick him hard enough to crack anything. If I had wanted to do that, he wouldn't have been able to sit up," Dorothy said in a serious matter of fact tone of voice.

"Did you see that?" Tony began to whine. "She could have killed me."

"You mean you are finally beginning to clue in to that fact? I mean, jeese, how dense do you have to be to blame someone else for your own stupidity." Ethan had been helping Tony to stand up but now he let go and Tony fell back to the ground.

"Hey!" Tony yelled out.

"Shut up, dummy. Don't you know how close to getting fired you just came?" Phil tried to caution him.

"Fired! Fired?" Tony was finally standing upright and tried to push his way in front of Dorothy but Ethan pushed him back towards Phil.

"Calm that temper of yours, Tony, or I will be forced to write you up for conduct un-becoming an officer." Ethan's own temper had begun to flare. Elva reached them as Tony was being rebuked.

"Sorry to cut your fun short, boss," Elva looked from Ethan to Tony and back. "But we got a call from the office. Seems old man Johnston has been using dynamite on his beaver dam again and his wife said he hasn't come home yet. She wants us to check it out. I figured seeing as we were close to his farm, we would stop on our way back into town." Elva glanced back over to Tony and sensed the tension.

"Hey Tony, how did you get that boot mark in the middle of your chest?" Elva's voice was childlike and innocent sounding. "And that blue paint, isn't that from Dorothy's team?" Elva had turned Tony around to inspect his backside like a mother would her truant child. Tony spun back to face her.

"Yes Aunty Elva. But she cheated!" Tony pointed to Dorothy with a sulky look on his face. Ethan took one look at the sorry looking officer in front of him and burst out laughing again. Phil and Dorothy joined in.

When Ethan was finally able to draw a serious breath, he turned to Elva with a wink. "Hey kiddo, good catch. Thanks."

Turning to Tony he tried to get serious but the smile on his face just wouldn't let him.

"Tony, I have a task for you. I want you to go with me to old man Johnston's and help me find him. You think you're up to it?"

"Aaahhh, sure." Tony answered. He was confused. He had been expecting to get reprimanded far worse than what he received but it didn't come. Instead he was being told to help with an active search. "I would like to help you, sir." Tony was all business now.

Phil took Ethan to the side and asked Ethan in a serious whisper "Are you sure? A moment ago you were ready to fire his ass." Phil inquired.

"Think about it, Phil. He walks into a public investigation with two paint ball stains on his butt and a boot print on his vest. How humiliating will that be?" Ethan winked at Phil. Phil's grin split his face.

"All right, seeing as we only have two vehicles, those who are not officially investigating the disappearance of old man Johnston, will leave in vehicle number two, and those who are will leave in vehicle number one with me. Phil, you're with Tony and me." Everyone began to move toward the lot where they had left their vehicles. Tony angled up alongside Ethan.

"I think I have a clean pair of camouflage pants in the truck, I'll get them out and be right with you," Tony informed Ethan.

"You don't have time to change. We're on a call out and the victim takes precedence over everything else. Got it?" Ethan stopped and poked his finger into the center of Tony's vest.

"But…." Tony began.

"But nothing! Move!" Ethan pushed Tony into the backseat of the black SUV he was driving and slammed the door. Climbing into the front driver's side, he waved at the ladies standing next to the other vehicle. "See you back at the office in a bit. I don't think it will take long to find him again this time. Old man Johnston does this every year." Dorothy nodded and waved as the black SUV drove off.

"Well, I arrived just in time." Elva said out loud with a smile.

"In time for what?" Dorothy turned to her.

"I think I saved young Tony from serious harm." Elva stood with her hands on her hips.

"Yep. He did have it coming to him," Dorothy answered.

"I would imagine he did. He never could get it through his thick head that he had the wrong impression of what women are capable of. I think that's his Dad's fault. Never did like the man even if he is my brother in law." Elva laughed as all four women got into their truck.

CHAPTER TWO

Ethan was driving with his siren on and as fast as he could go. His newest recruit in the back seat was whining about his butt, his chest, and the dust from the gravel road that funnelled in through Ethan's window. Phil looked at Ethan and just shook his head. Reading his thoughts, Ethan understood.

"He's wondering if we made a mistake in hiring this raw kid with the tough know-it-all attitude." Ethan thought to himself as he drove. As the SUV came up to the mailbox beside the quarter mile long drive way that old man Johnston had erected decades ago, Ethan slowed and turned left into the drive. He had to go slow but as they neared the house that looked like a log cabin, a plump woman in a cotton house dress came to the front step of the covered porch and started waving her broom. She stood of average height with a gray knot of hair adorning the back of her head. Mrs. Johnston was the perfect image of a farm wife in Ethan's mind. Gracious, quiet, unassuming, and she made a great cinnamon roll. Every time Ethan had to come to talk sense into Johnston, his wife always had fresh cinnamon rolls right out of the oven as if she were expecting him to call. This time, Ethan noticed she was extremely agitated and very worried looking. Ethan parked in the driveway and told Phil and Tony to find out where Mr. Johnston was while he talked to Mrs. Johnston.

Ethan didn't even get half way out of the vehicle when Mrs. Johnston came racing up to his door.

"Oh Ethan! I think he's finally done it this time. I heard an explosion over towards the beaver dam earlier this morning and Ben didn't make it home for his breakfast. I am so worried. He's never missed his breakfast before. And the explosion was larger than it has been in other years. It fair knocked the wind out of me it did." Ida was clinging to Ethan's left arm while she walked him over to the path that Ben's ATV took when he went to the dam. "Please go find him and bring him home to talk some sense into him." Ida pointed up the path that ran along a long barbed wire fence inside their property line.

Tony was hitching up his pants in a can-do style gesture and he rolled his eyes at Phil as he began to take the lead along the path. Not bothering to lower his voice, he began to swagger.

"I'll bet you ten bucks the silly bugger blew his foot off this time." Phil stopped as if rooted to the spot. Mrs. Johnston, shocked beyond belief, ran forward with her broom and whacked Tony over the head with it, dazing him before Ethan realized her intentions. Mrs. Johnston got a couple more good whacks in before Ethan and Phil both came to rescue Tony. All the while she was whacking Tony with the broom, she was screaming like a banshee and Tony was hollering in pain. To complete the pandemonium, Lazarus, the Johnstons' beagle, was howling at the top of his lungs.

Ethan finally got Mrs. Johnston's broom from her and Phil had Tony's arms locked behind him so he couldn't fight back. Lazarus, now awake after his morning nap, came down off the porch and bit Tony in the ankle for hurting his mistress. Tony kicked his foot out and howled again, catching Lazarus in the face and knocking him backwards. Ida, released when Ethan tried to stop the dog, brought the broom down once again upon Tony's head with an almost lethal thump. Tony went quiet with a surprised look on his youthful face, and slowly slipped to the ground out of Phil's grip.

"Oh oh, now you've done it Mrs. Johnston." Phil said with concern. Ethan reached over to feel Tony's pulse.

"Phil, get over to the truck and radio for an ambulance." Ethan straightened and looked squarely into Ida Johnston's frightened face and reached out to take both her shoulders in his hands. "Ida, calm down. You don't have to worry about this man. He'll be okay. But I do have to ask you not to hit my officers with that industrial sized corn broom any more. At least not until we've found Ben." Ida began to cry and she nodded as Tony slowly began to moan from behind them on the ground. Ethan hugged Ida and patted her on the shoulder. "Now shoo! Go on inside the house with Lazarus and make some coffee. I'll take care of this." Ida nodded and called to Lazarus who was busily licking Tony's face to wake him up. When Ida and the dog were out of ear shot, Ethan grabbed the collar of Tony's shirt and dragged him to his feet in one swift motion.

"If I ever hear you say or do anything like this ever again, you will be unemployed. Do you understand?" Ethan spoke softly and enunciated every syllable clearly. The anger was evident in his voice.

Groggy from the beating he took at the hands of Ida Johnston and her broom, Tony's eyelids fluttered and he looked up into Ethan's eyes. Slowly his legs straightened and he pulled away to stand on his own.

"Me? What I did? She beat me. I'm an officer of the law and she beat me. That is a felony." Tony's anger became evident from the spittle flying from his lips. Phil came back from the truck and stepped in between Ethan and Tony. Phil's aggressive stance and jutting chin warned Tony he was on dangerous ground.

"And what the hell did you do to her? She's worried sick about her husband and you insult her feelings and intelligence by your words and cavalier attitude, that's what you did. That kind of behavior is inexcusable and will not be tolerated by anyone. Do you understand me?" Phil's raised voice broke through the insolent stare Tony was sending Ethan's way.

"I only said what everyone was thinking," Tony returned.

"No!" Ethan stepped up. "You said what *you* were thinking. You were insensitive, overbearing, and totally out to lunch. Phil, why did we hire this man?"

Ethan looked at Phil and Phil looked at Ethan.

"Beats me. I think Elva recommended him," Phil shrugged.

Ethan looked at Tony and simply pointed towards the track that ran towards the beaver dam. The meaning actually sunk into Tony's thick head and he started to turn.

"Don't ever let me catch you doing that again, Tony, or I will have you up on charges." Ethan's voice had a ring of steel in it and it stopped Tony in his tracks. Shrugging his shoulders, he straightened and continued on along the track to the dam. Ethan and Phil let him get ahead for a minute or so and Ethan turned back to Phil.

"You watch him close. After today I don't want him doing anything on his own. He is on probation until I see a change in attitude." Phil nodded and went to join Tony on the long walk to the dam.

Ben and Ida Johnston had a beautiful little farm that used to be a very large farm. Through the years he had sold several acres off here and there and now, all that was left was a 360 acre parcel of land with approximately 120 acres of wooded area surrounding a little pond where water fowl and animals, fish and deer alike were known to be found. Ben had stocked the pond and the little creek that fed the pond and it kept him and his family fed for years. In the years of unusually large amounts of rain and snow, the pond became very large and threatened the safety of several water fowl habitats and Ben would blast the damn to let the level of the pond go down. It didn't take very long for the beavers to fix the damn but usually not until the habitat had become safe for the birds and their young.

Ben had gone out early that morning to place a small blast in the beaver dam along the end farthest away from the beaver house. He always gave himself time to get down from the dam and a good distance away. From what Ida had told Ethan, this time the explosion was larger than before and he worried that Ben wasn't far enough away.

"Stay on the radio!" Ethan called to Phil's receding back. Phil waved as he caught up to Tony and pushed him faster along the track. Turning, Ethan went up to the door of the house. The inner door was open so he called in through the wooden screen door.

"Ida, can I come in?" Lazarus came to the door to answer him. Whining with his tail wagging a million miles an hour, he placed his front feet on the door to push the screen open. "Hey there, Lazarus. Good boy!" Ethan opened the door wider and reached down to scratch Lazarus behind the ears. Ida came to the door and smiled at the dog.

"Here, Lazarus! Leave Ethan alone for now." Motioning to Ethan she beckoned him in to the kitchen. "Leave your boots on, I always do," she said as she led Ethan into the large country kitchen and he sat at the wooden table. Before Ethan could even remove his hat and place it on the floor beside him, Ida had a plate of cinnamon buns and a cup of coffee in front of him.

"Ida, you shouldn't have," Ethan grinned up at her. Ida moved to the spot directly to his right and sat down with a worried look on her face.

"It's no trouble, Ethan. Ben always did like cinnamon buns and coffee on a Sunday morning. You just happen to be here, that's all." Placing her chin in her hands she watched as Ethan took a healthy bite of the roll.

"Wow! That's delicious, Ida. As always," Ethan mumbled around the food in his mouth."

"You don't think Ben hurt himself do you?" Ida asked with a plaintive voice. "I don't think I could stand it if something happened to my Ben." Ida's blue eyes, though dim, were large and filling with tears at the thought of losing her one true love. She buried her face in her hands and let the tears flow as she sobbed.

Ethan tried to swallow but the sudden lump in his throat refused to budge. Taking a sip of the coffee he tried to wash it down. Slowly, he was able to clear his throat and reached out to touch Ida's shoulder as she sobbed relentlessly with her head on the table.

"Ida, Ben has had problems and accidents before. What makes you think he's hurt himself any worse than he usually does?" Ethan tried to console Ida in her grief.

"Because he was so angry this morning when he left! That man keeps calling him to buy our farm and Ben finally told him at six this morning that he could place the offer where the sun don't shine and hung up!" Ida raised her head to look right into Ethan's eyes. "The explosion was larger than usual. I heard the windows rattle. It never rattles the windows. Ben only uses one stick of dynamite and he knows where to place it. He has that fancy certificate and his permit. He never makes mistakes when he does this. He's been doing this for years!"

"Okay, Ida, I'll radio my men to check for anything out of the ordinary, okay?" Ida nodded as Ethan reached for the radio clipped to his shoulder. He started to ask Phil if he had reached the dam yet as he walked into the living room out of ear shot. "Phil, Ethan here. Are you at the dam yet?"

"Yeah. Just got here. Chief, doesn't Ben use only one stick of dynamite at a time when he's doing this?" Came Phil's question.

"Yeah, why?"

"It seems to me there's too much damage for just one charge. The whole dam and the beaver house have been blown to bits. I would say something is definitely wrong here." Phil answered.

"Keep me informed when you find Ben," Ethan's voice was short and clipped as he spoke into the microphone. A feeling of impending disaster settled on Ethan's shoulders and it was all he could do to turn and walk back into the room and sit by Ida's side and keep a neutral face.

Ida looked up and became alarmed. "What's wrong? What happened? Where's Ben?"

"Calm down, Ida. They haven't found Ben yet but that doesn't mean he's been hurt," Ethan tried to ease Ida's fears. "He's probably on his way back along a different route." Ida tried to smile.

"You're a good man, Ethan, and a terrible liar." Ida got up and went to the stove to pour herself a cup of coffee and came back to the table. Placing the cup in her spot she went down the hall to the washroom and closed the door. The sobs started to come shortly after the door closed. Ethan tried to endure them by picking up his cup and pacing while he drank. Minutes passed. The sobs slowly subsided and the door opened. Ida came back to the table with her face scrubbed clean and calmly sat at her spot at the table. Ethan just waited patiently and quietly with Ida for any news that came their way from the dam.

After about half an hour and two cups of coffee, Ethan was about to call on Phil again when his radio crackled.

"Chief, are you there?" Ethan walked out of ear shot and into the living room.

"I'm here, Phil, what did you find?" Ethan asked in a soft voice.

"Not much of anything, boss." Phil cleared his voice. "We did find Ben, sort of."

"What do you mean by that?" Ethan asked. An icy fear seemed to grip Ethan's chest.

"Are you alone?" Phil asked in return. The feeling of dread seemed to pour down from the top of his head and hit him in his heart. Ethan turned to the door into the kitchen and saw Ida standing framed in the light from the kitchen. Her arms were out to each side, holding her in place by the door frame. Ethan hesitated.

"No, just a minute." Ethan went out the front door onto the covered porch where he pictured Ben and Ida spending many a hot summer's eve. "Okay, go ahead."

"We found pieces of Ben, boss. We're going to need the ME," Phil answered.

"Are you sure it's Ben?" Ethan was desperately hoping for some good news.

"We're sure." Ethan closed his eyes and once again tried to swallow over the lump in his throat. From a distance the wail of a siren could be heard getting closer.

"Okay, Phil. I'll go talk to Ida and I'll send for the coroner. Stay there until he gets there, okay?" Phil signed off and Ethan turned to face the ambulance as it drew up to the front door.

"Just in time. Ida's going to need it I think." Ethan thought to himself. Going back into the kitchen, he approached a frighteningly white-faced Ida. A calm, quiet, stone-like Ida.

"Ida….Phil said he found Ben." Ethan carefully touched Ida's shoulder as if he were afraid she would break. She looked up into Ethan's face with eyes that tore his soul. Taking a deep breath he continued. "Ben will not be coming home tonight, Ida. I'm sorry." The tears started again as the EMTs came in through the door. Ethan pulled Ida to her feet and wrapped his arms around her. "It will be all right, Ida. We'll figure it out together." Ethan's mind went to Dorothy's face as he held the grieving Ida. *"I think I know how she must feel. If anything happened to Dorothy, I don't know what I would do."* His arms wrapped tighter around Ida at the thought of losing Dorothy. *"It'll never happen,"* he said to himself.

CHAPTER THREE

The ambulance attendants checked Ida Johnston out and gave her a shot to calm her. Her stressed-out condition had alarmed the physician online and he ordered her to be brought in. Ida refused. She was not going anywhere, she said, until Ben came home. Ethan understood but the attendants looked to Ethan for instructions. He quietly nodded and they let get up off the gurney.

"Ethan, I'm going to retire now. I think I need the rest. I'll be down in the bedroom at the end of the hall." She motioned to the stove and the coffee pot. "You people make what you need in the way of refreshments. Ethan, you make sure they get some coffee, you hear?" Ida was used to bossing a family of seven so talking in this way to the men standing in her kitchen attending to her needs seemed to help Ida much more than the shot to calm her.

"Yes, Ida. I will," Ethan said gently. Ida left the kitchen with her head raised but holding onto the wall for support. At the end of the hall she didn't hesitate to step through and close the door firmly behind her. One of the attendants looked at Ethan and spoke up.

"She should have someone here to watch her. Now that she's had that shot." The sound of an ATV sounded from outside and then silenced as it parked.

"I'll call someone to come out and stay with her until her own children can get here." Ethan said. The attendants began to pack up their equipment as Phil and Tony came in quietly from outside. Ethan nodded to each one of them in turn.

"Tony, do you want the attendants to check your head while they're still here?" Tony, in shock, looked at Ethan without understanding. His face actually looked green to Ethan. "Come here and sit down." The attendants closed in around him and Ethan stepped back.

"What happened, Phil?" He asked.

"I can't tell for sure, but I found this." Phil held out a small piece of plastic that had a wire leading away from it. "It wasn't far from where we found the first piece of Ben," Phil said in a hushed tone.

"That bad?" Ethan asked.

"Worse. We're going to need to spend some time searching for the rest of Ben. The dam is gone. Dead beavers in the pond, it looks like someone used at least a dozen sticks of dynamite." Ethan shook his head and reached for his cell phone.

"I'll call for help and see what Elva can do about getting the crime scene technicians here as fast as we can. I'm sure Dorothy will help with staying here with Ida until her family members can get here. You and Tony go back out once Tony has been taken care of and basically watch to make sure no one or anything contaminates the scene, clear?" Phil nodded and walked over to Tony while Ethan called for support. Once that was done, Ethan called Dorothy.

The EMTs were sent away and Ethan waited for Elva to send the crime scene out. While he did that, he searched the cupboards for coffee cups, coffee, and cream and sugar. He knew that whoever came to help with the "clean up" and investigation was going to need something stronger than water to help them get through the day. He concentrated on the little tasks he had set for himself to do until he heard the siren of the medical examiner's wagon and support personnel. Ethan squared his shoulders and went out to the front of the house so the noise would not wake Ida.

Ethan explained to the medical examiner where the scene was and off the examiner went with his crime scene technicians on a very somber trek to the beaver dam. He turned to go back inside when Dorothy showed up and parked out of the way by the barn. Approaching the front steps she stopped and looked at the silent Ethan on the top step of the covered porch. Both of them quietly stared into each other's eyes, taking in the seriousness of the moment. Ethan reached out to take her hand and draw her up to the top step to stand facing him.

"Is it bad?" Ethan nodded silently and embraced Dorothy in a fierce hug. Dorothy knew then how badly the emotionally stable man who engulfed her in his arms had been affected. He buried his head into the hair that fell down around her shoulders and held her tightly for a few more moments. "Ethan, let's go inside," Dorothy whispered.

They quietly went inside, away from the prying eyes of some of the technicians who had not yet left for the scene.

"Here, I made us some more coffee," Ethan's hand shook as he poured the coffee into Dorothy's cup. Dorothy took the pot from Ethan and finished the pour herself. They both sat at the table and Dorothy swallowed. It wasn't usual for Ethan to react this way. She knew she had to ask him why he was affected this way.

"Ethan, what is it?" Dorothy took one of his hands in hers. "What made you react this way?" Ethan's troubled eyes misted over as he fought through the emotional pain and looked away for a moment. When he looked back, his eyes held unshed tears.

"It's just, when Ida found out, she held onto me as if I was family. And I thought to myself, what would I do if I lost you that way? I can't even think of a day without you," Ethan's voice was quiet and shaky and Dorothy reached out to touch the side of his face.

"Don't worry, sweetheart, it will never happen. I'm not going anywhere, okay?" Dorothy's hand caressed his jawline. Ethan took her hand in his and placed a soft tender kiss in the middle of her palm.

"Okay. Please don't. I realized I need you more than ever right now." Dorothy's heart began to beat so rapidly her stomach began to flip flop. Just then, another vehicle pulled up into the yard. Ethan and Dorothy both stood up with tender smiles on their faces and went to greet the new arrivals.

Elva came with the police van, two waitresses from a local café, and lots of tables to set up. A small canvas gazebo was set up immediately to the left of the house in front of the driveway. Coffee for the workers, sandwiches from Maria at the Manor, and a huge pot of soup on a warmer were all set up. The usually efficient Elva had taken care of arranging for more food to arrive later if it was needed.

"Elva, I don't know how you arranged it so fast, but thank you," Ethan shook her hand gently. "You're amazing, you know that?" Ethan asked her.

"Just doing my job, boss. Besides, I never did like lazing around the office myself when I could be doing something more important like helping out here. How is Ida, Chief?" Elva enquired.

"She's inside laying down. Hopefully, the shot the ambulance attendants gave her will help. They did say that we should look in on her every once in a while to make sure. Why don't you and Dorothy go in and see if you can find out where her kids are and get their number. She's going to need them at a time like this." Both ladies nodded and left to go inside and carry out their tasks.

Ethan looked down the track of the path that led to the scene. Waiting for news wasn't going to be easy, but he knew Phil and Tony would be back as soon as they could. In the meantime, he knew he had to make some phone calls to the rest of the Johnston family before the news media found out about it.

Entering the house as quietly as he could, Ethan approached the living room and found Elva searching through the small desk in one corner.

"Did you find anything yet?" Ethan questioned.

"I think this is what we're looking for." Elva held up a small brown book with the words 'Address Book' on the cover. Opening it, she went straight to the name of Ida and Ben's son. Ethan took out his note book and wrote the name down and the number.

"That should be sufficient for now. I'll phone Brad so that he can call the rest of the kids and their families. Where's Dorothy?" Ethan asked.

"She's just down the hall," Elva said. "I'm going out to the coffee table and get some of that good stuff. I figure the technicians should be back before long and I would like to get some fresh coffee before it's all gone." Elva turned to leave. "Besides, you and your lady need to talk to Ida, I know that, but I don't think I can face Ida while you do that. Please be careful with her, Ethan. She's been through a lot in the last twenty years. And she's my friend." Ethan nodded as Elva left. Reaching for his cell phone, he called the number of Brad Johnston and listened to it ring.

"Hello?" Came Brad's voice over the phone.

"Brad Johnston?"

"Yes, who's this?" the tone of voice was surly and impatient.

"This is Ethan Barns, Chief of Police of Redwood," Ethan paused for the information to sink in on Brad's mind.

"Why are you calling me?" came Brad's question after a sharp intake of breath. "What's happened? What's Dad done this time?"

"I'm sorry to have to tell you this, Mr. Johnston, but there was an accident here at the farm, and your father was badly hurt." Ethan knew the easiest way for everyone was just to come right out and tell him.

Brad's silence stretched for a few moments longer than normal. A small moan sounded into the phone.

"Oh no. What happened, is he going to be okay?"

"Well, no, Brad, I'm sorry to say your father was killed. I'm out here at the farm now and your mother has been given a sedative for the moment. I think it would be a good thing if you called the rest of your family to give them the news as soon as possible and then come on out here. I can explain everything when you get here and possibly get you to answer some questions at the same time. Is that okay for you?"

"Chief Barns, I will be there as soon as I can make some phone calls and round up the family. Is mother all right for now?" Brad's voice was warbling and worried.

"Yes, Brad. But she needs you here as soon as you can get here, okay?" Ethan said.

"Okay. It shouldn't take me more than an hour to contact the rest of the family and drive over."

"That's good, Brad. I'll see you when you get here." Ethan turned off the phone and turned to face Phil and Tony as they came walking over from the track to the dam. They had returned and Tony's face was greener yet. Phil's wasn't as green but it was a pasty white.

"Phil? What have you got?" Ethan questioned his detective. Phil Harmon opened his case notebook and started to read his notes.

"First of all, the blast was a controlled blast, with more than one stick of dynamite. All the evidence is scattered to hell and back, and the scene technicians are still working on that. They did find the tracks of an ATV behind the dam coming from the opposite direction of this one here. It goes north and meets up with the cut line along the back of the Johnston property line. There is a cut in the barbed-wire fence where it came through and then continued on several miles along the cut line to a truck that was waiting. It appears the ATV was loaded onto a truck, and the truck was driven away. Technicians are taking pictures, taking impressions, and cataloguing everything they can find." Phil looked up from his notes. The rest was from memory.

"Ethan, it looks like someone set the charge before Ben got there this morning. It was deliberate, and even though it may not have been set to kill Ben, it did. Pieces of a timer were found and catalogued. Someone wanted to destroy Ben's dam, his pond, and ended up killing Ben as well." Tony nodded in agreement. Ethan turned to him.

"What do you think, Tony?" Ethan wanted everyone's impression of the scene before it was churned up by the masses.

"Ethan, Phil is right. I saw bits of a timer, and the explosive was placed approximately where it would do the most damage. They didn't care who they hurt, and what happened to anyone who got close to the blast. Whoever did this, wanted to destroy the pond. It seems to be draining quite rapidly at this point," Tony answered.

"So you think this was a deliberate attempt to destroy the water level of the pond?" Ethan asked him.

"Yes. Destroy the marshland, it won't be protected anymore," Tony nodded. Despite his green countenance, he seemed all business.

"I would like permission to use the laptop in your unit and check out something I think might have some bearing on this," Tony asked.

"Go ahead, Tony. Report back to me as soon as you know anything." Ethan instructed him. Tony left and walked over to the SUV they arrived in. Phil and Ethan watched him as he walked away with confidence.

"The boy has potential," Phil said quietly.

"Yep. Almost makes up for what he said earlier," Ethan answered. Both men turned towards the mess tent.

"Do you agree with his opinion?" Ethan asked Phil.

"I do. But that raises another question. Why now? Why would someone want to blow up the dam, destroy the marshland, and kill Ben?" Phil asked.

"I don't think they meant to kill Ben," Ethan answered. "Just to destroy the value of the property a little."

"What makes you think that?" Phil asked Ethan.

"Something Ida said earlier. We'll know more after Tony checks it out. He could be worth what we're paying him after all." Both Ethan and Phil accepted a hot cup of coffee and talked about the scene, motives, and evidence gathering.

"How long do you think it will take to find what's left of Ben?" Elva came over and sat with them.

"I think they should be done fairly soon. It's the other evidence I'm wondering about," Ethan said.

"Why would someone be so careful about placing the charge and leaving themselves enough time to get away, but leave a trail a dummy could find when they made their get-a-way?" Phil interjected after sipping his coffee.

"That's right. Either they are very dumb, or they want to implicate someone who is very dumb," Ethan turned to see who was driving into the yard.

"Okay, here's Brad." He stood up and motioned to the truck that stopped in front of him. "We'll finish this discussion later," Ethan told Phil. Phil nodded and turned to go back up the track to the dam. Or what was left of it. Ethan stood and walked over to the grey half-ton with the ATV in the back and reached out to shake Brad's hand.

CHAPTER FOUR

The day disappeared into darkness and the rest of the Johnston family arrived. Ida was kept busy inside by Dorothy as they reheated food that the neighbors started bringing by the truckload. Family members were questioned, and Ethan kept Phil on the crime scene investigation and kept Tony on the laptop doing the background information.

The last of the crime scene technicians left shortly after the medical examiner took Ben's body to their van and back to Redwood. The coffee tent was taken down and supplies were loaded back into Elva's van so she could take it back to town with her. Tony emerged from the truck as Ethan and Dorothy were saying their goodbyes to the family. The light from the porch illuminated Brad Johnston's outline as he leaned against the support column and watched Ethan and Dorothy walk out to their trucks. Dorothy looked back and saw the grief, the exhaustion, and the emotional pain the man carried after today.

"It will take a while," Dorothy said out loud as she walked with Ethan.

"What will?" Ethan asked as he opened her truck door for her.

"For this family to find closure and a bit of peace," Dorothy said to him. Ethan nodded and closed the door. Leaning in through the open window, he placed a gentle kiss on Dorothy's lips.

"You're right, but if I have anything to say about it, I will make sure whoever did this rots in jail for a long time." Ethan stepped back and waved to Dorothy as she drove away.

"Chief, I found something." Tony was carrying some papers he had brought with him from the truck. He handed them to Ethan.

"What do we have here?" Ethan started to read. "Why, it's an offer to purchase from the City of Redwood, which was turned down by Ben."

"Ben didn't like the amount they were offering him. Seeing as he is basically not three miles from the city, they wanted to buy it. Ben said no because he wants twice as much as they were offering," Tony explained the paper.

"Okay, and this is significant as to why?" Ethan asked Tony.

"This was rejected over six months ago. Didn't Ida say someone kept after Ben to sell him the farm just last week?" Tony asked Ethan. Both men and Phil climbed into the SUV and buckled in.

"That's true. So whoever made the offer from the City of Redwood, is not the person who made the last offer to purchase," Ethan surmised as he started the truck. "That's a good start, Tony. Keep digging when we get back to the office."

"Do you want us to keep at the paperwork for this, or finish it in the morning?" Phil asked Ethan. "It's after 9 now, and most of the technicians will have gone home by now."

"Okay, well then we get back at it early in the morning. I want those reports by 8 in the morning. How and when you get it done is up to you."

"You got it Chief," Phil answered.

"Chief?" Tony asked from the back seat. "Do you think it would help my situation much if I actually gave Miss Adams an apology the next time I see her?"

"For what?" Ethan glanced at Phil and winked.

"For being such an ass and letting my mouth get me into trouble," Tony answered.

"Well, when you say it like that Tony, I'm pretty sure she will take it in stride. Just don't say anything like that again," Ethan warned.

"Why is that? Is she going to kill me next time?" Tony said with a snicker.

"No. I will," Ethan answered in a firm voice. Tony swallowed hard and this time Phil did the snickering.

Ethan pulled up to the front door of the office and let Tony and Phil out then drove around the back. His parking spot was right beside the back door which led to a hallway straight to his office. It was easier for him to go in this way.

Turning his light on, he placed his hat on the coat rack and sat behind his desk. Phone messages adorned the blotter on his desk and the paperwork stack he had left on the far side of the desk was still there.

"Darn, how it never seems to file itself." Ethan muttered to himself. *"Never enough time to do the filing."*

Ethan spent all of ten minutes working on the pile of paperwork but his mind kept wandering to that moment when Ida had clung to him and he had vowed to never let that happen to Dorothy and himself. He had the pen poised over a paper but was lost in thoughts of Dorothy and himself making plans for the future. All of a sudden he realized he hadn't even asked Dorothy how her plans for the Bed and Breakfast were going.

Dorothy had started construction six months after Quentin Tallas had sold the land to her in exchange for Dorothy selling the family hotels to Quentin Tallas. Quentin was a real estate developer who had become entangled in the family business when two men, the Adams family lawyer and Darien Belknap had bilked him out of several million dollars in a real estate development deal. He had come to Redwood shortly after Dorothy and her family buried their father. In the tumultuous turn of events, Dorothy managed to help Ethan find out who her father's murderer was, sell the three hotels to Quentin in an amazing deal, and buy the property her family then turned into a memorial park. Two teens had died by Dorothy's side in a car crash many years ago, and Dorothy had taken responsibility for that and helped to give the teen's families closure by donating the park to the city in the teens' names. Of course, a building was erected as well which was used to give the youth of the city a place to go so they wouldn't turn to gang activity. On the lot next to that, was a huge building that Dorothy had also built on for herself. She had wanted to build a Bed and Breakfast she could run and operate while she pursued her real passion, writing. Lately, though there had been stumbling block after stumbling block. Permits were lost, licenses were denied, and paperwork was misplaced. Dorothy's frustration was at the boiling point, yet she still had enough compassion to come out to the farm when he called. Looking at the clock on his desk, Ethan decided it was too late to call Dorothy, so he turned off his desk lamp instead. He was going over to the Inn Hotel for a quick beer before he went home.

"I deserve that at least. Maybe it will help me to sleep." Ethan closed the door and placed his hat on his head. Going out the back way, he ran right into a whole pack of reporters with cameras flashing and microphones recording.

"Chief Barns, would you care to make a statement?" One female reporter asked as she shoved her microphone into Ethan's face. Struggling to control his temper Ethan shook his head.

"Yes I would," Ethan paused to give the cameras a chance to focus on him. Standing with his hands on his hips with his elbows out to give himself room, he cleared his throat as if he were going to say something momentous. "At this point, any and all information pertaining to the death of Ben Johnston is being kept quiet because of the on-going investigation. Other than that, I would also like to state, it has been a long day and I'm going home to bed." Brushing the reporters out of his way as if they were flies on the wall, he got into his SUV.

"*I wonder who told them,*" Ethan fumed to himself. There was to be a media ban on any active murder investigation unless Ethan made a statement himself. He pulled out of the lot and almost clipped a television van as it was pulling in. He laid on the horn and continued driving away with a fuming van driver behind him. "*They continue to drive like that and I will give them a ticket, not just a horn.*" Ethan cursed to himself and drove straight ahead.

CHAPTER FIVE

Dorothy parked in front of the huge building that was going to be her 'Bed and Breakfast'. Weariness seemed to seep into every bone in her body, rendering her immobile for a few seconds. Laying her head back, she closed her eyes and took a cleansing breath. The events of the day kept going through her mind like the fast moving blades of a windmill in a wind storm. Dorothy knew she needed to slow them down so she could relax.

She kept seeing Ethan's eyes as he admitted to her that the thought of losing her was more than he could bear. It was no surprise to Dorothy that he felt that way as she had been going through the same emotions. The two of them had clicked right from the time she had come home to Redwood; even when she was a suspect in the death of her father. Something drew them together and Dorothy knew she had found her soul mate. Opening her eyes, she got out of the truck and locked it before she carried her gear inside.

The house was a two-level building with eight bedrooms, six on the top floor, with three bathrooms, and two in the basement with two washrooms. The main floor held her office, a library, a television/entertainment room, and a small dining room attached to a fully professional kitchen. Dorothy had drawn up the plans herself when she was in her last tour of Kandahar. Her disjointed visions and dreams had gelled into one major vision and passion. She wanted to run a peaceful bed and breakfast while she did some writing on the side. That was why she had pressed on with permits, building plans, etc., even when it seemed to be an impossible chore.

The covered porch wrapped around the front and the two sides of a basically square two-story building. Large French doors opened onto the wrap around porch from the kitchen on one side of the entrance at the front, and a huge picture window all along the other side of the house, right to the back. French doors opened onto the porch from Dorothy's office at the back, giving her some measure of privacy and access to the outdoors. Upstairs, big beautiful windows let sun into each of the guest bedrooms and the main bedroom as well. Dorothy had a full bath with a soaker tub off her bedroom, and the other two bedrooms were marked Men and Women, with several shower stalls and toilets in each. That way it was easier for each guest to maintain some semblance of privacy.

The siding on the outside of the house was blue with the railing around the porch a contrasting white. During each phase of the construction, Dorothy chose the materials to be used not because she was cheap but because of the old-fashioned ambience she wanted to create. The building contractor approved of every choice she made, and together, they had finally stood proudly in front of the main door steps surveying it.

Now, though, the house was empty and dark because Dorothy had no guests yet. She was living in it, so she could continue to prepare for her opening day, but every time she went to set an opening date, one of the inspectors lost her permit, or City Hall would claim she didn't have one, etc. And while they investigated to make sure that her claims had validity, it took time. Dorothy's frustration was nearing the boiling point and she wasn't sure how much longer she could handle it.

Placing her gear on the floor beside her, Dorothy glanced around in the darkness before turning on the light. *"Maybe I should just cancel my plans, get married, and live happily ever after,"* She thought to herself. Then she laughed it off, turned off the light, and locked the door behind her. *"There is no happily ever after in the real world."* She said out loud.

It was late and she wanted to get cleaned up and off to bed. She hadn't had time to change before she got Ethan's call about going out to the Johnston farm. Throwing her gear back in her truck she had driven like mad to get there. "Poor old man Johnston," she said out loud. "Who could have hated him so much that they would blow him up like that? I know the Johnstons had a lot of problems there for a while, what with Ben sending Ida to the hospital several times, but the commotion had died down and Ethan told me Ben had done a complete 180 degree turn. He was as nice as pie and courteous to everyone to boot. Now, almost ten years later, someone has murdered him. I guess Karma is a bitch."

Wearily pulling herself up the bannister that led to her master suite, she froze when she saw the light under her closed bedroom door. Carefully she placed her gear bag down and stealthfully approached the bedroom door as she had been taught in the military. The paint ball gun was neatly tucked to her side in case she needed to use it like a baseball bat. It was useless otherwise. Her gloved hand reached out to the doorknob in front of her and she gently turned the knob clockwise. Pushing the door open with her shoulder she suddenly leaped into the middle of her bedroom with the rifle at the ready. In the light coming from the bathroom, she could see her jacuzzi tub full of bubbles and dear old Maria with her face in shocked surprise. Both of them were transfixed for a second until Maria screamed and sank beneath the bubbles of the tub.

"Maria!" Dorothy dropped the paint rifle and raced to the edge of the tub. "Maria, it's me, Dorothy!" She reached into the froth of bubbles and grabbed a handful of Maria's jet black hair and pulled upwards. Surging to the top, Maria smacked Dorothy over the head with a long handled back scrubber covered in bubbles.

Dorothy reeled back in surprise and promptly slipped on the wet floor and went face first into the tub with her feet up in the air. Maria, scared and not knowing who the intruder was, continued to hit Dorothy with the wooden handle until Dorothy was able to sit herself upright in front of Maria in the tub. Maria's hand froze in mid-air when she recognized Dorothy.

"Dorothy! What are you doing here?" Maria asked in surprise and relief. Dorothy paused, took a deep breath, and wiped the bubbles from her eyes.

"Well, Maria, it could be that it is my very own bathroom in my very own house!" Dorothy's voice began to raise as she raised her arms to survey her condition, as well as the condition of the floor surrounding the tub. Bubbles were everywhere!

"Don't you raise your voice to me, Dorothy. I came here to run you a bath with the scented bubbles you like so much, and it looked so good to me I decided to soak in it for a while! You did say you didn't expect to be home much before midnight," Maria's expression changed from indignation, to curiosity, and then concern all in the same sentence. "I just wanted things to be nice for you when you got home. And it looked so good, I put on my suit to join you." Now her tone was sulky. Dorothy placed her right elbow on the edge of the tub and rested her head on it.

"You know, Maria, you're right. It's not your fault I came home one minute early." Relief at the announcement that Maria had on her bathing suit was evident in Dorothy's grin.

"You mean its midnight already?" Maria looked up to the huge round gold clock on the wall and realized Dorothy was right. "Oops!" Realizing she still had the wooden back scrubber in one hand she quickly hid it behind her back. Maria was the family cook at the Manor, which was the family home. Occasionally, Maria would come over to the Bed and Breakfast to help with a few chores. Maria was also considered to be part of the family long before Dorothy left Redwood for the military life.

Dorothy began to shake her head and the laughter began. Softly at first, but when Maria joined in and covered her mouth with her hands in an utterly lady-like fashion, the absurdity of the situation made the ladies laugh so hard their stomachs began to hurt.

"I'm sorry, Maria, I'm just a little punch drunk after the day I had. And I did forget you were coming over tonight," Dorothy tried to apologize just as Temperance Adams, came rushing into the room wrapping her robe about her.

"What is all the commotion in here? Can't a lady get any sleep anymore?" Temperance was Dorothy's mother and when Temperance came upon the sight of her daughter and the family cook in the same Jacuzzi tub together, she stood frozen to the doorway with a hilarious look on her face. Her cook was in her bathing suit and in the bubble bath with her daughter, who was dressed in fatigues. Dorothy gave a whoop and disappeared underneath the bubbles.

"Don't give it another thought, Mrs. Adams, Dorothy is punch drunk," Maria emphasized her words with the back scrubber in her right hand, while carefully balancing the champagne flute she retrieved in her left.

Temperance shook her head to rid herself of the scene and turned with a slightly bewildered smile on her face.

"Perhaps you could tell my daughter it is okay to have a bath without her clothes on. And get her to sit up. She might drown soon if she doesn't." Temperance Adams was a very straight-laced and proper lady, a lady who knew how important it was to take strange and bewildering things in her stride. She left the bedroom to go back down the hall to her bedroom and Maria smacked the water above Dorothy's head like she was holding a magic wand instead of a long handled back scrubber.

"She's gone, kid," Maria poured more champagne into the flute. Dorothy sat up and began to sputter from all the bubbles. "She has a point, though." Maria intoned as she sipped and handed the bottle to Dorothy, who took it and raised it to her lips.

"Oh yeah? What's that?" Dorothy asked as she lowered the bottle.

"You could have taken your clothes off. Especially those boots! They are beginning to chaff my carefully sculpted pedicure!" Dorothy almost choked on the next swallow.

CHAPTER SIX

The sun rose on Redwood bringing with it a foggy haze from the river. It was thick and rolling and the sun was blocked by the rolling waves. Ethan looked up to the sun before he got in his car and shivered.

"It figures. This fog is not a good sign. There's going to be more traffic accidents today than usual." He let out a big sigh. "Guess I'd better get going."

Ethan started his car and pulled out into traffic for the trip to his office, and right at the first street light he saw a small fender bender. Nodding his head in affirmation of his previous prediction, he pulled over to the side, put his lights on, and got out to check and see if anyone was hurt.

The first responder at the scene recognized Ethan right away.

"Good morning, Chief. How are you today?"

"I'm fine, Doug, how are you?" Ethan recognized the officer as a long time employee with an excellent record. Seeing he had everything under control, he got back in his car and was about to pull away when the officer came over to speak to him through the window.

"Excuse me sir, but I was wondering about yesterday. Did poor old Ben kill himself this time?" He asked.

"What makes you ask?" Ethan was surprised the officer even dared to ask about an ongoing investigation.

"Well, it's just that, in the paper, it said he killed himself. And I found that unusual because I knew Ben. He's one of my neighbors. He was always so careful about what he was doing." Ethan studied the man's face as he listened to his words. He was genuinely concerned and confused.

"When you get back into the office, I want you to come and see me. We'll talk then." Ethan put the SUV in gear and drove away as the officer nodded. "*Okay, another reason why I don't believe Ben killed himself,*" Ethan said to himself. "*But somebody certainly tried to make it look like he did.*"

Parking in his spot by the back door, Ethan entered his office and found that the front lobby was crammed with reporters looking for information about the Ben Johnston story. Glancing at his desk as he sat down, he saw a copy of the morning paper and started to seethe.

Splashed all over the front page was a picture of a haggard looking Ida Johnston staring at the dirt track that led to the dam that had been blown to pieces. The headline stated "My Husband Killed Himself". Ethan began to go over the story when the com buzzed and it was Elva.

"Hey Chief, glad to see you're in. Would you like a coffee to go with your paper?" Her voice was light and cocky and that made Ethan suspicious that she was up to something.

"What will this show of good humor cost me?" Ethan began to smile.

"Wait until I bring you your coffee and donut, then we'll talk," Elva signed off.

"*Oh boy. It must be a pretty big favor she's going to ask me for if she's this nice.*" Ethan put down the paper and watched the door. Sure enough, Elva knocked and walked through the door with a coffee and *two* donuts for Ethan.

Ethan sat back and crossed his hands in front of him and waited for Elva to ask the question after she deposited the donuts and coffee in front of him. She saw him watching her and she stepped back.

"What?" she asked him. Ethan grinned even wider.

"Nothing. I'm just waiting to see what it is you want," Ethan answered.

"What makes you think I want anything?" Elva started to smile.

"Your attitude. You're never this nice to anyone unless you want something," Ethan answered.

"Okay, here it is," Elva paused and looked down to quickly collect her thoughts. "You know how I told you there has been a rash of minor thefts in the Loop neighborhood, right?" Elva asked.

"Right. Go on," Ethan answered, still in his relaxed mode.

"Well, there have actually been quite a few, but mostly clothes, food, minor articles, really. So I started tracking them on the map with dates, and locations." Ethan took a sip of coffee.

"Okay," He said. *"She must really want something bad. This coffee is fresh."* He thought to himself.

"I was wondering if I might be permitted to follow up on this. I have a half mile radius plotted, and after going to that training workshop, I think I know where the thieves are hiding. I would bet the little buggers are doing it for kicks," Elva's self-satisfied smile made Ethan wonder if she might be right.

Taking a bite of a donut, he considered her words then slowly lowered the donut back to the plate, drawing out his decision for as long as he could just to tease Elva.

"All right." Elva's fist struck the air in a gesture of triumph. "But I want you to keep me updated by the end of every day with reports. Got it?" Ethan said.

"Yes sir. Got it!" Elva saluted Ethan with a smile. "You won't regret it."

"I know I won't if you keep bringing me coffee and donuts like this. Can I get a refill?" Ethan offered the empty cup to Elva before she ran out. She paused and looked at Ethan with a smile.

"Pot's right around the corner, boss. Help yourself." And she was gone. Ethan was still sitting at his desk with his cup raised towards the door when Phil Harmon came walking in.

"No thanks, Boss. Already had one. Can we talk?" Phil closed the door and Ethan shrugged to himself.

"I knew it was too good to be true," Ethan said out loud as he set his now empty cup down. Phil reached over the desk and took the last donut and looked at Ethan.

"What was too good to be true?" he said as he took a bite. Ethan looked down at the empty plate and back up to Phil.

"That was the last donut," he complained.

"And it's good, too. What was too good to be true?" Phil asked again.

"Elva wants to run with the investigation into the rash of thefts in the community behind the Loop. She plied me with fresh coffee and donuts," Ethan sighed and sat back. "What would *you* like to talk about?" Ethan asked Phil.

"It's about Ben Johnston. I read Tony's background check on the entire family and it seems there's something strange going on," Phil stated as he glanced at his notes. "Remember when Ben was charged with domestic battery after Ida was admitted to the hospital with a broken arm and bruises?"

"That was some time ago, Phil. But I remember."

"Well it seems that the oldest son married and moved out to his own farm, but his wife has been to the hospital several times before he was charged with domestic battery. And Ben never touched Ida again after that first time," Phil paused as his meaning sank in.

"So what, do you think the oldest son was the one who was abusing Ida?" Ethan asked Phil.

"Yes, but there's more. Ben's mortgage on the farm is almost paid off, and with his death by accident, there is no more mortgage. Ida will be able to live off Ben's pension. But the oldest son is having huge money troubles. His farm is in danger of going under. He'll lose everything. And he owns an ATV." The noise from the front of the office began to swell at this point, distracting both men. Ethan used the intercom to call the receptionist.

"What's going on out there?" Ethan inquired.

"Just a bunch of reporters making a fuss because you won't come out and talk to them," came the answer.

"Tell them I will make a statement when I have something to report. And if they print anything other than an official statement before then, they will be barred from any further official statements or press conferences," Ethan barked into the phone.

Phil looked at Ethan and grinned.

"At least you're in a good mood," Phil laughed.

"How do you know that?" Ethan asked.

"You didn't threaten to incarcerate them like last time," Phil grinned. Ethan shook his head.

"Okay, where were we?" Ethan asked.

"Well, I had mentioned that Tony's background research revealed that Brad was the aggressor in the Johnston household just before he married, but Ben took the domestic abuse charge. Brad is now in trouble like before, and he's having money troubles as well. Brad knew where Ben kept his dynamite and blasting caps, and also knew how to set the charges. The life insurance policy Ida had on Ben said that if Ben died of an accident, Ida would have enough to pay off the farm and live comfortably ever after. But if Ben died by someone else's hand, Ida would get twice the amount, say," Phil searched the sheaf of papers he held in his hands. "Nearly $500,000 dollars. Now with Brad's history of abuse with his mother and his wife, I would tend to bet that Brad is the one who had a reason for wanting his father dead." Phil finished talking and Ethan took a few moments to consider Phil's idea.

"Do you have absolute proof that it was Brad who abused Ida and not his father?" Ethan asked him.

"No. The only way I could get that would be to interview Ida again, show her what we have in the way of hospital visits, etc., and get her to come clean. With a statement indicating who the actual abuser is from Ida herself, we could then concentrate on that theory," Phil answered.

"But you are assuming that it was someone other than Ben who set the charge. So check into Ben's medical records and see what you can come up with. Was he slowly dying, was he depressed, was there anything in his head that made him want to kill himself. We do know that the charge was too large for what Ben usually did, and that it *was* deliberately set. Then check into Brad's alibi for yesterday morning and see if you can corroborate it. I will go and talk to Ida." Phil nodded his agreement and got up to leave. Opening the door he poked his head out first to see if there were any more reporters out in the front lobby.

"It's all clear Chief. You may want to leave while the getting's good." Ethan smiled at Phil's departure and reached for the phone. First, he had a certain auburn-haired lady to call.

CHAPTER SEVEN

Dorothy picked up the phone after a quick scamper to her office. She had been in the kitchen with Maria, having her breakfast when the phone began to ring.

"Hello?" Dorothy asked with a smile. She knew who it was calling.

"Well hi there. How are you doing today?" Ethan's warm and inviting voice gave Dorothy a thrill right down to her toes.

"I'm fine," She said breathlessly. "I miss you." Those three words came out almost before Dorothy realized it. Ethan caught the breathlessness in her voice and smiled into the phone.

"Why are you breathing so heavy?"

"I had to run from the kitchen to answer your call in my office," Dorothy explained.

"I see. Anxious to talk to me, I gather?" Ethan chuckled.

"Yes. After yesterday, I realized how something could happen to either one of us and we could be separated. I didn't like that feeling," Dorothy explained in a rush.

Ethan's heart skipped and a lump formed in his throat.

"I feel the same way, my dear. And that is why I am calling. I would like to have dinner with you and discuss something that is dear to both our hearts," Ethan's words almost took Dorothy's breath away.

"What's that?" She finally managed to gasp. Ethan chuckled into the phone again. The rumble was low and deep.

"You'll see. Is seven all right? At your place?" Ethan asked.

"I'll be here," Dorothy promised.

"All right then, see you there," Ethan hung the phone up with a flourish. "Just wait until she sees what I bought her for this occasion." Sliding the drawer in the center of the desk open, he brought out a small velvet lined jewelry box and slowly opened the lid. Nestled inside was a beautiful half carat diamond engagement ring in Dorothy's size. Ethan had purchased it a month earlier, but had a hard time deciding when to ask Dorothy. "There's no time like the present." Closing the box he slipped it back into its resting place in the drawer and locked it.

"Time to get this day started." Picking up the phone, he asked the receptionist to put a call through to Ida Johnston's place.

"Hello?" Ida's tremulous voice came over the phone with a crackle.

"Ida, I'm sorry to bother you but there are some questions I have to ask you. May I come out to the farm?" Ethan asked. There was a pause while Ida considered the answer.

"I don't know, the family is still here and I'm having a hard time making arrangements," Ida's voice sounded as if it was coming through a long tunnel.

"Ida, have you had any sleep in the last little while?" Ethan was concerned for her.

"Not much, but Brad and his wife have been here helping out." Ethan's concern for Ida doubled at that statement.

"Well, I will be there in a little while and maybe I can help make this a little easier for you. Is that okay?" Ethan asked once again.

"Oh, okay. Sure. I'll have Anna put the coffee on. She's Brad's wife, you know?" Ida answered.

"Yes, I know. I'll be there within half an hour, Ida," Ethan said and hung up the phone. From the sound of Ida's voice, Ethan thought she sounded dazed and confused. If Brad had been the abuser, and Ben was now gone, it's no wonder she was sounding so distant. Brad's mother was fair game if Phil's theory was correct.

Ethan called the front desk and told the receptionist that he was going to be leaving and he could be reached on his cell. Picking up his hat, he left through the back door and jumped into his SUV.

Ethan got half way to the Johnston farm when his cell phone rang.

"Barns here," he answered.

"Chief, there seems to be a disturbance over at the Johnston farm. Brad called 911 and requested assistance."

"I'm half way there but send a squad out to cover me," Ethan put the lights on and floored the SUV.

Pulling into the yard, Ethan discovered several people out in the front yard. There was Brad who appeared to be holding his mother back from hitting his wife Anna. There was a lot of yelling and screaming going on and Anna seemed to be in a dazed state with a large red mark on the right side of her face with scratches and bruises on her arms. Anna's arms were up protecting her face and Brad appeared to be struggling to hold onto Ida while she was screaming at the top of her lungs. Several adults were on the porch watching while children were scattered here and there, crying in fear.

Ethan parked and jumped out of the SUV all in one motion and he came up to Ida and Brad in one smooth movement. Grabbing Brad by the wrist, he twisted it around behind his back and made Brad release Ida. Pinning Brad's other arm while Brad yelled at the top of his lungs, Ethan cuffed him and shoved him towards the porch steps and the other adults. Swinging around he saw Ida walk up to Anna and just stood staring at her. Anna slowly lowered her arms from her face.

Ethan checked to see Brad was secure, and forced him onto the top step as Brad stared in surprise at the sight of his wife and mother slowly reaching out to hug each other.

"You b—ch!" exploded from Brad as he launched himself off the top step towards the two women and Ethan caught him in a vise-like hold when another unit pulled into the yard. Ethan wrestled Brad to the ground as Tony came up with his Taser out and nailed Brad in the lower back. Brad made a few convulsive moves and then was silent except for a few moans. Ethan got up from the ground and glanced at the two women to satisfy himself that Anna was not in danger from Ida and noticed Ida seemed to be protecting Anna as she pushed her behind her. Glancing at Anna's shell-shocked face and the red bruise that seemed to be swelling at an alarming rate, Ethan knew he had tackled the right person.

"Tony, put him in the back of my unit. Then calm him down so I can talk to him," Ethan ordered. Tony nodded and hauled the now silent Brad to his feet and half carried him to Ethan's SUV. Looking up at the porch and the still silent adult siblings and their spouses, Ethan shook his head in disgust.

"What's the matter with you people?" Ethan yelled in frustration. "How could you let this go on?" The children began to wail louder and Ethan motioned to the children. "Go take care of your children and make sure they're okay. Nobody leaves! I want to talk to each and every one of you including the children." One of the men moved and nodded his acknowledgement and Ethan turned towards Ida and Anna.

Walking up to the pair of ladies he saw that Ida was still in a protective mode with Anna still standing behind her.

"Ida, what happened?" he asked gently. "Do you want to talk about it?" Ida nodded and moved to put her arms around Anna's shoulders.

"Come into the house, Ethan." Ida's hair had several tendrils whisping out from the carefully done bun at the back of her head. "It will be much better if we are sitting down for this." Ida propelled Anna forward and the crowd at the top of the steps seemed to part magically to let Ida and Anna through. Anna was now holding her hands to her face as if she couldn't bear to let anyone see her bruises.

Sitting down at the kitchen table, Ida sat to Anna's right and Ethan sat across from them. He watched quietly while Ida took the coffee pot off the stove in her right hand and poured three fresh cups of coffee. Then she added spoons, a creamer and a sugar container to the table, all with using only her right hand. She seemed to be holding her left arm close to her side. When she finally sat and cleared her throat, Ida looked straight into Ethan's eyes and began to speak.

"I did not hurt anyone, Ethan. I only tried to protect Anna." Ethan could see the knuckles of Ida's hands seemed to be scraped as if she was in a bare knuckle boxing match with someone. It was then that Ethan spoke.

"Did Brad hurt your left arm?" Ethan asked.

"He did," Ida answered. Taking the cup of coffee carefully into both hands, Ida seemed to hug it for its warmth.

"How did it all start?" Ethan queried.

"The children had all arrived so we could decide what we were going to do for their father's funeral and then you called. I told Brad you were on your way and he asked what for?" Ida swallowed some of the black coffee in her cup. The warmth seemed to put color back into her face.

"Brad started yelling about police interference and throwing things, so Anna tried to get him to calm down. That's when he hit her." Ethan glanced at Anna.

"Is that true?" Ethan looked into Anna's face. Instead of answering Ethan, Anna lowered her head to hide her eyes, seemingly to shrink in size right in front of Ethan.

"It's okay, my dear," Ida wrapped her good arm around Anna's shoulder and squeezed the girl in a semi-hug. "It's time to start telling the truth."

"Did Brad hit you?" Ethan had to get a verbal answer from the girl to confirm Ida's story. Slowly the girl looked up from her spot at the table and Ethan could see the fear in her eyes.

"He'll kill me if I say anything bad against him," Anna whispered. "I'm scared." Ethan's heart went out to the young mother. He understood how hard it was for her to speak against her husband with the fear of retribution in her mind.

"Let me assure you, Anna," Ethan reached out to cup Anna's tiny cold hands in his. "Brad will never be able to touch you again. I will make sure of that. But you must tell me in your own words what happened." Ethan's voice was warm and caring and the words seemed to comfort Anna. She nodded her answer and sat up a little straighter.

"Brad likes to get angry and hit me and the kids. At first it was just when he started drinking, but now it is whenever things don't go the way he planned. He's been losing a lot of money on the farm lately, and I can't seem to get anything right," Anna stopped to look at Ida for support.

"Good girl, keep going." Ida massaged the girl's shoulders in a motherly gesture of love.

"I just tried to get him to stop yelling at his mother and breaking all the dishes but he hit me. Told me it was all my fault things didn't go the way he planned. He said I was dragging him and the rest of the family down," Anna lowered her head and her voice trailed off into a whisper. She really felt as if it was her fault her husband was having money troubles. Ethan's anger began to build towards the bully that Brad had become.

"Ida, I want you to tell me, about ten years ago, you went to the hospital with a broken wrist, or an arm. Ben went to jail for domestic abuse. The truth now, did Ben do that to you?" Caught in Ethan's direct stare, Ida swallowed nervously and her face returned to a sallow color.

"No, Ethan. I'm ashamed to say it was Brad. I didn't tell the truth back then because Ben didn't want Brad's future to suffer for one little mistake," Ida began to shake her head back and forth. "It was the wrong thing to do and I know that now. He should have taken responsibility for his actions back then. Now, it's almost too late." Ida hung her head in shame. Ethan waited for a few seconds to let that realization sink into Ida's mind.

"Now Ida, after Brad hit Anna, what happened?" Ethan asked in a business-like manner.

"I tried to call 911 but Brad tore the phone out of my hand before I could say anything. He told the operator to get out here in a hurry. He said I was going off the deep end," Ida was still shaking her head and now she was crying at the same time. Quietly, Anna reached over for the Kleenex box and handed it to Ida. Ida looked at it in surprise then at Anna. "Thank you my dear. Thank you," Anna gave Ida a tremulous little smile.

"It's okay, Momma. I'll tell Chief Barns what he wants to know. He said he needed to hear it in my words, right?" There was courage in the girl's eyes and the way she sat beside her mother-in-law.

Turning to Ethan she straightened her shoulders.

"I would like to tell you my story now." Ethan nodded and took out his note book. For the next half hour, Ethan took notes on Anna's life with Brad for the past eight years. They had two children, ages 6 and 7 and both were girls. She explained how it was a fairy tale life at first, but things slowly began to change shortly after their first girl was born. Little things would start to bother Brad and he would drink. Then he started hitting Anna after he was drunk. He always promised to quit hitting her the next morning and that he was so sorry it happened in the first place. Then they started losing money on the farm because Brad seemed to be drinking all the time. This made matters even worse. Then when they received the call that Brad's dad had passed away, Brad did something so unusual, Anna was shocked. Brad gave her a hug and started to do a little dance around their kitchen after he got the call from Ethan. When Ethan heard that, he froze.

That was not the usual reaction for a grieving son. It was the reaction of someone who had been good at manipulating people through violence, and who knew they were coming into some money. Just then, Tony came in from outside.

"Sorry to interrupt, Chief, but another unit has just arrived and we would like to get started interviewing the rest of the family." Ethan looked up with a stone hard look on his face and Tony took a step back. "Uh, did I say something wrong?"

"No, you didn't. Where is the rest of this family?" Ethan's anger was about to come to a boil and Ida noticed it.

"Ethan, now you leave them alone. They didn't have anything to do with this." Ida called out to him as Ethan rose from the table. Ethan looked at her.

"And that's just the problem, isn't it?" Ethan's voice was raised. "They saw what was happening, knew what was happening, and didn't say anything," Ethan was seething with rage but kept his voice tightly controlled. "They are as responsible for not doing anything as Brad is for hitting Anna. If they see anyone in this kind of trouble, they have a responsibility to the family to help out where they can. Not to ignore it and walk away like it doesn't happen!" Ethan took a deep breath.

"Ida, I am sorry to say this, but you are just as responsible for covering it up so many years ago," Ethan said to the little lady sitting at the table beside Anna.

"No, she isn't. She was scared, just like me," Anna yelled out.

"That's kind of you child," Ida patted the hands of the young lady sitting next to her. "But he's right. If only I had said something years ago, Brad wouldn't be the man he is today."

Tony turned to Ethan and cleared his throat to be heard.

"Can we begin with the rest of the family?" Ethan nodded to him in frustration.

"Where are they? I told them not to go anywhere!" The rest of the house seemed so silent to Ethan.

"They're just in the next room. They were sitting there quietly waiting until I came in with the other two officers," Tony informed Ethan. Ethan hadn't even heard them and he jerked his head up in surprise.

"All right. Take their statements, and let them go." Ethan turned back to the two ladies at the table. "Brad will be going to jail for a few days, and he will be charged with domestic battery. I'm going to type up your statements for you and I want you to come down to the office and sign them. After that I want you two ladies to get a restraining order against Brad. If he gets out on bail I don't want him anywhere near you two ladies. Got it?" Ethan instructed the two ladies who nodded their heads in agreement.

"Tony, you and the other two officers will take the statements from the rest of the family into the office, type them up and file them. Make sure they know that Brad is not to come anywhere near these two ladies. I am making them responsible for Ida and Anna's welfare. Got it?" Ethan barked.

"Got it Chief. I'm on it." Turning, Tony went into the next room and he and the other two officers got started on their tasks.

"Ladies, I need you to stay here on this farm together. If you're together, you'll be a lot safer. Have one of your brothers go to your place, Anna, and pick up some clothes for you and the children. I don't want you to do it alone." Anna nodded.

"One more thing, Anna." Both of the ladies looked up to Ethan as he towered over them. "Where was Brad yesterday morning around six?" Ethan directed the question to Anna. Anna paused in confusion at the question.

"He was feeding the cows." She said. "Like he always does at that time of the morning. It was hard for him to get out of bed, though, he was up so late the night before. When he came home he didn't park the truck very well. I could tell he was gone from the farm because he never parks the truck in front of the house the way he did," Anna was speaking from memory and Ethan knew she was telling the truth.

"He was gone the night before?" Ethan's tone got very quiet.

"Yes, why?" The silence in the room stretched out very awkwardly as Ethan made notes in his book.

"Now Ethan, don't you go thinking that way! He didn't do it! He couldn't do that to his own father!" Ida's voice raised itself into a shriek. Walking away shaking his head, Ethan left Anna to sympathize with Ida as he got into his SUV with Brad in the back and drove away.

CHAPTER EIGHT

Maria poured herself a nice hot cup of tea in Dorothy's kitchen and sat down to read the newspaper. It was mid-morning after the two ladies had had their midnight tea party in the Jacuzzi, and Maria had been left alone by Dorothy for a little while. When the phone rang Dorothy ran to her office almost on the other side of the building. Laughing to herself and shaking her head, Maria opened the paper to the front page. What she saw shocked her.

Ida's picture was on the front page and she didn't look too good to Maria. Reading the story, Maria found out that Ida had decided that her husband killed himself by accident. Not on purpose.

"Well now, the way the reporter words the headline, it sounds like she thinks it is suicide until you read the actual story. What that man won't do to sell his papers!" Maria said out loud. Maria shrugged her shoulders. "Oh well. To each his own." Turning the page, Maria was about to get up and pour herself a second cup of coffee when she noticed a small story about how Dorothy was struggling to start her Bed and Breakfast but she kept making all the wrong moves, misfiling this report, and that report, and not being very organized right from the start. The story even said that Dorothy lost the paper application for her business licence, and is making a squawk at City Hall by blaming it on someone else. Maria's mouth fell open at that.

"Well! I am going to go down there and give that man a piece of my mind!" Maria slapped the paper down on the counter and was about to leave when Dorothy walked in.

"What's up?" Dorothy asked Maria. Instead of answering, Maria just pointed to the small story on page three. Dorothy read it and started to get red in the face.

"Oh no! Miss Dorothy, don't get mad and cause trouble!" Maria knew Dorothy could be a formidable opponent if she chose to be. Taking a deep breath, she looked at Maria.

"Didn't I hear you say you were going to go down there and give this man a piece of your mind when I came in?" Dorothy asked quietly.

"Oh yes, but that's because I'm me. You're you and that's different!" Maria tried to reach out and pat Dorothy on the shoulder.

"What?" Dorothy looked confused and shook her head.

"I mean, if I go down there and complain, maybe they will listen. But if you, the person mentioned in the story, go down there and complain, it could cause them to write another nasty story. I am a character witness. You are the character!" Maria tried to make Dorothy understand the ramifications of going down to the newspaper office and complaining on her own. Dorothy sat down with a dazed look and began to smile ruefully.

"You know, Maria, I think I understand what you're trying to say," Dorothy shook her head again. "At least I understand in a muddled sort of way."

"Okay! I will make more coffee, and we call Ethan, okay?" Maria patted Dorothy on her shoulder again. Dorothy shook her head no.

"Ethan is pretty busy with this death at the Johnstons, so that's out." Both women thought for a moment.

"Your mama! She would know what to do," Maria tried again.

"No, I don't want to bother her with this." Once again the kitchen was silent.

"Do you want to call your brother Matt?" Maria asked hopefully.

"No, he's too busy with his renovations," Dorothy answered. It was then that Dorothy realized, she didn't have too many friends in town. She still kept in touch with some of the ladies she served in the forces with, but they didn't live in town. Just then the phone rang and Maria pounced on it. Dorothy's eyes went wide with surprise at how fast chubby little Maria could move.

"Adams, Bed and Breakfast!" Maria said with as much dignity as she could muster.

"I was wondering if I could speak to Miss Dorothy Adams, please," The male voice on the other end of the phone seemed cultured and very business-like.

"Who's calling?" Asked Maria with a measure of distrust.

"It's Quentin Tallas from Toronto. Is she there?" Maria rolled her eyes at the name and looked at Maria. "Just one minute, sir, and I will see if she is available." Maria's eye roll alerted Dorothy of Maria's disapproval of the person on the phone. Placing her hand on the mouthpiece to muffle her voice, Maria whispered to Dorothy.

"It is that fancy pants man in Toronto. That Quentin Tallas guy. Do you want to talk to him?" This was another surprise for Dorothy at the sound of Quentin's name. Quentin Tallas had been the man who had basically traded land for land, and then paid cash for the three hotels that were on the land that Dorothy traded to him. It made the formation of a memorial public park and a youth center possible so that the youth of Redwood would have a place to go. Construction of the youth center went way over budget but Quentin had also matched dollar for dollar that the Adams family did to finish the building. Now the man was calling her almost a year and a half later, and Dorothy had no idea why. They hadn't been that friendly.

Motioning for the phone, Dorothy took it away from Maria, who promptly slipped into a few phrases of her native Spanish.

"Hello?" Dorothy said into the phone.

"Yes, hello. Dorothy, how nice to hear your voice again," came the cultured tone from across the country. "How are you?" Quentin asked.

"Confused as to why you are calling me. And for that matter, how did you get this number?" Dorothy asked.

"Dorothy, I have some very influential friends in certain areas and Redwood is no different." Dorothy nodded to herself. "The reason why I am calling is because there has been an incident here in Toronto that leaves me with a very bad taste in my mouth."

"What's that?" Dorothy was starting to get curious.

"Apparently, a small group of outrageous people here in Toronto have decided that my reputation is not the best and have been slandering me in the press, hoping to make people see that I am, and I quote, "An ungodly man with no fear of retribution because of his previous unclean life," Quentin said. "It's really quite annoying but not dangerous when one or two little stories pop up in the paper the way these have, but someone is also talking to my contractors, business contacts, and laborers, forcing them to turn their backs on me. I am not the only one they are doing this to here in Toronto," Quentin finished.

"Well what does this have to do with me?" Dorothy asked.

"You have been mentioned in the last little message they put in the paper. Apparently, they have quite a large following now," Quentin answered her. "A lot of this seems to be written by the same reporter. The son of the man that owns the newspaper in your city of Redwood." Now Dorothy knew the reason for Quentin's call.

"And you want me to go down there and read the newspaper reporter the riot act?" Dorothy spoke into the phone. "What makes you think they'll listen to me?"

"Good heavens no, Dorothy. I am just trying to warn you, and see if you can dig up any information on these do-gooder, burn-the-books crusaders. I am coming to Redwood myself day after tomorrow and I imagine it would be a good plan to get together and see if we can solve this problem without too many more delays for you and slander for me." Dorothy hesitated as she considered his proposal.

"How do we know if these do-gooder-book-burners wouldn't cause us more problems if we did have a meeting?" Dorothy asked.

"We don't, my dear. I just assume they will try and I would like to make sure they don't succeed in causing more problems for both of us. Two heads are better than one, as they say," Quentin's voice was low and firm. Obviously, he was not in a very good mood.

"Okay, Quentin. Give me the name of these people and I will try and check them out. Although, you usually know what's up before I do," Dorothy reached for a pen and paper. Maria had been listening and handed both to Dorothy.

"That's true, my dear. But these people are sneaky. So watch your back. They like to try and "convince" people to do their bidding by using something from their past against them."

"You mean they blackmail people?" Dorothy was horrified. Maria covered her mouth with both hands.

"Basically yes. They call it convincing people to do the right thing, morally."

"Yeah, right. Quentin, give me their names and I'll have a friend of mine see what he can come up with. Then when you get into Redwood, I should have something to give you by the way of information," Dorothy began writing and when she had finished, she looked up at Maria. "All right, Quentin. I'll talk to you when you get here."

"Thank you, Dorothy, I shall see you soon," Quentin hung up and Dorothy looked at the name of the group on the paper in front of her.

"What's wrong, dear?" Maria asked in a worried voice.

"I think I just found out who is trying to stop me from opening my bed and breakfast," Dorothy was fuming with anger.

"Who?" Maria asked.

"It's a group called the Puritans. They started in Toronto, apparently, and now they are here in Redwood. They basically persuade public opinion to turn against business people, by blocking their business licenses, liquor permits, restaurant licenses, etc. I ran into them in Toronto a couple of times and it seems they have followed me here to Redwood," Dorothy explained to Maria.

"Well, what do they want?" Maria's worried voice made Dorothy stand and go over to Maria to give her a hug.

"It's all right, Maria. If it's a fight they want, they've got one. I have some of the most wonderful people in my corner, right?" Maria pulled back and looked at Dorothy's face. There were little frown creases by the side of her eyes and Maria knew that meant she was worried too.

"You cannot fool me, Dorothy Marie Adams. I know you too well. You are worried too," Maria shook her finger in Dorothy's face.

"Yes I am, Maria. But I know something they don't know." Dorothy smiled.

"What?"

"I know that they've targeted me, and they don't know that I know."

"Huh?" It was Maria's turn to look confused. Dorothy reached out and hugged Maria again.

"Just to be on the safe side, perhaps I will tell Mother, and Matt, and the rest of the family. It's time to rally the troops! They may not be able to do anything, but they do have a right to know what's happening," Dorothy walked out of the kitchen and into her office with a purpose. She knew she was going to call her friend and former business partner Trevor in Toronto, and find out who the head of the Puritans was in Redwood. The more she knew, the better.

Maria stood staring at the swinging doors as they continued to move after Dorothy went through them.

A SILENT ENEMY

"*I think I saw a spark in those eyes,*" Maria nodded to herself. "*Whoever these people are, they are in for one big surprise. Dorothy Adams is a good girl and when she makes up her mind to fight for something, they had better watch out!*" Maria sat down and poured herself another cup of coffee. Sipping it slowly she smiled in satisfaction. "*This has made Dorothy want to fight! What a good girl!*"

CHAPTER NINE

Elva left Ethan's office and went back to her own desk. Picking up the map where she had plotted all the theft locations, she took out a pencil and drew a ring around all of them. In the center of that ring, there was a void. She knew from past experience, that thieves who are constantly looking for articles to steal and get away with it, did not steal in their comfort zone. Hard-core thieves, that is. Studying the map once more, and the list of articles, Elva had decided these thieves were probably just young kids stealing on a dare outside of their neighborhood, and did not know that Elva was on their trail.

"It's funny. The clothes are all of a small child's size, and the food that was stolen from the backyard gardens and fruit trees, are all easily edible without cooking. Hmmm," Elva said out loud to no one in particular.

"What clothes and what stolen food?" Tony had just come back from a lunch break and was going straight to his desk.

"Tony, look at this. Tell me if I am right. This list is a compilation of all the things that have been stolen in the back door community of the Loop. Always at night, and no one sees them. Am I wrong, or do you think this is the work of a bunch of young kids and not the idiots of a gang?" Elva offered the list up to Tony. Tony stopped and took the list and began reading it.

"Blankets, small shirts, a pair of pants, carrots, toys, potatoes, cherry tomatoes, more shirts, hey, even some socks! Sounds like your thieves are only stealing what they need to survive, Elva." Tony handed the list back to Elva. "What else have you got?" Tony asked.

"Well, here I have the map with each little star marked on it where items were taken," Elva passed the map to Tony.

"I see you have a diameter marked out here. Is that where you're going to start looking for the culprits?" Tony asked as he handed the map back to Elva.

"I thought I might," Elva said.

"Sounds like you know what you're doing, all right," Tony hitched his trousers up a little before he sat.

"Thanks Tony," Elva beamed at her nephew. If she wasn't sure before about what to do next, she sure was now. Grabbing her jacket from the hook beside her desk, she marked herself as out on the bulletin board. The new receptionist insisted on putting the board up so she could remember who was in and who was out. Elva thought it was a waste of time. If she couldn't remember who was where, why did she have the job? However, Ethan had okayed it as a good idea and Elva wasn't about to turn her promotion down. Dashing out the door she jumped into her car.

It didn't take very long to get to the neighborhood Elva needed. Parking in front of the first house, Elva went to the door and knocked. She was going to interview each person who had something stolen and make sure she had her facts right. The door opened to a young man in his teens and Elva could hear other family members in the house behind him.

"Can I help you?" The young man said politely. Elva had her uniform on and tried to sound professional when she showed her badge.

"I'm from the police department and I am investigating a rash of thefts in this neighborhood. I was wondering if I might be able to talk to your parents?" Elva asked.

"It's just my mom, so come on in. I'll call her for you." Elva stepped into the entrance and the boy closed the door behind her. "I'll be right back." The teenager left and suddenly a little boy about 8 years of age sprinted around the corner from a hallway and stopped short in surprise at the sight of Elva.

"Wow! Are you a real police officer?" He asked as his mother came around the same corner.

"Yes I am," Elva answered. Seeing the boy Elva realized he must be the boy who lost his shirt a while ago.

"Hello. I'm his mother." A fair haired petite lady held out her hand to Elva. Elva introduced herself and they shook hands. Taking out her note book, Elva declined the invitation to sit in the living room.

"I just want to ask a few questions then I will be on my way," Elva assured the lady.

"Oh, of course. Ask away," the lady answered.

"The items that you lost the other day, did they belong to your youngest son?" Elva asked.

"Yes, they belonged to Devlin," The woman nodded her head.

"Where were they when they were taken?" Elva asked another question.

"They had been hung on the clothesline overnight to dry. I prefer to air dry my clothes when I can. I was going to bring them in when I noticed they weren't there. They were on the end closest to the steps up to the platform for my clothesline." Elva nodded her head as the lady talked. She took notes, and by the time she was ready to leave, she knew she had been right. The thief wasn't much older than the eight year old Devlin who lived in the house.

"Could the thief have been someone who knew Devlin and had an ax to grind?" The other woman shook her head.

"Devlin doesn't have enemies. He's only eight years old. I have no idea who would steal his shirts, but just yesterday I was drying Devlin's favorite jean jacket and this morning it came up missing as well."

"Are you going to find my favorite jacket?" Devlin spoke up from behind his mother's legs.

"I'm definitely going to try," Elva answered him. As soon as Elva got a description of the new article of clothing that had gone missing, she went back out to her car. Plotting her course of action, she drove to the little wooded park that had the picnic tables, playground equipment, and a bath house for public use. Not far from the public washroom building was a small utility shed that housed some of the electrical and plumbing. It was only about thirty feet away from the bath house, but Elva also knew it was heated. If anybody was living in the park without detection, they would need to be invisible but warm. She remembered when the city had decided to leave the little public bath house open instead of tearing it down. The plumbing shed was renovated so the heating was more efficient. Now she walked slowly and as quietly as possible to the door of the little shed. The lock on the front of the door had been smashed with some sort of object. Reaching out to turn the handle of the door, Elva readied herself. Hand on her holster, ready to draw her weapon, she pulled the door open on rusty hinges. The noise startled the birds in the bushes beside the shed and Elva jumped and glanced up. All of a sudden there was an explosion of motion from inside the shed as two little brown bodies flew out through the open door and past Elva, fleeing down the path. Elva gave chase.

"Freeze you two. I said stop! I have a gun!" Elva caught up to the smallest and the slowest while another man stepped in front of the larger one and held onto him while Elva managed to wrestle the first one into submission.

"Whoa! Hold still you wiggly little worm. Nobody is going to hurt you," Elva tried to make herself understood but the little body in her grasp wasn't listening. The park manager who had caught the first guy was finally getting him under control when the boy started yelling in Spanish.

"Okay, stop! I won't hurt you!" She called out in Spanish to the two scared little boys. Almost immediately the wiggling stopped and the tears began. Elva stared at the two boys of Spanish heritage with dirt on their faces, bare feet, and tears streaming down their faces.

"Whew! You two are fast," She said in Spanish, trying to establish a connection of trust with the two boys.

"Yes. We are very fast!" The oldest one nodded with bravado. He reached out for his younger brother who wouldn't quit crying and Elva let him go. The oldest couldn't have been more than 8 years old and the younger one looked to be around five. Both looked very gaunt and tired, with dirt all over their little bodies. The oldest one wore only the jean jacket for a shirt and the pull up shorts taken from the clothesline. They youngest boy wore pants that were too big for him and the legs were rolled up past his ankles. A very large, filthy white t-shirt hung on his frame. Both boys had small round scars on several parts of their body that Elva could see.

Gasping in horror and outrage, Elva reached for the littlest one who shrank back in horror. The man who had helped to scoop up the oldest one couldn't believe his eyes either.

"Miss Elva, those are cigarette burns!" The manager helped to quiet the little one and Elva reached for his hand slowly. She spoke to the two frightened boys in Spanish and gently turned the boy's hand over, pushing the sleeve up above his shoulder.

"Oh my gosh!" Elva blurted. Scores of what could only be cigarette burns covered the arms of both boys, and continued down their backs.

Quickly, Elva removed her jacket and placed it over the youngest boy's shoulders and picked him up into her arms. The man standing guard over the oldest boy did likewise. The two boys went without a fight.

"Elmer, bring that little guy with you and we will put them in the back seat of my SUV. I need to take these little guys to the hospital." Elmer nodded his compliance and Elva noted the look of horror in Elmer's eyes. Elmer and Elva made sure the two boys were strapped into seat belts and covered with the jackets to keep warm. Looking up to Elmer for the last time that day, Elva asked him to leave the crime scene the way it was and she would have someone come down from the office and go through it. Elmer nodded and backed away as Elva drove away.

"Poor little jiggers," Elmer took of his ball cap and scratched the back of his head with the same hand. "Whoever done that to them should have their nuts cut out!" Shaking his head, the resident manager of the RV Park turned and made his way back to the office.

CHAPTER TEN

"Hello?" Dorothy could hear Trevor's voice had a hollow sound to it.

"Is that worry you have in your voice or are you on a satellite phone?" Dorothy asked her former business partner.

"Hey, Dorothy! Glad to hear your voice. I'm on satellite, yes. Are you coming back to work for me?" Trevor asked in jest.

"No chance, Trevor. But I do have a favor to ask." Dorothy's voice had become coy and inviting.

"I know that voice! Same old Dorothy. What's the favor?" Trevor asked with a laugh.

"Apparently there are some people in Toronto called the Puritans, giving some business people a bad time. What do you know about them?" Dorothy asked.

"Whoa!" Trevor answered. "These are bad people to fool around with. Very hard core. Tick them off, and show your ethics are the least little bit sketchy, and you're on their black list," Trevor drew a breath. "Why do you ask?"

"Remember the real estate guy, Quentin Tallas?" Dorothy asked.

"Yeah. He would definitely be on their hit list," Trevor answered.

"What do you mean "hit list?" Dorothy asked.

"I mean, once you make it to the black list, you are slowly and systematically eradicated in the business world. These people convince contractors, lawyers, and political affiliates to shun the people on the black list. It's either done legally, or by blackmail. I know of several businesses who have told them to go to hell and they ended up going out of business because the Puritans slowly destroyed their client list. One by one," Trevor answered. Dorothy was silent for a moment.

"How do they decide which person is on the list?" Dorothy asked.

"Usually the leaders of the group get together and have a meeting where they go over all the business people who have turned them down or made disparaging remarks towards them. The police here in Toronto are powerless to stop them because no one will testify against them," Trevor answered. "By the way, why are you asking?"

"Unfortunately there seems to be a group of these Puritans operating in Redwood, or so says Quentin Tallas," There was a long pause on Trevor's end of the line.

"Okay, I gather you need help in finding information on the Puritans!" Trevor hesitated again. "You do know that if we take them on and lose, we lose everything." Trevor's voice had become quiet but very deadly.

"I do, Trevor. But I can only be pushed so far. Tallas is coming to Redwood and we are going to need as much help as we can." Dorothy answered firmly.

"I think I need not worry about you, my dear, but for the Puritans. I just heard your fighting voice for the first time in a long time," Trevor's voice was now light. "And if there is nothing I like more than a fight it's a bigger fight." The excitement was evident in his voice.

"Let me get this little problem dealt with here, and I will be on the next plane to Redwood," Trevor almost chortled into the phone.

"No, really, Trevor, I think we can handle it on our own. We need you for the information," Dorothy protested.

"You need me there to help you strategize. These people are virtually untouchable in certain circles. I've dealt with them before. I can be more help if I'm there beside you," Trevor waited for Dorothy's answer as she digested Trevor's statement.

Dorothy took a deep breath and held it as she thought over Trevor's offer. Trevor and Dorothy had been slightly more than 'partners' when she was in Toronto, but they had parted as tried and true friends when they had both realized it wouldn't work. This weighed heavily on Dorothy's mind as she finally gave in.

"Okay, Trevor, on one condition. Hands off." Dorothy knew Trevor would understand. She had already told him of her personal situation when she had first come back to Redwood. Ethan's face swam before her eyes and she closed them. "I have a new man in my life now." She swallowed. Trevor would be a big help and she knew she could trust him.

"I know that, Dorothy. I've known almost from the first. So don't worry. I will be there strictly as a friend and former partner, okay?" Trevor asked.

"Okay, then you should get here the same time Tallas gets here," Dorothy answered with relief.

"On the next plane, boss," Trevor smiled into the phone. He hung up and placed the phone back in his lapel pocket. Glancing around he found the target he was looking for, and reached for the gun at his hip.

"*Safety first*," he said to himself as his target got closer. Reaching out with his right leg, he quickly hooked the left leg of his target and tripped him so he was on his face. Pouncing on top of him and swinging his arm behind his back while the man was still struggling on his face, Trevor slipped the cuffs on him. Reaching out for the duffle bag with the one million dollars of currency in it, he handed it to the cop who came running up behind him. Standing upright, Trevor wiped his hand across his brow.

"There you go, Sergeant. One bad guy down," Trevor shook hands with the man in uniform holding the duffle bag and turned to leave.

"Where do you think you're going?" The sergeant called out. "I need your statement!"

"I'll fax it to you. I'm on another case," Trevor answered as he climbed into his SUV and drove off in a cloud of dust.

The sergeant shook his head and handed the duffle bag to another officer.

"Where's he going?" the officer asked.

"He's got another case. Silly bugger said he would fax us his statement," the Sergeant answered.

"The DA ain't gonna like it," the officer voiced his opinion.

"The DA doesn't have to like it, but he will let it slide. He got the criminal and he's going to jail. Enough said now let's go." The two officers turned back to their vehicles, and Trevor was already half way to the airport.

CHAPTER ELEVEN

Dorothy hung up and clapped her hands together. Now she was definitely going to the newspaper office and asking to talk to the editor. She wanted him to know that she knew he was purposely twisting everything that happened lately in her life into a horrible view of an incompetent and immoral woman. Dorothy was going to correct that. Maria came into the office to ask Dorothy if she wanted more coffee.

"No, Maria. But please, sit down for a moment," Dorothy motioned to the chair on the other side of the desk.

"Uh oh!" Maria sat. "I'm not going to like this, am I?" Maria asked.

"Probably not. But please let me tell you everything I have to say before you react," Dorothy asked.

"Do I need coffee for this bad news?" Maria asked. Dorothy shook her head with an odd look.

"Cooking sherry?" Maria squeaked.

"Maybe," Dorothy nodded. Maria left her seat and charged into the kitchen and found the cooking sherry. Racing back to the office she poured one for Dorothy and one for herself. Maria raised her eyebrows and stood poised with the glass at half-mast, waiting for Dorothy to say something. Dorothy shook her head.

"Have you ever heard of the Puritans?" Dorothy asked Maria tentatively.

Maria's eyes went wide and she tossed the shot glass contents to the back of her throat. Sputtering and choking, she refilled her glass and took a deep breath.

"I've heard of them. They don't sound too bad," Maria responded.

"They are the ones behind all my setbacks and problems right now with the bed and breakfast," Dorothy explained.

"Why, you've done nothing wrong," Maria tossed back another one.

"Apparently, they think I have. I am an immoral person in their minds and I guess I have been targeted. Now Quentin Tallas has volunteered to come out from Toronto, and my ex business partner Trevor is on his way as well." Dorothy's eyes went wide with alarm as Maria threw back a shot glass at the mention of Quentin Tallas.

"Maria, maybe you should take it easy on the cooking sherry," Dorothy smiled a little.

"Why? I like it, and it is afternoon," Maria swallowed another shot glass of sherry for emphasis.

"You know it always gives you a headache if you drink too much," Dorothy said and she reached for the bottle. "Besides, I need your help to get a couple of rooms ready for my guests."

"You mean they're going to stay here?" Maria squealed. "What about that nice guy, the man you're going to marry? Isn't he going to be upset that they are staying here at the bed and breakfast with you?" Maria gulped a final shot glass of sherry before she gave it up to Dorothy.

"That's why I am going to call Ethan and tell him. So he doesn't get mad. And besides, he hasn't asked me yet," Dorothy answered and placed the sherry bottle on the desk. She sat back down in her chair.

"So you want me to stay and cook, and chaperone?" Maria asked. The thought of making sure neither one of the men touched Dorothy gave Maria a pleasant feeling.

Dorothy saw the hopeful look in Maria's eyes and she smiled.

"Okay, if you would do that, I would be grateful." Dorothy figured it would be easier to get Maria to go along with her living arrangements for the two men if she let Maria stay as well.

"Okay, I'll do it!" Maria stood and smiled at Dorothy. Maria loved Dorothy as if she were her own daughter. "What do I do first?" She reached for the sherry bottle. Dorothy started writing a list of things that needed to be done and carefully moved the sherry bottle out of Maria's reach at the same time.

"Here's a list of things we will need for dinner this evening. Just get it put on my account. I'm sure the grocery store won't mind and I will be down later to pay for it. Then we need to get three rooms ready." Maria reached for the list of groceries and glanced at it.

"Okay." She turned to leave and on a second thought turned back to Dorothy. "What are you going to do?"

"I am going to call Ethan and see if I can talk to him in his office, and let him know we are expecting company," Dorothy answered.

"Are you going to tell him about Trevor being your former boyfriend?" Maria asked. Dorothy's head came up with a snap.

"How did you know about Trevor?" Dorothy asked in amazement.

"The way your eyes got big when you said his name," Maria shook her finger at Dorothy. "I am not a dumb bunny, you know." As Maria left the room she reached for the sherry bottle and was gone.

"No, no you're not," Dorothy said quietly to the retreating back. Maria never failed to amaze her. Maria wore simple cotton dresses, sensible shoes, and her hair was jet black with a sprinkle of silver. When Maria got excited or upset, her hair seemed to spring up in snarls and frizzy lumps, even when it was held back in a bun. Maria wasn't skinny, but she was plump. Maria described herself as "comfortable" with a capital C. Her dark skin and eyebrows combined with her long black hair told people that she was from Mexico. Specifically, Mexico City.

Smiling at the simply adorned but beautiful lady that had just left the room, Dorothy picked up the phone once more. She punched in the number for Ethan and waited for him to answer his cell phone. It went straight to voice mail.

"Oh well. I guess I'll just surprise him with our dinner guests this evening," Dorothy said out loud.

CHAPTER TWELVE

Ethan was still fuming when he drove up to the secure entrance to the jail. It opened like a garage door and he entered into the first of three cubicles. Each prisoner brought in by a unit was brought in to the jail via the secure entrance. They were taken in through a series of secure doors released by an officer on the other side of a bullet proof glass window. They were then taken in to a desk to be searched by a jail attendant who entered all the information given by the arresting officer into the computer. Another attendant searched the prisoner, uncuffed the prisoner, and put them into a pair of coveralls and rubber slippers. Then they were placed in a holding cell.

Getting out of the driver's side, he slammed his door and went around to let the prisoner out. The officer behind the window buzzed him in, and heard the string of filthy language that seemed to come non-stop from the mouth of the prisoner standing cuffed in front of him.

"Here are his papers, and I want him kept in his shackles. If he gets violent again, I don't want him causing any more problems," Ethan growled over the bad language coming from Brad.

"Do you want us to muzzle him as well?" The officer was furiously typing into the computer in front of him. At that question, Brad fell silent.

"Only if he starts in again. Otherwise, keep him separate from the rest of the general population," Ethan's tone of voice was deadly.

"Yes sir." Taking the papers, the attendant came around to the front of the desk and took Brad by the elbow. "Come on, Brad. If I were you, I would keep your lips sealed for quite a while." The attendant started to lead Brad away through another secure door into the main booking room of the jail. Ethan slipped through another secure door on the way to the elevator and ultimately his office.

Smashing the heel of his hand firmly against the door of the elevator after it closed, Ethan realized he needed to control his anger before the rest of his officers saw him. Straightening his uniform shirt, he emerged onto the main floor of the administrative wing and went straight to his office.

Closing the door, Ethan went over to his desk and sat carefully, as if he were afraid his anger would be unleashed unless he held tight control over his actions. He sat back and put his boots up on the corner of the desk and let out a long slow sigh.

"At least this evening will be a great ending to a horrible day," Ethan said out loud. A small smile showed up on his face as he envisioned the look on Dorothy's face when he finally asked her to marry him. He pictured the scene as very romantic and uplifting. There would be candles, as always, Dorothy's favorite dish of the month, and peace and quiet. "No muss, no fuss, just us," Ethan murmured. Just then the phone rang.

"No! How did they figure out I was here?" Ethan fumed as he answered the phone.

"Barns here," Ethan snapped into the phone.

"Yes, Chief, I have a message for you from a Dorothy Adams, and one from the newspaper editor. He wants to speak with you as soon as possible. It is about a story he did on Dorothy Adams." Came the voice of their new receptionist. Carolyn was a very good receptionist, and her voice was a virtual monotone. Ethan had never heard her raise her voice at anything. Sometimes he wondered if she was emotional about anything. Still, she was a professional.

"Okay, I will talk to Dorothy later, and the editor tomorrow morning," Ethan spoke into the handset.

"Very good, sir. Are you leaving again?" Roxanne asked.

"Of course! I have a dinner to go to." Ethan wondered what she would say about that.

"Very good sir. I will see you tomorrow morning." The phone went silent as Roxanne hung up and Ethan smiled with a little nod.

"I don't think she knows any other tone." Hanging up he unlocked the top drawer of his desk and reached for the little velvet lined jewelry box tucked into the corner.

"Time to take a big step in my life." An excited feeling came over Ethan as he envisioned coming home to Dorothy every evening instead

of an empty apartment. He would wrap his arms around her, hold her close, and whisper warm little love sayings and never let her go.

Shaking his head, Ethan stood and walked around his desk as he pocketed his little treasure. Making sure the coast was clear, he went out the back way and claimed his vehicle in the covered parking lot. Driving over to his apartment, he went in, scooped the letters of the day from the floor inside his door, and placed them in the basket on his desk in his home office. Straight to the bathroom and a shower, and he came out refreshed.

While Ethan was getting changed and ready for his date with Dorothy, he missed the blinking light on the answering machine beside where he laid the jewelry box. When he was finished, he went and collected the box, all the while he was whistling the same tune.

Ethan arrived at the Bed and Breakfast and the good mood he was in disappeared with a thump. There were two strange SUVs parked beside Dorothy's with a news crew from the local television station parked beside that. People were milling about, waiting for someone to come along so they could get a lead on a story, and when they saw Ethan, they charged his vehicle.

"Chief Barns, can you tell us why Quentin Tallas is here in Redwood?" One young red-headed female managed to get her microphone in through the rapidly closing window. Ethan's eyebrows raised in surprise and outwardly he appeared totally calm. Behind his mirrored sunglasses though, his eyes were sparking and a muscle along the bottom of his jaw line started to clench.

"*Tallas is in Redwood again, eh?*" Ethan lowered the window again so the reporter could get her microphone back. "*I wonder why Tallas is here and why Dorothy never told me,*" Ethan thought to himself. His thoughts went from happy to stormy in the space of a few seconds. Ethan sat and contemplated the situation until his cell rang. Reaching into his shirt pocket, he fished his phone out and looked at the caller ID. It was Dorothy.

"Hi there. I see we have some company," Ethan breathed his anger into the phone before Dorothy could say anything.

"Yes, they arrived about an hour ago. Did you get my text?" Dorothy felt Ethan's anger through the phone. Glancing at his phone again, Ethan saw that he had two messages, both from Dorothy.

"No. Not until just now," Ethan's anger didn't dissipate at all.

"I sent you the first one this morning, but you didn't answer, so by coffee break this afternoon I sent you another one," Dorothy held her breath. Ethan nodded and his other hand scratched the back of his head.

"Okay, so what does this mean?" Ethan was loathe to say too much because he didn't want the press to hear their conversation.

"Are you going to come in?" Dorothy couldn't understand Ethan's anger. Worse yet, she couldn't understand why it was directed at her for no reason. She had sent him notice on his cell, and it wasn't her fault he didn't look at it. Dorothy's chin began to set in that obstinate way she had when she began to get angry. The two men sitting across from the desk looking at her, began to smile. They knew exactly what was going through Ethan's mind. Looking at each other, the smiles grew.

"Is there any point in my coming in or is Tallas leaving any time soon?" Ethan's gruff voice began to be irritating to Dorothy.

"Of course there's a point. Quentin and Trevor have a very interesting story to tell and I think you should be in on it," Dorothy almost barked into the phone.

"So it's Quentin now, is it?" Ethan barked right back.

Yes, Quentin AND Trevor," Dorothy's voice was beginning to rise to match Ethan's. There was a pause on the other end of the line and Ethan's voice came back in a surprised tone of voice.

"Quentin and Trevor?"

"Yes, Quentin and Trevor," Dorothy's voice lowered a notch. "Now will you come in? Maria has dinner ready and it's going to get cold," Dorothy almost slammed the phone down on the desk.

"Gentlemen, if you will follow me I will show you to the dining table and then meet Ethan at the door." Dorothy rose and walked around the desk to lead the men out to the dining area. Just as they arrived there together, Ethan came bursting through the door and had to push his weight against it to close it. Dorothy went racing over to help while the other two men stood and watched the little drama with grins still glued to their faces.

"Where did these people come from?" Ethan strained to get the locks set so they could stop pushing.

"They came with Quentin and haven't left. I hope they leave soon," Dorothy explained. Turning towards the dining table and the wonderful smells coming from the kitchen, Ethan spotted the two men. Curious as to who Trevor was, and what he and Tallas were up to made Ethan move towards them.

"Ethan Barns, Chief of Police," Ethan extended his right hand in offering.

"I'm Trevor Wright." Both men shook and Ethan turned to Tallas. "I know you. Now what in the hell are you doing here?" Ethan asked Tallas. Just then, the swinging doors to the kitchen admitted a beaming Maria with her famous pot roast, potatoes and vegetables on a platter. Ethan's attention was diverted by the smell of that heavenly aroma.

"Maria, let me help you dear," Ethan moved to take the platter from Maria and she smiled her appreciation.

"Why thank you, Ethan," Maria patted him on the shoulder and sent a scathing glance at the other two men. "At least *you're* a gentleman." Both men lowered their eyes as if they had been chastised by their own mother.

"You sit down and I will be right back with the wine," Maria smiled at Ethan. Ethan placed the platter in the middle of the table that was set with five plates. There were wine glasses at each setting and Ethan was surprised. Dorothy never usually had wine with her dinner.

All four sat across from each other and waited Maria's return. Dorothy sat beside Ethan, and across the table, Trevor sat beside the polished Quentin.

"I was just wondering who the fifth person is going to be at the table?" Quentin tried to ask politely. There was a loud crash from the kitchen at that very moment. Maria's loud voice shrieked and then she started to laugh.

"It's okay, it's okay!" Maria called from the kitchen. "I'm okay."

The swinging doors opened once more and Maria came to the table with the wine cooler with a bottle opened inside it. Quentin's eyes met Maria's with surprise as she put it down beside Ethan.

"What happened to the wine I brought?" Quentin asked in a quiet voice.

"Well, I'm sure you probably heard, there was a little accident in the kitchen." Maria looked at Ethan and placed a kiss on his cheek. He smiled at her. Trevor and Dorothy had a hard time to keep from laughing.

"That was a $5000 dollar bottle of wine!" Quentin almost shouted as he half raised to his feet. Trevor reached out and grabbed his hand and motioned for him to sit back down.

"Really? Well this is a $15 bottle of wine and I'm sure it tastes just as good as the other one." Maria went to the vacant place at the table and sat. Tallas's eyes almost popped out of his head.

"Do you plan to join us for the meal as well?" he blurted.

"Why?" Maria asked with her sweet little smirk. "Aren't you good enough to eat with me?" At that moment, Dorothy, Ethan and Trevor started laughing and couldn't stop. Quentin looked at Dorothy in confusion.

"But she's the help," Quentin said.

"And you're the uninvited guest, but you don't hear me complaining." Maria's head perched on the top of her neck like she was daring mega millionaire Quentin Tallas to say anything else. Quentin just sat and swallowed. Dorothy reached over to hold Maria's hand.

"Thank you, Maria. Dinner looks delicious." Dorothy said to Maria. Turning to Quentin she smiled with tears in her eyes. "Quentin Tallas, this is Maria Gonzalez. She is a member of our family, as well as an excellent cook." The redness started to leave Quentin's face and he began to smile a rueful little smile.

"I am sorry if I insulted you, Ms. Gonzalez. Please forgive me. The shock of finding out the loss of my expensive wine addled my mind for a moment." Quentin picked up his fork and reached to the platter in front of him.

"No!" Maria's sharp rebuke called out to him and stopped his reaching for the platter.

"What?" he yelled in surprise.

"In this house, we say grace before our meals." Maria's stare was deadly and definitely unfriendly as she reached for the hands of the people on both sides of her. With an imperious nod at Dorothy and Ethan, everyone joined hands as Maria said grace.

"Amen," Four people chorused when Maria finished.

"Thank you, Maria. That was wonderful," Dorothy thanked Maria and reached for her glass. "Ethan, would you please pour me a glass of wine?"

CHAPTER THIRTEEN

Dinner was somewhat tense for awhile as topics were brought up and quickly dismissed. All of the diners were preoccupied with their own thoughts.

Dorothy was wondering if the night would ever end. *"I know this isn't the dinner Ethan wanted, but I didn't have a choice. And it's not like I didn't let him know."*

Ethan was wondering if he had possibly made a mistake about proposing to Dorothy as he glared at the other two men at the table. *"I wonder why they didn't stay someplace else instead of here."*

Quentin ate slowly and contemplated that he maybe should have made a reservation at one of his own hotels in Redwood. *"I wonder what is exactly going on between the Chief and Dorothy. Maybe that's why that fiery little Mexican woman keeps glaring at me with those daggers in her eyes."*

Trevor was slowly chewing his food and knew that someone had to break through the ice surrounding the people at the table. *"I know Dorothy has feelings for this big jerk sitting beside her, but why did she want Quentin and me staying at her place instead of somewhere else?"*

Maria, of course, was happily chowing down in her own delicate way, while sipping her way through a second bottle of house wine. *"That's my girl! Keep them guessing. But I think Dorothy should have told Ethan in person instead of sending a message to that stupid phone these young kids use all the time. And that Tallas guy, oh if I had my frying pan handy, what I wouldn't do to him!"*

Finally, when Trevor could stand it no longer, he stood up and proposed a toast.

"Ladies and gentlemen!" He raised his half full glass. "I would like to say that this is not the liveliest dinner table I have been at before, but it is the most sombre one. We need to get some things straightened out here." He turned to Maria. "Thank you for this lovely meal and the wonderful wine." A choking sound was heard from Quentin beside him. Trevor turned to Dorothy across from him. "And to our wonderful hostess, who should have really let us stay at one of Quentin's hotels." A choke sounded from Ethan across the table from Quentin. "And to Quentin Tallas, my fellow guest here, who is going to fund the quest to bring these Puritan buggers to justice." There was another choking sound from Quentin. Trevor downed the remainder of the wine in his glass, as did the others. Maria reached for the bottle and shook it to see how much was left.

"Oh dear. It's all gone. Let me get another one," Maria wobbled as she stood up and then giggled a little. All the men around the table rose as one as Maria tried to walk away from the table in a dignified manner.

"Ahh, excuse me, my fine lady." Quentin went to her side. "Allow me to assist you."

"I don't need your help Mr. Tallas. I can do this all by myself. I may be an immigrant from Mexico, but I am not ignorant, nor am I incapable." Maria raised her shoulders and set them with pride as she took a step forward.

"I did not think you were, my dear. I think you have put me in my place quite eloquently, though. My only desire is to make sure you are able to enjoy the rest of the evening with us. May I escort you to the wine cellar?" Quentin offered his arm for support and Maria sniffed.

"There you go, putting on airs again. We do not have a wine cellar. Just a wine cupboard in the kitchen." Maria latched onto Quentin's arm as they walked through the swinging doors into the kitchen. Trevor, Dorothy, and Ethan were still laughing long after the doors stopped moving.

"I think your little speech came through loud and clear, Trevor. Thank you," Dorothy said with a smile. Reaching out with her hand she touched Ethan's which lay next to hers on the table. "I'm sorry. I should have made sure you heard it from me in person. I didn't realize you had such a rough day."

Ethan blinked then swallowed over the lump in his throat.

"I guess I shouldn't have come on so strong with you over the reporters and these two guys. I feel a little ashamed of myself," Ethan enfolded her hand in his and squeezed to show his understanding.

Trevor began to smile as he realized how important this relationship was to Dorothy.

"*Well I'll be. She finally bit the bullet. I wonder if she even knows.*" Clearing his throat, Trevor stood again.

"If you guys will excuse me, I will go and find Quentin and Maria in the kitchen. You two need to be alone," Trevor turned to leave.

"But what about the talk we were all going to have?" Dorothy objected. Ethan started to eye her with suspicion again. "You know, our brainstorming session about the Puritans."

Trevor continued to walk through the doors into the kitchen and was gone. Ethan turned to Dorothy and smiled. He understood Dorothy's motives for having the two men stay at the Bed and Breakfast. A wave of relief washed over him. Then a wave of guilt washed through him. He knew then, that he should have trusted Dorothy more.

"Dorothy, I have something I would like to talk to you about," Ethan reached out and touched Dorothy's finely featured face and caressed her jawline with his thumb. "It's really quite important."

Uhhh...," Dorothy swallowed. "Okay. What would you like to talk about?" She asked in a nervous little voice as she turned to look into Ethan's eyes. Dorothy saw it there. The love, the tenderness, the faith, and the trust. Mostly the love. She wasn't afraid anymore because she knew Ethan was the right man.

"I bought this a while ago and wanted to ask you, but I could never find the right time," His hand came out of his pocket bearing a velvet ring box tied with a red ribbon. "And today, I realized, there is never a right time. So I am going to do it now," Ethan lowered himself onto his right knee beside Dorothy and held the box up to her with his heart in his eyes.

"Dorothy Adams, I would like to marry you. I want to grow old with you, dream with you, and build wonderful things with you. I never want to lose sight of you for the rest of my life. And if you will have me, you would make me the happiest man ever," Ethan held his breath and waited. Dorothy's eyes filled with tears as she reached out and took the box. Opening it, she saw a wonderful ring nestled inside.

"Oh Ethan, it's beautiful," Dorothy put her hand up to her mouth in an effort to stop herself from crying with joy but it didn't work. The tears began to fall.

"Is that a yes?" Ethan asked with joy.

"That's a yes," Dorothy nodded. The sound of a loud cheer came from the direction of the kitchen but went unnoticed as Ethan swept Dorothy up in his arms in a crushing embrace and kissed her lips tenderly. Holding her face in his so tenderly, he tried to catch his breath.

"That day at the Johnston farm, I almost went crazy with fear over losing you like that. Then I realized, I hadn't even gotten up the courage to ask you to marry me." His lips caressed hers once more then travelled down her jawline to the nape of her neck. "I don't ever want to have that feeling again," Ethan murmured into her neck as his hands started to wander.

"The ring! Don't forget the ring!" Came Maria's voice from the kitchen.

"Ssshhh!" came from both Quentin and Trevor at the same time.

"Ethan, I think we should take this conversation upstairs," Dorothy whispered through her laughter and her tears. Ethan stepped back but did not release Dorothy.

"Maria, Quentin, Trevor, will you quit hiding behind that door and come out here?" Ethan called. All three of the eavesdroppers came out with sheepish looks on their faces. Maria was supported on both sides by the two men. She also had a bottle of wine in each hand.

"Oh Maria! Two bottles of wine?" Dorothy admonished.

"Never have you minded me!" Maria slurred her words and pointed to the ring box Dorothy still held in her hand. "You put that ring on her finger before you take advantage of her!" Maria looked at Ethan.

"Quite right, Ethan old boy," Trevor grinned at him. Ethan looked at Quentin and saw a similar grin. Turning back to Dorothy, he saw nothing but love.

Ethan took the little box carefully and removed the ring. Placing it on Dorothy's finger, he once more kissed Dorothy on the lips very tenderly. The other three cheered again, and Maria popped the cork on the champagne in her right hand.

"Let's celebrate!" Maria called out to the others and began to pour. Trevor helped her to aim properly at the glasses and Quentin shook hands with Ethan once he let go of Dorothy.

"Listen, you two. I'm sorry my presence dampened your plans, I am going to take Trevor here, and we will go to one of my penthouse rooms at the Inn."

"Thank you, Quentin," Dorothy still had tears in her eyes. Maria handed out a full glass to each of the people in the group. Raising hers high in the air, she grinned again.

"I knew the two of you were right for each other the moment you met," Maria giggled then tossed back the full glass.

"Come my dear lady, I think we should go to the penthouse suite, the three of us, and relax with a hot tub, and silk sheets for the evening. These two need some privacy." Quentin took the now empty glass from Maria without a fuss. Nodding, Maria allowed Trevor and Quentin to lead her towards the front door. "You will lock up behind us, won't you, Ethan?"

"Of course, Quentin," Ethan answered in a rueful tone of voice and looked down at Dorothy and smiled.

"Good night Maria!" Dorothy called out.

"G'night dear. Sleep tight!" Maria called. Then they were gone and Ethan left Dorothy's side long enough to lock the door. Back at her side, Dorothy couldn't help laughing at Maria.

"Do you think she'll have a hangover in the morning? I've never seen her so blitzed before."

"Let's not worry about her right now. Tomorrow will be soon enough," Ethan swept Dorothy up into his arms and started up the stairs.

"Who's going to do the dishes?" Dorothy asked with laughter.

"I will. Starting tomorrow," Ethan said with confidence. The both of them were wrapped around each other by the time they reached the top of the stairs. The lights went out, and the two of them made their way to Dorothy's room in the dark.

"Oh Ethan, I love you," Dorothy murmured as she lay beside him.

"I love you too," Ethan answered.

Outside, Quentin sat behind the wheel while Trevor helped Maria into the back seat of the shiny black SUV. All the reporters had disappeared and all was quiet. Quentin pulled his phone out and started to talk into it. Finished with his conversation, he turned to Trevor who was just getting into the passenger side in the front.

"We have the penthouse suite at the Inn. That okay with you?"

"Sounds good to me," Trevor answered with a smile.

Before Quentin started the engine and drove off, he shook his head.

"I didn't know Ethan was going to ask her to marry him. If I had, I would have done this sooner."

"That's okay. I came here with the intent of helping her, and possibly winning her hand in the process," Trevor said. Quentin's head shot up to look at Trevor.

"Well I think I could have given you a run for your money, dear boy!" Quentin's smirk was obnoxious to Trevor.

"No way. You're not her type!" Both men laughed as the SUV pulled out of the lot. Maria was happily whistling the wedding song from the back seat.

CHAPTER FOURTEEN

Elva took the two little boys to the local community hospital. The youngest one began to cry and held onto the oldest with both arms. Parking at the entrance to the emergency doors, Elva got out and went around to the back passenger door.

"Okay, you two," she said in Spanish, "You have to come in here to this place and let the nice people examine you to make sure your health is good," Elva explained in Spanish again. "Do you understand English?" she asked the older boy. He nodded and looked down.

"My brother, not so good," He said in a muffled voice.

"That's okay, we won't separate you two." Elva reached for the smallest one and he pulled back. The older boy translated Elva's words and took his brother by the hand. Jumping down from the back seat, the older boy turned and held his arms out for the youngest one. He just stared at Elva and his tears started to run down his cheeks. It broke Elva's heart to see the tears on that young boy's face where there should have been laughter and smiles at his young age. Bending down so that she was on the same eye level as the youngest child, Elva spoke slowly and confidently.

"I promise, no one will ever hurt you again. I will stay with you until we can find someone to take care of you." Elva's eyes began to water with tears as she once more held out her arms to the little boy. He was smelly, dirty, his ribs were sticking out, and his tears left a trail down his little cheeks. Elva wanted to reach out and grab him to hold him close and never let go, as if her promise and her love could erase the hurts that were showered down upon this boy. That little gesture won her a little bit of trust as the young boy held out his arms in turn. Scooping him up, Elva closed the door and turned to hold out her hand to the other boy. Together they walked in the hospital door as it noiselessly slid open. The nurses took one look at Elva as she walked in with the two boys. Speechless, they stood stunned.

"I think these two brave young men need to be taken a look at, and then cleaned up. Can you ladies help me out?" Elva's question seemed to mobilize everyone into action. One nurse turned to the computer to start typing in some information, another went into a curtained cubicle to get it ready for the boy's examination.

"Over here, Elva," The floor nurse called to her. "Do you want both of them on the same gurney?" Elva nodded and carefully placed the five year old on the gurney. He clung to her and held tighter until Elva explained she would be right there with him until he told her to go. After that, things went a little smoother.

Nurse number two came into the cubicle and started asking Elva some questions but Elva saw she was bothering the children.

"I'll come out and answer your questions soon, Gerda. I think we need to get these children settled first." The nurse nodded and left quietly. The first nurse had her stethoscope out and was looking at the older boy's chest first. She flinched when she was the cigarette burns all over most of his back. Elva let the nurse continue to work. First, she would check the older boy's heartbeat, then the youngest boy's. She checked the older boy's eyes, then the younger boy's. This went on until both boys had been thoroughly examined.

"Okay, boys, I am going to take you two into a little room with a big tub. I'll put bubbles in the water if you two will take a bath for me."

"Nancy," Elva tapped her on the shoulder. "Maybe we should wait until they have been examined by the doctor."

"Oh I think we'll be okay, Elva. We're buddies by now, aren't we?" Nancy smiled at the boys. Both of them nodded at once. Elva stepped back and watch Nancy work her magic as she escorted the two little brown bodies into the room where they kept the tub. Gerda caught Elva's attention as she followed Nancy down the hall. Going over to the desk, Elva was handed a large clipboard with some forms to fill out.

"I gather they're runaways?" Gerda asked.

"I don't know, actually. I found them as the result of a minor theft ring investigation. Scared the bats out of my belfry when they came charging at me from inside that little pump house." Elva exclaimed. While Elva filled out the forms, she informed Gerda of the events leading up to their arrival at the hospital.

"And that is how I came to bring them here. Where they came from, I have no idea," Elva finished the forms and her story at the same time.

"Well don't you worry, we sent for Doctor Beans. He's the best children's doctor we have," Gerda smiled with her answer.

"Does he speak Spanish?" Elva asked with some trepidation. "The little one doesn't speak much English and the older boy has to translate for him."

"I have no idea. But Nancy does, and she is handling the two of them quite well as you can hear," Gerda referred to the happy little screams of laughter coming from the room with the tub. "How much do you want to bet those two boys haven't had that much fun since the day they were born?" Gerda took the forms from Elva and began to process them.

Elva took that opportunity to call into the office and let them know where she was. She moved the truck from the emergency entrance and notified the security detail where she had parked. Just before she walked back into the emergency wing of the hospital, her cell rang.

"Elva here," She answered.

"Elva, Tony here," came the voice of her nephew.

"What's up?" Elva asked.

"Those two boys have not been reported missing, but I remembered when I first joined the force about six months ago, there was a foster family that was busted for having several unexplained children at their residence," Tony informed Elva.

"Okay, so what does that have to do with these two?" Elva asked. "They can barely speak English." Elva said.

"That's just it," Tony explained. "The extra children were all of Spanish heritage. And one of the older children said there were two missing when we scooped them all up." Elva's heart began to beat a little faster. If the children she had here were the missing ones, then she knew she was sitting on a powder keg about to explode.

"If these boys are who you think they are, the DA will want to question them about the leaders of the human trafficking ring. Those dudes are bad news." Something occurred to Elva all of a sudden. "Wait a minute, some of those cigarette burns look too recent to have been made six months ago." Elva tried to think of some rational explanation. "If these are the "Pablo Ring" boys that went missing, either they have been at large for over six months, or someone has been holding onto them and they got away." Tony could be heard typing away into his computer at the other end of the phone.

"Right. And someone will be looking for them either way," Tony's voice became urgent. "I want to send a squad car over there immediately before anyone becomes aware of who we have here," Elva nodded.

"Send it over but send it silent." Elva directed Tony. "I don't want anyone knowing they're here just yet. Tell the Chief what it is we think we have and get back to me as soon as possible." Elva ended the call and turned just as two shiny clean little boys came out of the room with Nancy dressed in boys pajamas that fit them perfectly.

Back up on the gurney, the two boys were laughing with Nancy as she tried to take their blood pressure. They weren't protesting just pretending to. Elva walked into the cubicle and closed the curtain.

"Nancy, do you think these two boys would like some ice cream?" Elva asked with a big smile on her face. Two little heads nodded their answers and Nancy went to find some ice cream. Elva walked up to the oldest boy and smiled.

"Do you feel like talking now?" Elva's urgency seemed to convey itself to the two little boys and the youngest clung to the older one. "I just want to find out what your names are," Elva tried to sound nice and cheery.

The oldest boy looked down at his younger companion then looked back at Elva.

"If I tell you, you'll send us back to the farm where we were," The boy's voice was low and panicked.

"No I won't. I won't ever let you go to that place again. I am here to protect you so you don't ever get hurt again," Elva leaned a little closer. "Can you please tell me just your names?" Elva pleaded to the little man.

"I am Juan, and I don't know his name. Either does he. I just call him brother." Juan sat straight and tall with his arm around the younger boy, showing the entire world that he was there to protect the younger boy at whatever cost.

"Thank you Juan. Look, here's Nurse Nancy with the ice cream," Elva straightened as Nancy came in with a tray filled with foods the boys would love to eat.

"I'm just going to be outside by that desk over there, Juan. I won't be far, okay?" Elva said. Juan nodded and accepted a huge bowl filled three different kinds of ice cream.

Outside the cubicle, Elva closed the curtain and almost staggered over to the nurse's desk. The minute she heard the names Juan and Brother, she had felt an icy fear trace down her back. Feeling a little nauseous and excited at the same time, she knew without a doubt that the two little boys were the ones that had gotten away six months ago. Not only was the DA looking for them, but the entire police force had been looking for them. Elva knew the Pablo Boys trafficking ring didn't just traffic in drugs, they trafficked in human beings. The most expensive ones were the little boys and girls. They would scoop them up in Mexico before the parents had a chance to find them missing, and transport them here in Redwood somehow before placing them in homes of immigrants who were blackmailed into caring for them until a permanent use could be found for them. The leaders of the ring had been arrested and charged, and were being held without bail pending their trial, but one of the young abductees had told a tale of two of them being missing. The search had covered the entire Province but nothing could be found. The RCMP even became involved. Several foster families were busted because of their willingness to hold onto some of these abducted children.

As the case against the human traffickers stood, they were about to go to trial, but the DA wasn't sure if they still had a slam dunk or not. They needed more eye witness testimony against the Pablo boys and the foster families, so finding the two missing boys would certainly help the DA.

The Pablo Boys needed to make sure those two little boys never saw the light of day, and they would certainly be after them. Ethan would not like the way the events are turning out. Elva being the one who found the two boys would be like a punch in the nose to the RCMP but Elva knew she didn't care about that. The two boys and their safety were all that mattered to her.

"Tony, this is Elva. I want those two squad cars here on the double," Elva barked into the phone.

"Elva, I sent one, are you sure you want another one?" Tony queried. "You know how Ethan hates us working overtime."

"Just do it. And find Ethan! Now!" Elva snapped into the phone.

CHAPTER FIFTEEN

The reporter with the camera waited in the bushes at the side of the Bed and Breakfast until Quentin and Trevor left with Maria in the back seat. The lights in the entire downstairs went out and he waited a while longer to make sure the remaining two subjects were upstairs. Creeping up to the window he had been trying to look through earlier, he saw a table in the middle of a large dining room full of dirty plates and half eaten meals. There were half full wine goblets scattered throughout the mess, and the door to the kitchen had been propped open, but the reporter was unable to see. He took several pictures with a special lense, and then circled back around the front porch to peer inside the window of the kitchen. There was a bottle of wine smashed in the corner, drawers were open all over the place, and the remnants of a large meal on the counter had not yet been put away. The reporter grinned at his luck. Taking more pictures with the special lens, he started to chuckle. When he was handed the assignment this morning after his boss had found out Quentin Tallas was going to be in town, he knew he was going to have a streak of good luck.

Backing away from the windows, he circled around to the back porch off the French windows leading into some kind of office. Luckily the owner of the establishment had not locked the door properly or he never would have been able to gain entry. As silently as he possibly could, he went over to the desk and started taking pictures of the documents left in neat little piles on top of the desk.

Upstairs, Ethan paused in his efforts to placate a willing and vivacious Dorothy, and he raised his head to look at the closed door of the bedroom.

"Ethan, what's wrong?" Dorothy raised herself up on her elbows with a frown on her face. "What is it?" she asked in a whisper.

"There's someone downstairs," Ethan held his fingers to his lips as he whispered his reply as quietly as he could. Easing back into a sitting position, he hitched up his pants and went over to the door in bare feet with no shirt. His sandy blond hair had been given a good tousle from Dorothy and stood at every angle possible.

"Give me about ten seconds then call the police on your phone," Ethan cautioned Dorothy with another finger held to his lips then carefully and noiselessly opened the bedroom door and slipped through. Dorothy launched herself for her cell phone and dialed 911 as fast as she could. She knew Ethan had no gun with him and no weapon of any sort.

"911, what's your emergency?" came the operator's bored voice.

"I have someone breaking into my house downstairs and my boyfriend just went down to see who it is," Dorothy spoke as loudly as she dared without notifying the intruder downstairs that they were on to him or her.

"You say you have an intruder in your house?" came the voice with a little more excitement.

"Yes!" Dorothy's voice was little more than a hiss.

"Would you like me to call the police for you?" Came the dispatcher's voice. Dorothy shook her head in amazement at the silly question. Of course she wanted the police to come.

"Yes ma'am, if you wouldn't mind. And could you hurry it up?" Dorothy whispered.

"What is your address?" The voice was now very business-like and professional.

Dorothy gave the address and was told to remain on the line. Tossing the phone onto the bed, Dorothy sprinted for the door when she heard a crash and some yelling coming from downstairs. She flung open the door and with her heart in her mouth she flew down the stairs in bare feet and her clothes in disarray. Just as she came to the bottom of the stairs, she saw a light coming from the open door of her office. Dorothy stopped short at the sight of a half-naked Ethan holding a man in a vise-like choke-hold from behind.

The papers on Dorothy's desk that had once been neat and tidy, were now strewn all over the floor of her office. The weasely little man was starting to whine and was trying to extricate himself from Ethan's grip. He stood around five foot three, was built small and compact, and had greasy black hair falling forward over his forehead. The man's complexion was oily and his clothes looked like he had been sleeping in them for a week.

"I'm not going to ask you again, asshole. Who are you and what are you doing breaking into this office?" Ethan let up a little on the choke hold so the man would answer him. All the man did was start whining louder.

"Dorothy, did you call 911?" Ethan looked at Dorothy as he asked the question and loosened his hold still more. The little weasel took that opportunity to elbow Ethan in the ribs rather unexpectedly. Grabbing his camera where it had dropped onto the desk, he charged forward at full speed.

"Dorothy!" Ethan bellowed and reached out for the little man but missed. Dorothy watched the man come flying towards her and stepped to the side at the last second. With a coolness she hadn't felt in a long time, Dorothy stuck her leg out in front of the man and tripped him so he fell flat on his face, with the camera skittering along the hardwood floor like it was on ice. Calmly and with a determination that amazed Ethan, she sat on the man's back and put her own version of the choke hold on the man.

"Aaaaak!" The man squawked.

"I believe the man asked you a question. If you don't answer him, I won't be so nice," Dorothy's voice was well heard over the frightened sounds coming from the little man pinned to the floor.

Ethan stood with a little smile on his face. Rubbing his ribs where he was elbowed, Ethan walked up to Dorothy with a rueful look on his face. Dorothy looked up with a grin.

"Would you like to take over, dear?" Dorothy asked in all her sweetness.

"No, I think I should go and get some more clothes on before the boys get here. Do you mind?" Ethan was laughing.

"Not at all. But you'd better hurry though. I can hear the sirens already," Dorothy sat calmly upon the man's back as if she were sitting on top of a trophy.

Ethan raced up the stairs and was back just before two cars pulled into the lot with their lights flashing and their sirens wailing. He touched Dorothy's shoulder and made her release the man to him so she could at least do her blouse up. After she did just that, Dorothy went to the door with a nice serene smile on her face while she was in her bare feet, and let the four uniformed officers in.

"Hello boys. Hey, Kathy, how are the twins doing?" Ethan smiled at all the officers as they were met with an incredibly bizarre scene.

"These two people were abusing me and their brutality was unconscionable," The little guy screamed and beat the floor with his fists.

"Knock it off or you'll put scuff marks on the finish. I just had these floors done!" Dorothy screamed back.

The female officer reached down with a set of cuffs and put them on the man and made him sit up.

"All right, now. I want everyone to just settle down here!" Dorothy recognized the officer talking and smiled at him.

"Hey, Herb. They've got you on the night rotation again, eh?" She reached out to shake hands with the man.

"Well hello there, little lady. So this is where you've gotten yourself off to these days. You know your mother told me you were building a bed and breakfast thing. Is this the place?" Herb was smiling and laughing, Dorothy was smiling and laughing, the other three officers were smiling and laughing, and Ethan was smiling and laughing. In fact, the only person who wasn't smiling and laughing, was the smelly little photographer who was trying to squirm around and get out of his cuffs.

"I wouldn't try to get away, if I were you" the tallest of the officers stood six foot six and weighed in at 280 pounds. He stood right in front of the little man and glared down at him. The reporter looked up in fear and almost swallowed his tongue, silent at last.

Ethan satisfied himself that the reporter was under control and started in on his explanation of what was happening and how everyone came to be in this spot at this time.

"Harold, this fellow here broke into the office through these windows here," Ethan gestured to the windows behind him and then continued. "Then proceeded to snoop into things on the desk."

"He made a mess of my office and scared us half to death," Dorothy stood rooted to her spot in anger and Ethan moved over to her and began rubbing her shoulders.

"I did not break in, the doors were wide open, and to me that is an invitation if I ever saw one!" Squaring his shoulders, the reporter sat up a little straighter.

"Do you know who you are talking to?" Harold stepped up to question the reporter.

"Obviously a good friend of yours," The reporter's words seemed to spurt out of his mouth. "I'm going to get a raw deal out of this one, I can tell you that."

"Who the hell do you think you are to think you can just walk in to someone's home and start snooping through someone's personal things? That's called breaking and entering," Dorothy's anger was not dissipating at all, but she was really beginning to enjoy the way Ethan was rubbing her shoulders.

"I am a reporter and I have the ID to prove it," The reporter almost snarled.

"I want to see that ID so where is it?" Harold, obviously the one in command, held his hand out to the reporter. Looking at the outstretched hand in disbelief, the reporter sneered at Harold in contempt.

"You obviously think I have more than one pair of hands." the dry tone finally touched a nerve in Harold.

"No, no, I do understand that snakes don't have hands, you little shit, now where is your ID?" Harold's comment went a long way to disarming Dorothy's anger as she heard the quiet laughter coming from the other three officers. Even Ethan was laughing. The reporter hung his head.

"It's in my left front pocket in my jacket," The reporter answered in a sullen tone.

"You two guys go and retrieve that camera over there and see what kind of evidence is inside it. You never know what they can hide in those things nowadays," Harold's commands were met with smiles from the two male officers as they went to pick up the camera. The reporter began to sqwak again.

"You can't do that!" He cried out. "That's covered by the first amendment! If you open that I will lose. . ." The reporter's nasal whining was stopped in mid- sentence when the tallest guy hit a button and the camera popped open. "Oh my God! You people don't know who you're dealing with!"

Ethan stopped massaging Dorothy's back and approached the reporter sitting in his chair against the wall.

"Suppose you tell us?" Ethan said in a quiet voice. There was dead silence as the little reporter weighed his options in his head. Deciding he had the upper hand, he smirked and sat a little taller in his chair.

"I don't have to tell you anything. I was just passing by when I noticed the open door, and decided to investigate because all the lights were out."

"Sure, sure," Harold nodded his head and the female officer was writing in her note book. "Stick to that story if you want." Turning to Ethan who was just straightening he smiled and winked so that the reporter couldn't see it.

"Okay, I guess we have to take him down to the station, so do you want to press charges, boss?" Harold asked.

"I think we should ask Dorothy here. It's her property," Ethan stepped back and motioned to Dorothy, who stepped forward.

"Yes I do," She had seen the wink and was going to play along.

"You can't charge me with anything. I told you, I was walking past when I saw the open door and I decided to investigate." The whining began again.

"You two go outside and check the perimeter and bag any evidence you find. Take that camera with you as well," Harold directed the two male officers outside. Dorothy, disappointed that Ethan had stopped that delicious back rub, sat down behind the desk and began to enjoy the scene playing out before her.

"Kathy, take Dorothy's statement and the boss and I will begin filling out the forms so we can get this little shit down to the cells. It's late and I'm off shift in ten minutes." Harold started writing in his own notebook as Ethan and Harold stepped off to the side so their discussion couldn't be heard. That left the little reporter sitting with his head hanging and wishing he hadn't heard of this assignment. Large paycheck or not, this kind of trouble just wasn't worth getting his press pass pulled. Suddenly he sat up with a jerk and looked over to Ethan and Harold.

"Hey, wait a minute, what did you call that guy officer?" Harold turned to face the reporter.

"Who, this guy?" Harold approached the man in the chair. "You mean you don't know who this man is?" Harold looked down at the ID he held in his hand that he had fished out of the reporter's pocket. "Hank, you are a reporter, and you didn't do your research too well," Harold shook his head. "This is my boss, the Chief of Police of Redwood." The reporter turned a sickly kind of greenish white and he almost collapsed. Leaning back against the chair, he began to moan.

"Now I've done it!" The reporter named Hank seemed to wilt right in front of everyone's eyes.

"Now you've done it is right," Ethan approached him again. He reached out a hand to check the pulse of the man to make sure he wasn't having a heart attack and Dorothy watched that large, strong, sexy hand touch the skin of the reporter's wrist.

"*There has got to be something wrong with me.*" Dorothy's tongue slowly wet her bottom lip as she thought to herself. "*I'm consumed with the man, no matter what he's doing.*" The female officer noticed the wetting of Dorothy's lips, the ring on her finger, and a knowing smile blossomed on her face. She continued to take notes.

"Well, at least you are not having a heart attack," Ethan said as he stepped back. "Now let's have it. And be quick about it. I may change my mind if you give me a reason to."

The reporter's greasy hair fell forward onto his brow and he seemed to cringe. If possible, it seemed he got a little greener.

"I checked my emails yesterday in my home office and there was one with a job attached. The instructions attached were to come here to Redwood, find this address, and do some snooping, take lots of pictures, and write a very ugly story about the person living here." Dorothy almost jumped over the desk and Kathy had to hold her back.

"Who was it?" Dorothy demanded. The reporter saw the anger in Dorothy's eyes, and looked at Ethan with an appeal for mercy in his own.

"I didn't know who you were! I needed the money. And besides, I was told that if I did this job well, all the money I owed would be wiped out, and the pictures they had, would be destroyed." Tears were actually appearing in the corners of the filthy man's face.

"What pictures? Who told you to do this?" Ethan placed his face right in front of Hank and stared into a weasel's eyes. "Tell me or I'll take you to jail right now!"

"Okay, okay!" Hank put his hands up to ward Ethan off. "It was the Puritans," He wailed. Dorothy jumped and gasped at the same time as if she was physically hit.

"Who?" Ethan did reach out to grab Hank's collar. Pulling him up almost to his feet, they were nose to nose. "How do you know?"

"The email they sent me had a letterhead emblem from them I recognized. And it had attachments," Hank's voice was almost inaudible and his greasy face was now a mottled greenish white. Ethan released him and as he collapsed in the chair, Ethan turned to Dorothy.

"Get those two buddies of yours on the phone and get them over here. I think it's going to be a long night, sweetie." The rueful smile on Ethan's face did nothing to cover the disappointment Dorothy felt at the statement. Nodding, she picked up the phone on the desk.

"Kathy, get one of those court reporters or stenographers over here on the double," Harold motioned to Kathy. "I'm going out to the men outside and see if they've found anything." Kathy nodded at Harold and spoke into the microphone attached to her shoulder.

Ethan shook his head as he looked at Hank and then turned back to Dorothy as she put the phone down.

"They'll be right here," Dorothy's disappointed tone came through loud and clear to Ethan.

"Aww, honey, I'm sorry. We'll just have to finish what we were doing at a later time," Ethan began to massage Dorothy's shoulders again and she began to smile.

"Promise?" Dorothy purred into Ethan's shoulder.

"Promise," Ethan purred right back as both arms went around Dorothy in a quick hug.

CHAPTER SIXTEEN

The time seemed to go by so slowly and Dorothy was determined not to let the mess they were all in get her down. She went into the kitchen and made some fresh coffee. Putting out some cold-cuts, cheese, and fresh fruit, she also put out cream and sugar for everyone. Then she went upstairs to get properly dressed and when she came back down, the office seemed full of police milling around and snooping through everything.

"Hey, guys," she called out. "If you're that bored, come and have some coffee and something to eat. And keep your hands out of my private things!" She demanded and invited at the same time.

"Sorry about that, little lady. We actually have to check to see if anything is missing. Kathy here, volunteered to help you clean up when we're done," Harold motioned to the other officers to go into the kitchen and help themselves.

"Well, Harold, looking to see if anything is missing is my job," Dorothy stood with her hands on her hips and admonished him. "Now go and get some coffee." Dorothy motioned towards the kitchen.

"Yes ma'am," Harold left the messy office with a little grin and joined his fellow officers in the kitchen.

Dorothy surveyed the mess in the office and cringed. The reporter was nowhere to be seen and neither was Ethan. She assumed he had gone to the office to interview the reporter himself. In her opinion, that would be a wrong move. Ethan should let someone else do the interview so there would be no question of impropriety.

Without touching anything, Dorothy closely scrutinized the entire area of the desk top and did not see anything missing. Next she checked the pullout drawer in the middle of the desk top and it was filled with fingerprint dust but did not seem to have been touched. Going over to the closet she noticed the door of the closet had been pulled back on its sliders. Knowing that the noise that alerted Ethan was probably the grating sound of metal grating on metal, Dorothy checked the tracks on the sliders both up and down. Sure enough, they were off track. She had never fixed that after the contractors brought it to her attention, but she had installed a lock, which Dorothy saw was jimmied with some sort of metal object. The finger print dust covered most of the frontal plate of the lock, but not the scratches that were showing.

"Hmmmm!" Dorothy thought out loud and put a finger to her lips. "Someone was prying a little too deeply for a reporter." The filing cabinet behind the door had been opened and several files had been pulled halfway out.

"He got to my files with the permits and licenses," Dorothy gasped out loud. Knowing that if the manager at City Hall could prove that Dorothy was operating without proof of licence, she would be charged for operating the Bed and Breakfast without a proper licence. Turning to run out the office door she came full tilt into Ethan who had come back in through the front door.

"Whoa!" Ethan barked. "Slow down. What's wrong?" Ethan queried as he held Dorothy back from him. Dorothy's eyes had a wild look in them and she tried to look over Ethan's shoulder into the cars parked outside.

"Where is he? He has my copies of the original licences and permits for development. Without them, I can't open the Bed and Breakfast!" Dorothy's wild utterance made Ethan's eyes disappear into mere slits. Pushing Dorothy back a step he held up his index finger and cautioned her with it.

"Wait right here. I'll be right back!" Ethan turned and sprinted for the door before the squad car with the reporter could actually get rolling out of the parking lot. Dorothy was left standing there with tears in her eyes as Ethan disappeared out the door.

"Wait!" Ethan yelled at the marked squad car that had just started to back out of its spot. "Wait just a darned minute!" Reaching with his right hand in the air, he managed to attract the attention of the officer behind the wheel. The officer opened his window and waited for Ethan to say what he wanted.

"This little snake in the grass has something tucked in his clothing somewhere. I want him pulled out and searched," Ethan's voice roared off into the black of the night and the officer jumped out of the car immediately and opened the back door, as if afraid to fail Ethan's command.

"Come here!" The officer pulled the reporter out of the car and made him lean against the back fender facing the car.

"I have rights, you know! This is abuse!" The little man began to whine as he spotted the news van coming in through the parking lot driveway. "You can't do this!" He said loud enough for the news people inside the van to hear.

Ethan stood back and waited so no one could say he had actually touched the little rat after the officers took custody of him. When the driver of the city police car moved his hands up near the waist band at the back of his pants, the reporter began to squirm.

"Got something here, Chief!" The officer brought out several sheets of paper folded in half length-wise and examined them. Ethan stood there and seethed with anger as the news van parked and two reporters piled out beside them with microphones at the ready.

"What do you have, officer?" Ethan's voice was deadly quiet. The officer took a step over to the yard light so he could see better.

"I have some building permits, some applications that are approved for a restaurant and hotel establishment, and a couple other letters of reference," the officer held them out to Ethan. Ethan didn't move.

"Did you search this man before you put him into your squad car?" Ethan's voice had a ring of steel as the anger registered with the junior officer.

"No sir. The sergeant inside said he was already searched, sir." The junior officer swallowed the lump in his throat.

"What is the department policy?" Ethan now stood with his hands on his hips and his feet spread out at a 45 degree angle. The junior officer lowered the offered papers down to his side and visibly started to shake.

"Department policy states that I am to search my prisoner myself before I place the man in the back of my unit for transport." One of the reporters had sidled up beside Ethan and shoved a microphone into Ethan's face as he started firing all sorts of questions at Ethan. Ethan's head turned to the reporter with a steely gaze.

"No comment." He turned his head back to the junior officer and pushed the microphone to the side. The other reporter had just placed his microphone into the reporter's face who was handcuffed and spread eagled over the trunk of the car.

"Can you tell us what kind of abuse you have experienced at the hands of the Chief of Police?"

The reporter was just starting to say his first word when the officer being addressed by Ethan shot his hand out and took the microphone and the hand holding it and whipped it behind the man's back and cuffed his wrists together.

"Hey! Hey!" The second man being cuffed that evening looked at the third reporter, who cautiously backed away to a safe distance. "You can't do that! I have freedom of speech!" He screamed.

"Freedom of speech doesn't mean freedom to obstruct an investigation, no matter which way you look at it!" The young officer looked up to Ethan, who was standing there with a huge smile on his face. Retrieving the papers from the ground where the young officer had dropped them he held them out to Ethan once more.

"These were found on the burglary suspect under his clothing, sir." This was said loud enough for the third reporter to hear. Ethan took the papers with a smile and glanced down at them. While Ethan looked over the papers, the two men in handcuffs were calling out to the third man still holding his microphone. "Be quiet you two or I'll find another crime to charge you with instead of obstruction of justice and burglary in the second degree." The young officer began to search the second reporter and turned to look at the one standing directly behind him now.

"What do you want?" He almost snarled.

"Easy, officer, easy," Ethan put his hand on the other officer's shoulder in a friendly gesture. "When you finish searching these two "reporters" call another transport unit out for pick-up." Ethan turned to go back into the Bed and Breakfast.

"Sir, would you like me to put those into an evidence pouch?" the young officer asked politely.

"Do you have a spare one?" Ethan turned back.

"Certainly sir."

When the searches were over, and Ethan said "No comment" for what seemed like a dozen times, he went back into the Bed and Breakfast with the evidence sealed and secure in its own little pouch.

Dorothy met him at the door and stood there with a question in her eyes. Ethan held the clear pouch up so she could see the documents inside but couldn't touch it.

"Now we know what he was after, my dear. Your permits and licenses." Dorothy reached for them and was surprised when Ethan pulled them out of her reach. "I'm sorry Dorothy. These are evidence," Ethan began to fold them in half and put them in his brief case which rested on the dining room table.

"I need those to prove that I have all the permits filed," Dorothy explained.

"I have to log these in as evidence, dear. I don't have a choice," Ethan's shoulders raised and then lowered. "I'm sorry," he said with concern.

"You're sorry?" Dorothy's anger at Ethan's stubbornness was quite evident in the way she put her hands on her hips.

A sound came from the doorway and a reporter tried to push his way in through the door past the young officer who had cuffed the second reporter.

"I said stay out! You are on private property!" he pushed back with both hands.

"This is a public building and I can come in!" the reporter yelled back at him.

"You move one more inch and I'll pull this gun and shoot you right in the microphone!" Ethan yelled over the voices of the two wrestling in the doorway. There was instant silence as the two noticed Ethan was actually resting his right hand on his holstered gun.

"I told you not to come in," the young officer pointed out.

"Officer, take this man in for trespassing on private property," Ethan relaxed his stance as the young officer reached for Ethan's own pair of handcuffs. Several officers came out of the kitchen with cuffs out and helped the young officer. The Sergeant poked his head out of the kitchen to see what was going on.

"And just what are you doing in there, Sergeant?" Ethan's temper had not improved with the last reporter's antics.

"I'm recording the state of the kitchen on the camera, sir." The Sergeant came out with a camera in his hand and Ethan just shook his head. Rubbing the back of his neck with one hand and bracing his back with the other, Ethan longed to go back to the moment when Dorothy had said yes to his proposal.

"All right, all right," Ethan squared his shoulders and tried to stand straight, but his weariness was evident. "Finish up in the kitchen and then get the suspects squared away at the office," Ethan directed.

"Suspects?" the Sergeant looked confused.

"Two reporters out there came along when I tried to re-question the first guy. They stuck their microphones in our faces and Thompson took charge." Ethan indicated the open door. "Remind me to give him a pat on the back when I see him next."

"Will do, Chief," The Sergeant ducked back inside the kitchen and Dorothy could hear him taking several more pictures.

"Dorothy, I do have to take these in to the evidence locker. At least this proves that someone is after you, and they are trying to close you down one way or another." Dorothy's anger towards Ethan began to cool when she realized that what Ethan was saying was right.

Temperance Rose Adams walked in the front door as if she owned the Bed and Breakfast and went straight to Dorothy to enfold her in a warm and understanding embrace.

"Mom! What are you doing here?" Dorothy tried to talk through her mother's shoulder.

"Sweetheart! You poor thing. Ethan called me and told me what was going on. I think you should come home with me to the Manor this evening. Apparently Maria is still out of commission at the moment and you shouldn't be alone at this place until all this snooping business is taken care of." Temperance held Dorothy out at arm's length. "What do you think?" Dorothy never dared to argue with her mother and she just nodded.

"Okay, I'll help you go upstairs and pack a few things and we'll lock up for tonight. We can come and clean in the morning, okay?" Dorothy nodded a second time, too numb to argue.

"Ethan, do you have keys?" Temperance directed this question at the haggard looking man beside Dorothy.

"Yes, ma'am. I can lock up for you. As soon as my men have everything sorted out, I'll lock up and you can come back in the morning like your mother said," Ethan directed this last part to Dorothy who seemed to be clinging to her mother with her knuckles turning white.

"All right dear. I'll talk to you tomorrow," Dorothy said in a tired and resigned voice. Temperance directed Dorothy up the stairs and into her bedroom. Quickly, before her daughter could change her mind, Temperance packed an overnight bag, then took her daughter by the hand. Dorothy followed Temperance down the stairs and into the sleek little sportster beside her black SUV.

"You've got a new car?" Dorothy said in surprise as she saw the small red car and she shook her head.

"I'm just borrowing it for a while until mine gets fixed, dear." Temperance tucked Dorothy into the front passenger seat and closed the door. Getting into the driver's seat, she started the car and drove away in a cloud of dust. Ethan stood waving to them as they drove away and then gave a big sigh.

"Oh man!" What a night!" Ethan wiped a wearied brow and went back into the Bed and Breakfast. "Sergeant! Are you done yet?" he yelled towards the kitchen.

CHAPTER SEVENTEEN

Elva's eyes came open in the semi darkness of her bedroom and she realised she hadn't slept much all night. Weariness that went right through her seemed to make her want to roll over and smash the alarm clock right off the end of her nightstand. Instead, she rolled out of bed and placed her feet on the floor, silencing the alarm with one hand and trying to hold her head up with the other. Scratching the top of her head, she tried to clear the grogginess by yawning.

"*What is it that kept me awake all night?*" She asked herself in confusion. Then her mind cleared and she knew. Sprinting into the shower, Elva wanted to make sure she checked on the status of the two little boys she had taken in to the station last night.

"Lord I hope I don't lose my job over this." Elva was out of the house ten minutes later with her coffee in one hand, and car keys in the other when a large black SUV rolled past the front of her house. All the windows had been blackened including the windshield, and the licence plate was covered with mud. Elva froze with one leg in the car and one out. Dropping the keys to her unit, she slowly moved her right hand down to her holster. Elva's heart began beating faster as the window in the front on the passenger's side began to go down.

Elva ducked down and drew her weapon in one smooth motion. The gun muzzle that appeared in the open window began to fire as if everything was in slow motion. It was an automatic weapon and Elva had no chance to return fire when she felt the burn of a bullet in her lower left leg which was exposed. Crawling into the unit she reached for the radio and keyed the microphone. Sweat trickled down her brow and between her eyes. Wiping it away with her gun in her hand she yelled into the radio.

"Officer down! Officer down!" Elva screamed her name and dropped the microphone as another barrage of bullets came from the automatic weapon. Glass exploded all around her and suddenly, for Elva, all time seemed to stop. A bullet had ricocheted off the top of the hood and hit Elva in the center of her vest as she tried to raise herself up high enough to fire back. She felt the slug hit with enough impact it threw her against the ground outside the door of the car. Unable to breath because of the pain and the pressure, Elva's gasps were heard by the dispatcher.

"Hold on, Elva, we're sending units, they should almost be there!" The dispatcher called out. "You hear me Elva? Hold on!" The dispatcher could hear the squeal of tires and sirens in the distance. "Elva, what's your status?" The dispatcher called out in fear when Elva's gasping became louder and suddenly stopped.

Tony's unit was the first one to arrive on scene and he leaped from his car with his weapon ready. Crouching and running at the same time, he tried to aim at the disappearing SUV but couldn't make a clear shot. Holstering his weapon he focused on the licence plate but couldn't read it because it was covered with something.

"Elva!" He screamed when he saw her legs sticking out from under the car with glass and blood all around her.

Another car arrived with two officers who had their guns trained on the disappearing SUV.

"You two clear the house! Make sure there's no one hiding in there," Tony reached Elva's side and called her name again. Fear for his Aunt's life coursed through his veins and his hands were shaky. He heard a few short gasps and grunts as he began to pull Elva out from under the car. Detective Phil Harmon was suddenly beside them and helped to finish pulling Elva out so they could check her wounds.

"Tony, we have an ambulance on the way," Phil reassured Tony. Tony was hurriedly unstrapping Elva's vest, trying to figure out where the blood was coming from. The slugs didn't come from the chest wound, but a cut on the back of Elva's head where it hit the cement before she rolled herself under the car for protection. Tony examined her leg wound carefully while Phil scanned the area around them. Elva was still unconscious when the ambulance pulled up and Tony felt more fear when he saw Elva's lips turning blue.

"She can't breathe, Phil. She' going blue!" An EMT tried to pull Tony back from Elva so he could place an oxygen mask on her but he refused to let go.

"Tony!" Ethan had come up behind Tony and grabbed his shoulders to pull him back. Phil helped to move Tony back. The EMTs worked fast and were able to stabilize Elva's breathing. Ethan held on to Tony even tighter when Elva was loaded onto a stretcher. "Tony, if you want to go with Elva, go ahead but stay out of their way," Ethan said into Tony's ear.

"Thanks, Chief," Tony held Elva's hand as the doors closed and the ambulance sped away.

Ethan stepped back and surveyed the scene before him and knew that Elva had stumbled onto something that had almost gotten her killed. The blood and broken glass was scattered all over the inside and the outside of the unit. Most of the blood was on the ground under the car where Elva had managed to crawl for protection after the slug hit her in the vest. Ethan's jaw tightened and his hands went to his hips and one glance at Phil told him the crime scene was in good hands.

"Detective Harmon," Ethan called out to Phil.

"Yes, Chief?" Phil's eyes looked at Ethan and Ethan saw the tears.

"I want this crime scene gone over with every available man. The house, the unit, and her phone, got it?" Ethan ordered.

"Her phone?" Harmon questioned.

"We need to know who let these Pablo Brothers know where Elva lived." Phil nodded. Turning to go back to his own unit, Ethan had a sudden idea that almost scared him. With all these police units hunting down and tracking the shooters of one of their own, who was protecting the two little children at the station? Surely the Pablo Brothers wouldn't be so bold or stupid enough to try and steal the children out of the holding cell they had been placed in for their own protection.

The pandemonium around him seemed to increase as Ethan's fears seemed to escalate. Turning back to Detective Harmon he called out again.

"Harmon!"

"Yes Chief?" Harmon's eyes were looking right at Ethan with anger in them.

"I hadn't finished reading the reports yet, when this all happened. We just went through a shift change, are the two children still at the station?" Ethan's sense of urgency conveyed itself to Detective Harmon.

"I think they are. In one of our holding cells, why?" It suddenly dawned on Detective Harmon what Ethan was leading up to. "Good God! You don't think. . ."

"I don't think, I know!" Ethan sprinted for his unit and Detective Harmon gave fast and detailed instructions for his crime scene technicians, then he too raced for his unit.

CHAPTER EIGHTEEN

Ethan pulled up to the police headquarters with a squeal of tires and smoke. Phil Harmon wasn't too far behind him. Racing through the back door closest to his office, Ethan, with Detective Harmon close behind, slid to a quick stop behind the security door with the bullet proof glass in the top panel. From their vantage point, they scrutinized every person in the main office. Most of the police officers that were sitting at their desks were focused on the paperwork in front of them. There didn't seem to be any sense of urgency or alarm in anyone's deportment. Even so, Ethan motioned to Phil in sign language to precede him by a few seconds and he ducked down behind the glass. Phil nodded and quietly opened the door into the main office. Stepping lively as if he hadn't a care in the world, Detective Harmon went straight to his office and opened his door with his key. Not one person seemed to look his way or even acknowledge his presence. Several officers even looked away. Stepping inside his office he sat down behind his desk and picked up the phone to talk to the new receptionist.

"Redwood Police, how may I help you?" came the new girl's strained voice.

"It's Phil Harmon. Can you talk?" Phil asked in a quiet voice. From his office he couldn't see the receptionist's desk.

"I'm sorry, sir. We don't offer that service at this point in time. Perhaps you should call the town office and inquire there." Phil immediately mumbled a thank you and hung up. Pulling his cell phone out of his pocket, he called Ethan and told him of the receptionist's answer.

"Well we definitely know that there is someone in the outer office near the receptionist who is not supposed to be there. Smart girl, answering like that." Detective Harmon said in a quiet voice. "What do you want to do?" he asked Ethan.

"Call down to the holding cells and tell them to sit tight. We need to find out where they are in the building," Ethan answered.

"Ethan, if they are anywhere near the security center and can see the camera monitors, they know you and I are here," Phil said with some urgency. "Maybe you should go out the back door again and circle around to the front."

"Okay. Good idea. That will leave at least one of us out front to follow them when they leave. But I don't like the idea of leaving everyone exposed," Ethan answered into his phone as he turned to leave.

"If you stay out front, and I'm back here, we can catch them in between us," Phil outlined his plan.

"The kids would be with them, no doubt. I don't want those two kids hurt," Ethan fairly hissed into his phone. All of a sudden there was a commotion that came through the doors from the holding cells.

"Ethan, they're coming out. Quick! Get out front." Ethan flew through the back door, into his vehicle and was just swinging into the front parking lot when Tony's unit and two others came up on both sides of him.

"Tony, we have to keep them pinned between the two security doors. And no firing, got it?" Ethan called through the mike of the radio.

"Got it," Tony slammed his transmission into park and was immediately aiming his weapon through the driver's side window towards the front door of the police station. It was the shot gun that was supplied with the unit.

Sweat rolled down Ethan's brow as he took up his position behind the open door of his own unit. There were two men with masks on their faces, and a third in civilian clothing pushing the two children towards the front door of the station. Seeing the four squad cars, police officers, and the police chief aiming their weapons at them they froze.

"I want you men to lay your weapons down, release the two boys, and come on out with your hands up!" Ethan's voice came through the loudspeaker and almost deafened the men on either side of him. Hearing the command yelled at them, the men turned to scramble back through the other door when they spotted Phil and several other officers pointing their weapons at them. The door remained locked when they tried to push through.

A SILENT ENEMY

"You heard me, I'll give you thirty seconds to do as you're told or we'll open fire." Ethan yelled again. Tony's surprised face looked over at Ethan.

"Chief. . . ." Tony began.

"Tony, shut up. Keep your weapon on those men!" Ethan growled at him. Tony looked back at the men with their hostages and aimed his shot gun at them once more. He was visibly shaken.

"Hey Chief, you shoot at us and you'll kill the hostages. What kind of Chief of Police would you be if you let that happen?" The man without the mask yelled back at Ethan. He pulled the youngest boy to him and pointed his gun at the kid's head.

"What kind of an idiot would you be to do that?" Ethan yelled back. "I have marksmen on three different vantage points aiming their rifles at your heads right now. You wouldn't get ten feet and you'd lose your life," Ethan answered.

Ethan could see the three men craning their necks to look around at the taller buildings across the street.

"Ten seconds, dirt bag," Ethan called once again. Looking at Tony's look of anger he barked an order.

"Count it down, Tony." Ethan calmly reached into the back of his unit and pulled out his hunting rifle and scope. Making a big show of brushing it off and loading his weapon so the three men caught between the security doors could see him, Ethan aimed, adjusted his sights and waited.

"5, 4, . . ." Tony counted. The men hesitated.

"Which one of you wants to go first?" Ethan called out. The three of them were startled and looked out the glass of the door and saw Ethan adjusting his scope.

"3, 2, . . ." Tony continued.

"All right! All right!" The first man raised his hands and dropped his gun. The second one did the same.

"One!" Tony finished counting.

The third man let the youngest boy go and put his hands up into the air as well.

"Drop the weapon!" Man number three dropped his weapon. Twelve police officers converged on the security doors with their weapons drawn with Ethan in the lead. A buzzer sounded and the two doors opened simultaneously. Scooping the two boys up and returning with them to his SUV, Ethan calmed them down while Phil Harmon issued orders for the three men to be taken into custody.

"Ethan! Ethan!" Tony came running back to Ethan's side. The two boys were crying with huge tears running down their cheeks. Other than that, they weren't making a sound, just shaking uncontrollably.

"What, Tony?" Ethan looked up into the red rimmed eyes of his newest member.

"We were coming back from the hospital to tell you that Elva is going to be okay. Her vest stopped any slugs and she has a few stitches in her head. She'll be on crutches for a while as well. They want to keep her in the hospital overnight for observation." Tony was worked up with sweat streaming into his eyes and dirt all over his uniform.

"You came back at the perfect time, Tony. Good job!" Ethan paused and looked at the children. "These two are scared to death, and I have nowhere to put them right now. Any suggestions?"

Tony looked down at the two little boys shaking uncontrollably in the back seat of Ethan's vehicle and suddenly he began to smile. Looking at Ethan he nodded.

"I do. But she won't like it," Tony continued to smile at Ethan.

"Oh no!" Ethan began to shake his head. "I'm not going to ask her after last night!" Ethan continued to shake his head.

"What's up Chief?" Phil asked as he walked up to the two men.

"Tony wants me to ask Dorothy if she will take care of these two young men at her place." Ethan stated flatly.

"Sounds like a good idea to me," Phil answered. Ethan looked at Phil in confusion.

"You like that idea?" he asked.

"Sure. It would solve two problems. Dorothy knows security, and she knows Spanish." Phil and Tony both nodded. Ethan shrugged in resignation and turned to the two boys.

"How would you two boys like to stay with a very nice lady who will keep you safe and warm?" Ethan gave them a little smile. They weren't crying any longer but they were still shaking. Taking a blanket out of the back Ethan covered the two boys.

"Tony, go over there and tell the boys to charge those idiots with kidnapping. Phil, I want you to find out how they actually got into the main office so easily, and I'm going to call Dorothy. Go on now, move!" Ethan pulled out his phone and called Dorothy.

A SILENT ENEMY

CHAPTER NINETEEN

Dorothy woke up to the sound of a knock on her door. As soon as she opened her eyes she remembered where she was and what had transpired the night before. She had a headache that was pounding right behind her eyes and she slowly sat up. Holding her head to stop the throbbing she called out.

"Whoever is knocking on my door, please come in," She said in a sheepish voice. The door began to creep open and Dorothy watched it with an amused smile.

"Good morning Dorothy." Dorothy's mother, Temperance Rose Adams, poked her head around the door and smiled. "Do you feel like joining me for breakfast this morning?" Dorothy's hair was tumbling over her shoulders and she glanced down at the t-shirt she was wearing. Looking up at her mother she smiled and nodded.

"Can you give me ten minutes and I'll come down and make some pancakes and eggs just for the two of us?" Dorothy quickly kicked the covers back and swung her legs over the edge of the bed. Temperance came all the way in the door and suddenly Dorothy could smell bacon cooking and coffee perking all the way upstairs. She also saw her mother standing beside the bed with a bottle of Tylenol and a glass of water. Dorothy's mouth dropped open.

"How do you do that, mom?" Dorothy asked in amazement.

"Do what dear?" Temperance asked as she handed the pills and the water to Dorothy. Dorothy took them and looked up to her mother.

"Read my mind like that." She swallowed the pills and downed the entire glass of water.

"Oh it's not hard, dear." Temperance reached over and patted Dorothy's shoulder. "Maria came in this morning with the same kind of headache I'm sure you have." Waving her hand under her nose as if to repel some awful smell, Temperance sat beside Dorothy. Dorothy began to laugh a little despite the headache.

"I think Maria may have had a hangover, Mom. She drank more than the rest of us put together."

"Well she also said that you and Ethan had something to tell me this morning, but I'm afraid I can't get in touch with your young man to invite him over for breakfast. Some sort of emergency at the office." Temperance shook her head. "He seems to have an emergency every other day there. If you ask me, he doesn't have time to start a family." Once again Dorothy's mouth fell open as she looked at her mother. "Close your mouth, dear. You'll catch flies." Temperance rose and went to the door. "If you don't hurry you will miss watching Maria scramble those eggs. You know how hard it is for her to scramble eggs when she's had a good time the night before." Temperance smiled then and her whole face lit up.

"Mother, you look so beautiful when you smile," Dorothy walked over to her mother and gave her a hug. "I'll hurry. I don't want to miss the show." Temperance went out and Dorothy had a quick shower. It was ten minutes on the dot when Dorothy walked into the kitchen all fresh and full of energy.

Entering the kitchen she stopped in mid-stride as she saw Maria trying to whisk the eggs in the bowl. Temperance rose from the kitchen table and gently took the bowl and the whisk from her hands.

"That's okay, Maria. I think you've suffered enough. Have a seat and Dorothy will get you a cup of coffee."

"Oh yes! Thank you Dorothy. Thank you so much," Maria crossed to the table and sat down very carefully while Temperance scrambled the eggs and Dorothy poured the family cook a large cup of hot coffee. She placed it on the table in front of Maria and smiled. Maria looked up and watched Dorothy bounce over to the fridge for the cream for Maria's coffee. She screwed up her face and stuck her tongue out at Dorothy's back.

"Now Maria, don't be like that. Dorothy's night wasn't as hard as yours was. She can't help it if she's so happy." Maria watched Dorothy pour the cream into her coffee and stir it for her.

"She can't help it if she's so happy!" Maria mimicked Temperance. Slowly she took a sip of coffee and a small smile began to form on her lips. Dorothy and Temperance were truly amazed at the transformation in Maria's face.

"Thank you Dorothy. You're a good girl. Ms. Adams, I'm sorry I was unable to perform my duties," Maria gave Temperance such a look of woe that both Dorothy and Temperance began laughing.

"It's okay, Maria. You don't do this very often so you just sit there and enjoy your coffee. Dorothy and I will finish breakfast."

It wasn't too long before all three of them sat at one end of the huge table and said grace over the food in front of them. After all the pancakes and eggs, and bacon had been passed around, Maria looked again at Dorothy and smiled her biggest smile.

"What is it Maria?" Dorothy asked before she took a bite of her breakfast.

"Did you tell her?" Maria smirked into her coffee mug. Temperance glanced sideways at Maria and then at Dorothy.

"Tell me what, Dorothy?" Temperance stared right into Dorothy's eyes. Dorothy put her fork and knife down and sat back in her chair. A little nervous because of the hard stare she was receiving from Temperance, Dorothy took a deep breath.

"Mother, Ethan and I had dinner together last night," she began.

"Yes I know, Maria told me that already. That's why she was drinking so much last night. Those other two men from Toronto joined you and Maria said it was very hard to create a good meal for those two 'heathens'." Temperance took a sip of her coffee while she rested her elbows on the table.

"No, Mom, . . ." Dorothy tried again.

"Tell her about the wine, and how I smashed it on the floor so Quentin couldn't lord it over the rest of us with his fancy stuff." Maria was smiling and nodded at Dorothy while she pulled on Dorothy's sleeve.

"Please, Maria, let me tell it, okay?" Dorothy delicately plucked Maria's fingers from her sleeve and turned back towards her mother.

"I mean honestly, Dorothy, you should have told those two men to stay at the Inn instead of with you at the Bed and Breakfast," Temperance said as she took another sip of her coffee.

"That's what I said! But would she listen to me? No!" Maria threw her hands up in the air and then flattened them on the table as if she was upset.

"Maria, please! Let me tell it," Dorothy pleaded.

"Sure, sure. Go ahead!" Maria beamed and sat back with her arms crossed. Dorothy looked back to her mother again.

"You could have even let them stay here if you needed a private place to have a meeting, but at the Bed and Breakfast? I don't think so." Temperance shook her head and took another sip of her coffee.

"That's what I told her!" Maria threw her hands up in the air again.

"Mom, really, will you two let me tell you about last night or do I have to tie Maria down and tape her lips together?" The other two women at the table looked at Dorothy with shock in their eyes. "Well?" Dorothy stared right into Maria's eyes and Maria sat back with a sullen look on her face.

"Dorothy, that was not nice. Now you apologize this minute!" Temperance scolded Dorothy.

"Ethan asked me to marry him," Dorothy was so perturbed, she let the words just pop out of her mouth. Temperance froze and Maria jumped up and leaned over to give Dorothy a hug.

"Well, I guess that's a good thing, Dorothy. It took him long enough," Temperance took another sip of her coffee with a smile on her face. "What did you tell him?" She put her cup down and whisked an imaginary crumb off the table before her.

"I said yes, Mom. I'm going to marry him." Dorothy's smile not only lit up her entire face, it made her eyes shine.

"Oh sweetheart, I'm so proud of you. Congratulations, dear, he's a good man." Temperance rose to give Dorothy a hug. They clung together for a moment.

"He has to be to put up with her shenanigans." Maria mumbled and walked over to the kitchen sink.

"Maria! Why would you say that?" Temperance turned to Maria.

"I'm just saying, she has a strong will, that's all," Maria shrugged and put her hands up in the air. Looking straight at Dorothy she reached out to hug her again. "I couldn't be more proud of how you turned out." All three ladies were hugging when Dorothy's cell phone went off.

"Hello?" Dorothy answered.

"Dorothy, Ethan here." Dorothy immediately lost the happy look on her face at the sound of Ethan's urgent voice. "I have a problem and I need your help, immediately."

"What is it?" Dorothy's tension conveyed to the other two ladies that something was definitely wrong. Maria took a step back and put her hand to her mouth.

"All right, I'll be right there," Dorothy turned to her Mother with a look of fear on her face. Putting her phone in her pocket, Dorothy began to speak in a hurried tone.

"There was an attack on the police precinct where they were holding those two little boys that Elva found yesterday. And they even showed up at Elva's house to shoot her down as she was getting into her vehicle. They took her to the hospital and Ethan arrived at the precinct in time to prevent a blood bath there." Dorothy walked as she talked and the other two ladies followed. "Ethan needs me to take the boys over to the Bed and Breakfast and get Trevor to help me look after them in case those idiots the Pablo Boys try again," Dorothy halted and looked at her mother. "Mom, I'm scared for Ethan." Temperance reached for her daughter and held her. Stepping back after a few moments, Dorothy tried to smile.

"You go, Dorothy. Get those two little boys and take care of them like they were your own. You can do it. Maria and I will go and do some shopping and come over to your place as soon as we can. Okay?" Temperance took charge and tried not to let Dorothy see her own fear.

"Here, take your jacket, and get going. Maria and I will make sure we get everything they will need, right Maria?" Maria nodded and patted Dorothy's shoulder as Dorothy slipped into her jacket.

"Okay, mom, and thanks." Seconds later Dorothy was out the door of the manor and Temperance and Maria stood in the door to watch her go.

"We have to get moving, Ms. Adams," Maria gently took her employer and long-time friend by the arm and led her up the stairs. Now that Dorothy was gone, Maria knew Temperance was getting scared.

"You go and get some things together. I will clean the kitchen and call your sons and other daughters. This family always does things together. Don't we?" Temperance took a deep breath and nodded.

"Yes, you're right, Maria. Call the family and tell them what is happening. Dorothy needs our help right now. No wait! Tell them to stay home and stay safe." Temperance flew the rest of the way to her room and Maria rushed to the kitchen and the phone to make some calls.

CHAPTER TWENTY

Trevor looked out the window in his room and tried to figure out why there was a man lurking by the light standard across the parking lot. He held a camera and looked through the viewing lens. The man raised the camera and pointed it at the window of the room next to his. Quentin's room. Nodding with the knowledge the man was a snoopy reporter, he turned to go back into his room and finish dressing. A knock sounded at his door and Trevor quickly slipped up to the door and looked through the viewer. It was Quentin, all dressed in a three piece suit with his hair slicked back in the business-man's cut that he liked so much. Opening the door, Trevor smiled and held out his hands to shake Quentin's offered hand.

"We must hurry, Trevor. All hell is breaking loose in this city and we need to find out what it is." Trevor watched in stunned fascination as Quentin Tallas turned and continued to walk down the hallway to the stairs.

"Where are we going?" Trevor called out, still motionless.

"I will meet you in the coffee shop downstairs in ten minutes. We need to have a plan of attack and our two friends are so busy they don't have time to help," Quentin had turned to look back at Trevor as he spoke. Trevor noticed his features seemed a bit hard and determined. The dark suit looked brand new with no wrinkles; Italian cut with a slimming effect.

"I will be there." Trevor closed the door to his room and was on his cell phone before he even got to the bed. "Trixie, I need Thomas to call me as soon as he is able. I need some info and I need it fast." Ending the call, he finished dressing and left the room with a sense of purpose.

In the café, he sat at the same table that Quentin was sitting at and waited quietly for Quentin to begin.

"There have been a couple of developments through the night that we have to keep in mind," Quentin said in his controlled voice. Taking a sip of his coffee, he looked right at Trevor so Trevor could see his eyes. There was an attack on one of Ethan's officers this morning, and a kidnapping attempt at the main police station this morning." The only change in Trevor's face was a tightening of his jaw-line and his eyes began to squint.

"Go on," Trevor said in his own dangerous voice. The waitress who was pouring his coffee hesitated. Trevor nodded at her and then she left.

"Last night's little adventure was recorded and sent via the internet to the newspaper here in Redwood. The resulting story is not very good." Quentin handed Trevor the story and Trevor scanned the headlines.

"ADAMS FAMILY OPERATES BED AND BREAKFAST ILLEGALY"

Last night the owner of the new Bed and Breakfast in the city was throwing a lavish party for friends and supporters even while they had been warned not to operate without a licence."

Trevor placed the paper down on his plate and reached for his own coffee cup. Taking a sip he looked again into Quentin's eyes.

"We are going to have to fix this ourselves, Quentin," he said.

"There is more. Someone broke into the Bed and Breakfast last night after we left and tried to steal the original copies of the licences and permits. I had a communique with one of the officers involved in the investigation this morning. The officer who was shot at found two children who had been missing in the Pablo Brothers case. They were the ones who were being kidnapped this morning. Someone in the police department is on the take to the Pablo Brothers." Trevor's jaw began to bulge at this information.

"And you know this because?" Trevor was starting to doubt this man's word. In his mind, Ethan was not a man who would allow something like this to happen in his city.

"I know who the mole is, and I can prove it," Quentin's deadly tone told Trevor he knew Trevor was finding it hard to believe what Quentin was telling him.

"Okay, let's have it. Why do you know who it is and how did you find out?" Trevor asked.

"Have your breakfast, Trevor. Then we'll go over to the Bed and Breakfast and clean up the mess that was left last night. We owe that much to Dorothy and Ethan. After we finish we can have a strategy session." Trevor nodded his agreement to Quentin. "I don't think I have to tell you that we should sweep the Bed and Breakfast for any listening devices as well," Quentin added.

"I'm on it," Trevor said. His cell phone rang and Quentin sat back to finish reading the paper while Trevor talked on the phone.

"Trevor here."

"Hey, boss. You called?" Thomas' voice spoke through the phone.

"I need you in Redwood immediately. We have a complication here," Trevor said quietly.

"No problem. Where are you at? I will be there in minutes." Trevor was doubtful Thomas could be that fast.

"Where are you, Thomas?"

"Just getting off the plane at the airport," Thomas answered.

"You anticipated?"

"Just like you taught me. I have some info, and some equipment you may need." Thomas's voice was point blank.

"There is a new Bed and Breakfast in town. Find it and be there in ten." Trevor said and ended the call.

"You have some very good employees, Trevor. I gather he'll meet us at the Bed and Breakfast?"

"Yes, Quentin, and I have to tell you, I am not sure working with you is going to be such a boost to my business." Trevor had finally mentioned what was bothering him about the 'friendship' between them.

"I think you have the completely wrong impression of me, my friend." Quentin folded the newspaper, placed it beside his plate and stood up.

"I am not your friend. Not by any means." Trevor stood and stared right at Quentin.

"Is this really a good time for a showdown between us, Trevor?" Quentin's cultured voice asked. His face was inscrutable and his eyes were hooded.

"I don't believe so. But when this whole mess is cleared up for Dorothy's sake, we will talk," Trevor answered. Quentin nodded and

A SILENT ENEMY

led the way out of the café and into his SUV. There was complete silence between them as they travelled to the Bed and Breakfast.

Quentin pulled up to park beside a black vehicle with Thomas unloading equipment out of the back. Before he got out, Quentin motioned to Thomas.

"Is this your man, Trevor?"

"Yes." The resentment still remained between them and Trevor's answer was short. Trevor climbed out of the SUV and walked over to Thomas.

"Got your sweeping equipment in the first case, and some files in the second." Thomas pointed to the two cases on the ground. He pulled a third out of the truck and grabbed one on the ground. "Do we have keys for the front door?" Thomas asked as he walked on ahead.

"No. But then, you don't really want to let that bother you, do you?" Trevor answered as he picked up the case on the ground and followed behind Thomas.

Quentin paused after getting out of the truck and noticed that there was no greeting between the two men. Both of them were focused on the task at hand of clearing the building before them of listening devices. He slowly followed behind the two men and admired their work.

"By the way, Thomas," Trevor said as Thomas quickly unlocked the front door.

"Yes?" Thomas asked as he looked over his shoulder and entered through the open door.

"There's a security alarm on the wall to the right of the door." Trevor instructed. Thomas stepped over to the security pad as Quentin entered through the door behind Trevor. It only took a few seconds and Thomas had the alarm disabled.

"Dorothy should know better than to use these ancient things for protection," Thomas said over his shoulder to Trevor.

"True. But her mind has been preoccupied for some time lately and she didn't have the same security conscious mind that we all know and love," Trevor stated flatly. Quentin turned to Trevor with a raised eyebrow.

"Come now, Trevor. Don't tell me you're jealous?"

"Not in the least. Just wondering what other things Dorothy let slide in the last couple of years," Trevor intoned in that quiet voice he had.

"I'm going upstairs to look around and make sure no one broke in while we were out." Trevor said as he picked up the bag with the sweeping equipment. Both of the other two men nodded at him silently when they understood his meaning.

"I'll start cleaning in the kitchen." Quentin took off his jacket as he went through the swinging doors to the kitchen. That left Thomas with the office and the rest of the main floor. Twenty minutes later, Trevor came down the stairs with his hand held sweeper and motioned for Thomas to come over to him. With a finger held to his lips, he showed the three little electronic devices out in the palm of his hand. Thomas nodded and pointed the way to the office. Trevor followed him and Thomas pointed to the lamp shade of the floor lamp behind the desk.

"Trevor, I have cleaned up in here and would you like me to go and help Quentin in the kitchen? I don't think he's used to scut work." Thomas grinned.

"Okay. I'll just take a look at Dorothy's paperwork and file it for her." Trevor said, then motioned with the sweeper to cover the desk. Thomas left the office and Trevor was able to find three more bugs in the office. Next he covered the lobby area and found two. He went to the dining area and found another two. Going through the swinging doors into the kitchen he found another three. The other two men had their sleeves rolled up and were silently cleaning the kitchen and washing dishes.

"Well, it looks like the two of you are doing okay in here, I need to use the washroom. Be right back, okay?" The other two nodded and smiled. Trevor had just told them that the house was clear except for the washroom. Still, they didn't say a word, they just continued to clean until Trevor came back in.

Placing the little electronic devices on the table in front of him, he was joined by Thomas and Quentin. It was obvious that there were two different types of listening devices on the table. That meant there were two different people trying to listen in on the conversations that went on in the Bed and Breakfast. Trevor held up two fingers so the other men could see what he was thinking. Both of them nodded. Going over to a drawer that held cooking utensils, Trevor took out a meat mallet and began to systematically smash each and every one of the devices into tiny little pieces.

"Well that looked like fun," Thomas smiled at Trevor.

"It was," Trevor looked at Quentin and noticed a little smile on Quentin's lips.

"Now we can converse in complete privacy." Quentin motioned to the table. "Please sit. I have some coffee ready." Thomas looked at Trevor and raised his brows in a silent question. Trevor nodded and both men sat. Quentin poured the coffee and all three men began to talk about strategy. After an hour they came up with a very good plan.

"So then you two want me to place listening devices at the newspaper, on the newspaper editor's phone, and at the church pulpit, and the Pastor's office for the Puritans?" Thomas checked off the list in his head.

"Should we bug the police chief's office?" Quentin asked. Trevor shook his head.

"Under no circumstances are we to bug that office. But we do want to do a sweep in case he has been under scrutiny," Trevor answered Thomas nodded and did another mental check.

"How will Thomas be able to do that?" Quentin asked.

"Don't ask, Quentin. Thomas has certain abilities that no one knows about," Trevor answered.

"All right. I'm just not used to this type of heavy security measures. I didn't even know there were people here in Canada who knew how to do this type of espionage." Quentin's little smirk brought Trevor's stare up to Quentin's eyes.

"And just what do you mean by that?" Trevor asked.

"Easy, Trevor, easy! All I meant was I have only seen espionage tactics like this on the big screen or in the States. I didn't mean that as an insult." Quentin raised his hands up in front of him as if to ward off an invisible enemy.

"Oh well, of course you didn't," Trevor grimaced. "Who the hell do you think taught the actors and the States all about security?" Thomas smiled at that and looked down at the hand sweeper on the table. Quentin laughed out-right.

"Of course you did. Well, the next thing we have to discuss is how we are going to keep those two safe until this is resolved?" Quentin stated.

"I think you're talking about Dorothy and Ethan. So we had better wait until we can talk to them alone. They're a little busy right now, but if we do something before they know about it, they could get a little miffed at us," Trevor said. Quentin nodded.

"Trevor knows that from experience," Thomas smiled.

"Is that right?" Quentin was smiling as he asked the question.

"Save it, Thomas. We need to find out what is going on down at the station house where Ethan is. Any ideas?" Trevor asked. Quentin took out his cell phone and punched in a number. The two other men watched him closely.

"Hello my dear. Quentin here. Can you tell me where you are right now and what you are doing?"

"Why?" Dorothy's voice carried to Trevor and Thomas on the other side of the table.

"I have you on speaker phone and I have Trevor and Thomas with me. We are having a strategy session and we were wondering if we could expect you at the Bed and Breakfast any time soon?"

"Thomas is here too?" Dorothy's voice was alarmed. "Why, what's happened?"

"Perhaps it would be best if you just came over as soon as you are able to," Quentin cleared his throat. "And bring Ethan as soon as he can get here, okay?" Both Trevor and Thomas nodded at that last statement. There was a pause as Dorothy digested this information.

"All right. But expect Maria and my mother any time soon. They were picking up a few things I need and they should be there any minute. Oh, and I will have a police escort with me until further notice." She ended the call and all three men looked at each other in alarm.

"It's serious," Trevor's understatement made the two others nod.

"Okay then, I'm off for the newspaper," Thomas rubbed his two hands together in anticipation. "I assume you don't need me for the next couple of hours, eh?"

"No, go ahead. Quentin and I have something to talk about." Trevor looked right at Quentin and his stare made a shiver go down Thomas's back.

A SILENT ENEMY

CHAPTER TWENTY ONE

Ida Johnston hung up the phone and stared with amusement out the window as her two grandchildren played in the grass in the back yard.

"Who was that, Momma?" Ida turned to look at Anna who was standing at the stove making cinnamon buns. Ida had promised to show Anna how to bake them.

"A man from the city. He wants to buy the farm from me," Ida watched Anna's back when she said that. She knew Anna was thinking what she was thinking. It was human nature, after all. Anna slowly turned to look into Ida's eyes.

"So, are you going to sell?" Anna asked with trepidation. If Ida sold the farm, Anna would have nowhere to go. She couldn't go back to the farm with Brad. He would kill her if she did.

"Not yet, my dear. The price he is offering isn't what I want to make selling worthwhile." Anna watched a slow smile spread over Anna's face.

"Would you like a cup of coffee when I take these out of the oven?" Anna asked Ida as she indicated the cinnamon buns in the oven.

"I would love one, dear," Ida answered and she smiled in return. "I think we should start getting some things packed that we want to take with us when we leave, though. I don't think it will be too long before we get that decent offer." The two women smiled at each other across the table.

"I really don't want much from this life, Momma," Anna said.

"I know, dear, but we do have to be circumspect and careful with our cash until we're gone," Ida instructed the younger girl. Anna nodded.

"Of course, Momma," drying her hands on a tea towel, a timer went off on the oven.

"Oh good!" Anna clapped her hands together. "I'll call the kids in to wash up." She said as she took the buns out of the oven.

"Oh Anna," Ida said quietly. "We don't want to speak of this in front of the children, do we?"

"No momma," Anna caught the warning that was sent her way. "I understand."

CHAPTER TWENTY TWO

Ryan sat in his office with sweat pouring down his forehead. The air conditioning was off again and it didn't help his disposition any as the technicians seemed to think the problem was in his vent. For over an hour he had to put up with a technician climbing up a ladder and working over his desk. Ryan even had to move his desk so the technician could reach the vent.

"Could you hurry up? I need to get *some* work done today," Ryan's irritated voice reached the technician on the ladder.

"Sorry, sir. I'll just be another minute." The technician reached into his utility belt and took a small electrical bug and placed it carefully where the other one had been hidden. "There! All done, sir." Thomas climbed down the ladder and smiled at Ryan. "Whew! You're right. It sure is warm in here." Going over to the thermostat on the wall, he clicked it to automatic a/c and a hum was heard from the vent.

"Thank goodness," Ryan exclaimed. "We've had more than enough trouble with that unit since they installed it six months ago." He wiped his brow with a handkerchief.

"And I'll bet that bug has been there since they fixed it." Thomas said to himself as he pocketed the little electronic bug in his utility belt. "Well, I guess I'm out of here," Thomas smiled and nodded, touching the brim of his cap like so many of the people in Redwood did. Collecting his equipment and his ladder, he went out the way he had come in. When he had first arrived at the city hall, he had gone in the back door after he found out they had lost their air conditioning at City Hall. Ryan had met him at the main door and escorted him into Ryan's office as Thomas had used the bug sweeper and pretended to be looking for a short in the electrical system for the air conditioner. Stopping just under the vent in Ryan's office, he announced success in finding the short. A few tweaks and the new bug was set where the old bug had been.

Getting into his truck, Thomas neutralized the old bug and slipped it into his pocket. It looked exactly like one of the other bugs they had found at Dorothy's.

"Well, well. Ryan is important to someone's plan here in Redwood. I'll bet it is the Puritans." Thomas said to himself. He drove out of the parking lot and over to the address of the church he had been given. Parking so he could see anyone coming and going through the front door, he sat and watched for a while. There didn't seem to be anyone suspicious but still, Thomas decided to wait until dark to plant his bug.

CHAPTER TWENTY THREE

Dorothy bent down to look at the two little tear streaked faces on the back seat of Ethan's truck. She reached out to touch the shoulder of the littlest one and he shrank away.

"He is scared, miss," The older one said in Spanish as he held onto the younger boy.

"I would imagine so are you?" Dorothy looked at Juan and tried to smile. The fear and the pain those two boys had gone through just about tore her heart out. It was a second or two before Juan had realized Dorothy answered him in Spanish. Juan nodded and started to smile a little.

"Would you two like to come to my place for a little while?" Dorothy asked when Juan smiled. Juan looked at Brother and whispered something into his ear. Brother nodded and started to slide towards the end of the seat with Juan. Dorothy held out her arms to Juan, who hesitantly accepted her help. Then she helped Brother down and as soon as she set Brother down beside Juan, Juan put his arms around Brother. Bending down on one knee in front of the two boys she asked a very simple question.

"Can I trust you two to keep a secret?" she asked in a conspiratorial voice. Both boys nodded. "I've been a little scared myself lately. Do you think we could help each other out and protect each other? I don't think I could do it alone." Dorothy's admission of being scared made a connection to the two boys, and asking them for help had let the two boys puff up with pride. Little Brother slowly let go of Juan and reached for Dorothy with both arms. Ethan saw it but he didn't believe it. He couldn't hear what Dorothy had said to the two boys, but she turned and came towards him where he stood on the sidewalk with Brother in her arms, and Juan's hand in hers.

"I'm going to take my boys home now," Dorothy said in a tone that defied argument. Ethan nodded and tried to smile over the lump in his throat. For someone who was scared of children, Dorothy sure had a way with them.

"Dorothy, there will be a police escort with you wherever you go, 24/7, okay?" Ethan said as he tried to clear the tears from his eyes before his men saw any sign of weakness. Dorothy nodded and put the two boys in the back seat and latched their seat belts. Climbing into the front seat, she waved at Ethan and drove away while the two boys stared at him silently from the back seat.

"How did she do that?" Detective Harmon came up behind Ethan and asked over his shoulder. Ethan shrugged.

"I don't know. There are some things she does that are still a mystery to me," Ethan answered as he watched a squad car pull in behind Dorothy's truck.

Dorothy pulled into the parking lot of the Bed and Breakfast a few minutes later and saw the vehicles. Turning the ignition off, she turned to the two boys in the back seat. She wanted to assure them that she knew the people inside the house and they didn't have to be scared.

"Okay, Juan, Brother. I know all these people in the big house over there. They are my friends, okay?" the two boys silently nodded. "Do you trust me?" The two boys nodded again. "Good. Then I trust you. Those people in there trust me, too. So I want you two to be brave and come in with me, okay?" They nodded a third time in unison as Dorothy got out of the truck. The front door opened and Quentin Tallas stood there tall and strong. Quentin glanced around and motioned to Dorothy to come in. She nodded and opened the door to the back seat.

"Okay, here we go." Dorothy carried Brother while Juan held onto her hand and they went into the house. Quentin closed the door behind them as the cruiser pulled up in the parking lot. Dorothy set down Brother beside Juan and straightened up.

"Are you two hungry?" Dorothy asked. She could smell tacos cooking in the kitchen. Two little heads nodded and smiles spread across their faces. This was something they were familiar with. Eating tacos. "We have to wash up first. I'll show you the washroom." Trevor came out of the kitchen and smiled at the two boys.

"I can take you two boys to clean up if you want." The two boys looked at Dorothy with a question in their eyes.

"It's okay, boys. You go with Trevor. You can trust him." Trevor took the two little hands offered to him and with a wink directed towards Dorothy, he led them to the washroom. When they were out of ear shot, Dorothy turned to Quentin.

"What is going on here?" she demanded. "Where are Maria and my mother?"

"Easy, Dorothy. Maria is cooking up a storm in the kitchen. When she heard you were bringing the two little boys here, she started cooking right away," Quentin tried to use a soothing tone of voice.

"Where is my mother?" she demanded again.

"Upstairs getting a room ready for the two of them," Quentin answered.

"Who did the cleaning around here?" Dorothy looked around in surprise when she noticed the spotless office.

"We did it after the sweep for bugs had been completed," Quentin answered.

"Bugs?" Dorothy's horrified voice made Quentin smile. Dorothy didn't like bugs.

"Not real bugs, electronic bugs," Quentin reassured Dorothy. Dorothy slumped down into the chair behind the desk and let out a sigh of relief.

"Wait a minute, electronic bugs?" Dorothy sat up straight in her chair.

"Two different kinds from two different people," Quentin explained. "We have everything taken care of for now. You and the two children will be safe here."

Dorothy sat in her chair behind the desk for a few seconds before she said anything.

"You realize who the Pablo Boys are, don't you?" Dorothy asked in a quiet voice. Her eyes were pleading with Quentin for understanding. "I mean, you came here to take care of one thing, and end up in the middle of what could possibly turn into a fire-fight." Quentin smiled his reassurance.

"Dorothy, you are a friend in need. I have never turned away from a friend when they needed my help, no matter what the circumstances. Now come," he reached out his hand beckoning her to come into the kitchen. "We have two little children to feed." Dorothy smiled her relief and got up to walk ahead of Quentin into the kitchen. Trevor already had the two little boys settled at the table. The youngest one, was sitting on two very thick phone books so he could reach the table top. He actually had a smile on his face and when Dorothy entered, he turned and waved at her.

"Well look at this!" Dorothy exclaimed loudly for everyone to hear. "My two boys are eating very well, Maria. May I join you?" Maria and Temperance were both fussing over the meal and the children; they both turned at the same time and smiled their happiness at Dorothy.

"Oh Dorothy, it's been so long since I've been able to play with grandchildren," Temperance gushed and ran over to Dorothy who was standing with a surprised look on her face.

"Grandchildren?" Dorothy stammered as her mother wrapped her in a tight embrace. "Mom, these aren't your grandchildren." The two boys looked at Dorothy when she said that and watched her with expectation. Temperance stepped back and smiled at Dorothy, bringing Dorothy's attention back from the hurt stares of the two little boys.

"Well, dear, they may as well be. You know once Maria gets attached there isn't anything you can do to change her mind." Temperance patted Dorothy's shoulder and turned back to the table.

"Well, Maria, shall we serve the adults as well?" Temperance inquired.

Maria looked at the stunned expression on Dorothy's face and began to smile. She knew all about Dorothy's health problem where children were concerned. Dorothy couldn't have any. Dorothy and Ethan would never be able to have any children of their own, but right in front of Dorothy was the perfect solution, and Temperance had set the wheels turning in Dorothy's head by that one little statement. From the look on Dorothy's face, Maria surmised the idea hit home pretty hard. A slow smile started on Dorothy's face as she began to think about the two boys. By the time she had advanced to the side of the two boys sitting at the table, Maria knew that the two boys had found their forever home.

"Yes, ma'am. Breakfast is served!" Maria placed the bowl in the middle of the table and took her place. Quentin and Trevor had already sat, and Temperance made sure Dorothy could sit in between the two boys. She watched Dorothy interact with the two boys and knew she had done the right thing by planting the seed in Dorothy's mind. The look in Dorothy's eyes was almost luminescent as the meal progressed to its conclusion. Even Trevor and Quentin were impressed with the instant change in Dorothy.

CHAPTER TWENTY FOUR

Ethan was in his office when he got the call from Ida Johnston. His officers were still cleaning up the mess after the kidnapping attempt and Detective Harmon was looking into how they had gotten into the precinct. The new receptionist came into the office with a worried look on her face.

"What's up?" Ethan looked up from his paperwork.

"You have a call from Ida Johnston. She won't talk to anyone but you," Came the reply. "She won't talk to Detective Harmon, or Tony." She waited for Ethan's reply.

"Put her call through. I'll talk to her," Ethan directed her. The receptionist nodded and walked back to her desk. Ethan was wondering why she didn't just use the com phone when his call came through.

"Ethan?" came Ida's querulous voice.

"Yes Ida, it's Ethan. How are you doing?" Ethan asked in a gentle voice.

"Brad is out and he is coming here later to get Anna and the kids. He says a piece of paper will not keep him away from his wife and children." The panic conveyed to Ethan over the phone was very real.

"I'll have someone out there as soon as I can Ida. Just stay inside and lock your doors. If Brad tries to get in, hide."

"Okay, Ethan." The phone line went dead and Ethan called the receptionist over the com.

"Yes Chief?" came her voice.

"Send a unit out to the Johnston farm immediately. In fact, send two. I want to make sure that Brad Johnston does not harm that family any more than he has."

"Yes Chief," Came the clipped reply.

"And notify Phil Harmon if he needs me, I'll be at the Bed and Breakfast." Ethan signed off on the com as he heard the receptionist reply.

Getting up and picking up his hat from the coat rack in the corner of his office, he looked forward to seeing how Dorothy was dealing with the children. He knew Dorothy couldn't have children and that she seemed terrified of even babysitting, but he knew he really had no choice when he asked Dorothy to take the boys. And in an amazing turn of events, Dorothy didn't even blink an eye when he asked for her help. Life was certainly getting interesting.

It didn't take Ethan long to get to the Bed and Breakfast. When he pulled up he saw the extra vehicles and realized that Temperance and Maria must be there along with Quentin and Trevor. Shaking his head at the thought of having to trust the two men who had arrived to help Dorothy and Ethan out of this mess really wasn't something Ethan wanted to do. But Dorothy trusted them, and he trusted Dorothy.

He was at the front door and ready to go in when he noticed the security camera out of the corner of his eye. It hadn't been there last night. *"It must be Trevor's doing,"* Ethan thought and tried the knob. It was locked tight. And Ethan didn't have a key. He knocked in annoyance and waited for an answer. It only took a few seconds but in those few seconds, Ethan's short fuse had been lit.

"Well good morning, Ethan," Quentin Tallas said as he offered a hand in greeting. Ethan shook it and brushed his way past Quentin's shoulder to find someone he didn't know leaning up against the wall next to the open door of the office.

"Who's he?" Ethan stopped with his hand on his holster.

"Easy, my friend. You wouldn't even get that weapon drawn before you were shot. This is Thomas, an associate of Trevor's. He's the one who installed the security system we are now using here," Quentin explained.

"We?" Ethan asked as he turned to Quentin, grimacing at Quentin's use of the word we.

"Of course. Dorothy asked for our help with this mess that has developed and we said we would lend her a hand," Quentin answered. "We can protect her and the boys much easier if we all stay here." These words were said in a much lower tone of voice so only Ethan could hear them. Just at that moment, Dorothy came through the doors from the kitchen and her yes seemed to be shining.

"Ethan, oh how wonderful!" She quickly embraced Ethan and kissed him gently on the cheek.

"How are you this evening?" he asked as Dorothy led him into the office. They sat in the two chairs across from the desk and Dorothy closed the door so they could have privacy.

"Dorothy, I am so sorry last night turned out the way it did," Ethan began as he held her two hands in his. He was standing directly in front of Dorothy with his heart in his eyes. Dorothy smiled and shook her head.

"You have nothing to be sorry for. It wasn't your fault that reporter broke in. It wasn't your fault Elva was shot, and it wasn't your fault someone tried to kidnap the boys. You're just the one who has to clean up everyone else's mess. I knew that about you before you even asked me to marry you. This family will have to remain strong and independent with you continuing to work in law enforcement." Ethan sank to his knees and drew a deep breath. He liked the sound of the word 'family'.

"Dorothy, I know you can't have children, and I was wondering how to bring this up, but I don't mind adopting, or even just being a foster parent. You were the only one I could think of when I had to place the boys in a safe house." Dorothy reached out and cupped Ethan's strong jawline and smiled with tears in her eyes.

"Ethan, that is the second time I've heard someone say that, in a way," Dorothy began to chuckle a little.

"Second time? Who said it first?" Ethan asked with a smile.

"My mother remarked how much she enjoyed playing with grandchildren. I just naturally assumed she would at least wait until we were married," Dorothy chuckled and Ethan joined her.

"I gather she wants us to consider taking the two boys on as foster children?" Ethan could hardly contain his joy.

"Yes, but Ethan, we have to be careful with the boys. They have been hurt, abused, and there are some very powerful people after them right now. I don't want them to think they will be here forever, if the DA is going to move them around from safe house to safe house. That would hurt them very much." Dorothy's face showed her happiness as well as caution. Ethan stood up and pulled Dorothy to her feet. He pulled her close and pressed his lips to hers, while his hands began to massage her shoulders. Looking into her eyes he made her a promise.

"Dorothy, my love, if you want these boys, I will make sure we get these boys. But perhaps we should give ourselves a little time to decide. See how we get along with them." Dorothy started to cry when she realized Ethan could fulfill that promise. She buried her head into his shoulder and mumbled.

"Oh Ethan, I want it to work out so much," She cried. Ethan held her closer and felt her begin to shake.

"Dorothy, it will. We'll make it work out. I love you so much," Ethan started trailing kisses along her jawline and down onto her lips. Passionate, hot and wet kisses like he couldn't stop.

"Ethan!" A knock sounded on the door to the office. "I think you'd better come out here," Came Trevor's voice from the other side of the door.

"Sounds like a call to work." Ethan gave Dorothy one last fleeting kiss and then released her from his embrace. "We will talk more about this when the mess is cleared up, okay?" His eyes held a promise to Dorothy for the future. She nodded, speechless with joy.

CHAPTER TWENTY FIVE

Ethan opened the door to Dorothy's office and Trevor stood there motioning to the windows that overlooked the parking lot. It seemed to be filled with a large number of people from all professions, not just reporters. The on-lookers were all watching a gentleman who stood on the steps of the front veranda and he was speaking in a rapid and aggressive manner, pointing at the Bed and Breakfast. He started to shake his fist at the sight of Ethan and Dorothy emerging from the office. Ethan could see several of the people nodding their heads and glaring angrily at the reflection of Dorothy and Ethan in the windows.

"It didn't take them long to figure out I was here. Dorothy and I weren't in the office very long and they weren't here when we went in." Ethan seemed stunned at the amount of people that accumulated in so short of a time.

"They flowed down the driveway like a tidal wave, Ethan," Trevor said, shaking his head. "The man preaching to them is the good Reverend Banks. He is the head of the Puritans here in Redwood and they followed him here."

Ethan's steely gaze focused on Reverend Banks as he watched the man's wildly waving arms as he spoke.

"He looks like he is ready to take off like a helicopter." Dorothy came up beside Ethan and slipped her arm around his waist. "I would like to meet this Reverend Banks," Dorothy said out loud. She waved with her free hand at the man in black standing on her front steps. When Reverend Banks saw the gesture, he seemed to puff up with his anger and his face turned red. He walked over to the door and tried to open the door. When the knob wouldn't turn, he started to shake the door, trying to open it.

"Not right now, Dorothy. The man is trespassing on private property, instigating a riot, and they probably don't even have a permit for this little event," Ethan spoke out. Taking his cell phone out of his pocket, he called the office.

"It's Ethan. I'm at the Bed and Breakfast over here and I have some people trying to have a gathering without a permit. Oh, and they are getting a little agitated. They are on private property and I want some units over here, they have to be dispersed."

"Ethan, if we could get Reverend Banks in here, alone, perhaps we could find out what he is actually up to. Without him out there prodding and pushing, we might be able to diffuse this without much hassle." Quentin had come up behind the rest of them as they surveyed the parking lot of people in front of them.

"You're right," Ethan nodded. "That's why I am about to invite Mr. Banks in for a little conversation." He pointed at Reverend Banks and crooked his finger as the Reverend smiled in victory. Banks turned to the crowd and clasped his hands together above his head as a sign he had won some kind of victory over the minions inside the building behind him. Ethan went and unlocked the door as Dorothy turned towards the kitchen. Maria and Temperance were inside there, keeping the boys busy with something and she did not want to be present in the office with Ethan or the Reverend in case she got physical.

"Good afternoon, *Mister* Banks, how are you this day?" Ethan greeted the man with a handshake and a smile after opening the door. "How would you like to come in and have a little talk?" Ethan stepped back and opened the door wider to let the man in.

"I'm fine, thank you." The man was short, about five and a half feet, and his black frock coat went to his knees. He had on a clerical collar over a black shirt and his hat was a bowler, also black. He had a long thin face and nose with a little bump on the end, giving him the look of a vulture with his dark hair and black eyes. "My friends here would like to come in and join us," Banks motioned to three very large body guards dressed in black as well except for the white shirts. All had sunglasses and very big muscles. Ethan blocked their entrance by holding up his hand.

"Sorry fellas, only the good Reverend here is allowed in. And you can tell the rest of your friends that holding a public gathering without a permit is against the law and they should disperse immediately, or I will haul them all into my jail and process them when I can find the time." He closed the door in the faces of the body guards and turned to Reverend Banks's surprised countenance.

"They have to come in. they're my body guards," Bank's voice was starting to whine when he realized he had to face Ethan alone.

"Mr. Banks, if you wouldn't mind coming and sitting in the office, I'm sure you will find yourself very safe with me." Ethan gestured for Banks to lead the way. Reverend Banks hesitated then seeing he had no alternative, he preceded Ethan into the office. Behind them, out in the parking lot, two police units pulled in and began to disperse the people in the crowd. Quentin and Trevor looked at each other and smiled. Ethan had that little problem under control.

The two men went into the kitchen to see Maria, Temperance, and Dorothy sitting with the two little boys at the table, and they were all coloring with crayons. The two little boys were smiling and laughing and didn't have a care in the world other than finishing their pictures.

"Dorothy," Quentin began. "We are going to leave just as soon as that crowd in the parking lot is gone and we'll be back for dinner," he announced. Dorothy looked up from the picture she was helping Juan to color and she nodded.

"Okay, but maybe you should call before you come in, just so we know who it is coming through that door," Dorothy mentioned.

"Of course, my dear." Quentin smiled at the sight before him. Going around the end of the table to where Maria sat with crayons in hand and took her hand in his. Bowing like a gentleman, he raised Maria's hand to his lips and kissed it gently. "Until we see each other again, dear lady." He went to where Temperance was sitting and did the same. Both the ladies began to get a little red in the face and stammer.

Trevor and Quentin went out the back door when the coast was clear and left the three ladies staring at each other. Dorothy shrugged her shoulders and smiled, then went back to coloring. "Don't look at me, he didn't kiss my hand," Dorothy said.

"I do believe that man likes you, Maria," Temperance smiled. The two boys covered their mouths and giggled into their hands. Dorothy looked at them with surprise.

"Did you understand what my mother just said?" she asked in Spanish. The two little boys grinned at each other and began to nod. "So you can understand English?" The boys nodded again. Dorothy turned to her mother and Maria and smiled. "I think these two young men have been keeping a secret from us," Dorothy said in English.

"What's that?" Temperance asked.

"They can understand English." Dorothy announced with a smile. Temperance turned to Juan and smiled at him.

"Do you really understand me?" Temperance touched Juan's cheek gently as she asked the question. Temperance clutched her hands to her chest at the mention of 'Grandmother'.

"Did you hear that, Dorothy?" Temperance gasped. "He called me Grandmother." Temperance literally had stars in her eyes.

"I heard that," Dorothy said with tears in her eyes. "Ethan and I had a talk, and we have decided that once we are married, we would like to keep these two boys with us. Not as Foster parents, but adoptive parents." She turned to Brother. "Would you like that?"

Maria and Temperance were starting to cry as well.

"Well it's about time, the way you two were gallivanting around and taking all the time in the world, I didn't think you would ever settle down," Maria said.

Brother looked deeply into Dorothy's eyes and saw the love there. He also saw what a little boy his age needed the most. Security. He reached out to Dorothy and Dorothy took him into her arms and hugged him so tight the little boy almost squealed. Juan jumped down and went to Dorothy, throwing his arms around the two of them.

"Well I think that is a yes, don't you Maria?" Temperance clapped her hands together. "Now we can start getting ready for the wedding. Have you two set a date yet?"

"Not yet. We seem to keep getting interrupted." Dorothy hugged both boys again. Looking up to her mother she saw the joy and love in her eyes. "I think we should ask Brother what his real name is before we adopt him, though." She turned Brother to look at her. "Can you tell me your real name?" Brother shook his head no.

"He doesn't know his name. We were both in that house for such a long time on the farm. He doesn't even remember his mother or father. I was all he had because I took care of him." All three women were shocked and upset at that long statement by Juan.

"Would you like me to pick a name for you?" She asked with a smile. "I know a good one you would like." Brother looked at Juan who nodded his answer to the silent question in Brother's eyes. Maria and

Temperance held their breaths waiting for the little boy to make his decision. Finally, he nodded and began to smile.

"Okay." he said in halting English.

"Your name is going to be Samuel. That's a good strong Christian name. We can call you Sam for short if you like. But you are going to have to talk a little bit more so you can get used to speaking with the rest of your cousins." Juan gave Samuel a big hug and a pat on the back.

"You are now my brother Samuel," he said with laughter.

"I don't know about you but I think I'm getting hungry again." Maria said with a smile. "Who wants spaghetti and meat balls?" At the blank stares she received from the two boys, Maria put her hands on her hips. "Don't tell me you've never had spaghetti and meatballs?" she asked. The two boys looked at each other and their eyes got big. Looking back at Maria they shook their heads no.

"All right, one gourmet meal of my spaghetti and meatballs coming right up!" Maria cheered. "That used to be your mother's favorite meal you know."

"Really?" Juan asked.

"Really!" Dorothy answered. "It still is."

Temperance began putting the coloring books and crayons together in the box and clearing the table.

"You two boys should go upstairs for a while and try on some of those new clothes I put in your bedrooms. Dorothy, why don't you go and help them do that?" Temperance seemed to be choking on something as she tried to talk. Dorothy smiled and took the two boys by the hands and walked them up the stairs. When they were gone, Temperance put a Kleenex to her eyes to clear the tears.

"She looks so happy with those two boys," Temperance said when Maria came over and took her by the shoulders.

"She is happy. And with the Good Lord willing, a few prayers, and a lot of work, she will stay happy." Maria gave Temperance a quick hug. "Now quit crying and make yourself useful. I need some onions chopped," Maria said.

"Oh no! Not the onions again. I did those last time and I had tears in my eyes," Temperance objected.

"Well you already have tears in your eyes so what's the difference?" Maria chuckled as she placed a chopping board, onions, and a large knife next to Temperance on the counter.

"Oh well, I guess you're right," Temperance picked up the knife and began to peel the onions under cold water.

"This wedding is going to be a big humdinger, isn't it?" Maria said as she started to brown the meat.

"Maria, you're right there. I think everyone in Redwood is going to want to come," Temperance answered her.

"Everyone except the Puritans," Maria interjected.

"Maria did you have to go and ruin a perfectly good joyful moment by saying that?" Temperance began randomly chopping the onions into tiny pieces. Maria stared at Temperance's angry glare for a moment.

"Remind me not to get you mad at me again. The way you're chopping that onion, I pity the person who does get you mad." Maria turned back to the stove and her pasta sauce.

CHAPTER TWENTY SIX

Ethan had the Reverend Banks sit in the chair in front of the desk while he sat in Dorothy's chair. Once the Reverend was seated, and Quentin and Trevor who had quietly come in behind them and shut the door, Ethan looked right at Reverend Banks and smiled.

"Thank you for coming inside for this impromptu meeting, Reverend." The Reverend glanced around and noticed Quentin and Trevor standing at the door with their arms crossed.

"Thank you for having me inside like this. I didn't know you were going to be here, what with all the trouble at the precinct," Reverend Banks admitted.

"Oh? You mean you planned to come here because you thought Dorothy would be alone here with the two boys?" Ethan seized on the information immediately.

"No, I was actually having a meeting at the church when one of my parishioners came in and complained that there was nothing being done to conclude the problem at the Johnston Farm," Banks cleared his throat and sat a little straighter. "One thing led to another and the next thing I knew, almost the whole congregation was at the church and we decided to come here and protest about that woman who owns this place and why she gets such special attention."

"Who was your parishioner?" Ethan leaned forward and asked in a menacing manner. This made Banks try to swallow over the fear in his throat.

"What do you mean, who is the parishioner? I have hundreds of parishioners in my church." Reverend Banks sat back. "You should come to one of my services and you'll see."

"I meant, who is the parishioner who came in to complain to you about the investigation into the Johnston case?" Ethan countered.

"Oh, well, I do believe you will need a warrant for any of the names of my parishioners. Am I not correct in that?" Reverend Banks was too full of his own importance.

"You're right, of course, but in the spirit of generosity that brought you here to have a conversation with me, I thought you might like to know 'that woman' happens to have had a break in here last night. The police precinct was invaded by three men with guns, and you happen to be trespassing on private property by staging this "meeting" without a permit," Ethan informed the Reverend.

Reverend Banks looked at Ethan in surprise. He hadn't counted on Ethan being at the Bed and Breakfast and it seemed that Ethan now had the upper hand. He could have done some miraculous work if Dorothy had been here herself. He may even have been able to get her to pack up and leave town, but now he was stymied by one very particular cop who happened to be very infatuated with the immoral woman called 'Dorothy'. Ethan was still waiting for a response from Reverend Banks and he had to admit to himself, that he would have to back up a little in order to appear to be a reasonable man. Reverend Banks knew that would ingratiate him with his followers.

"I think you're right, Chief," Reverend Banks smiled at Ethan. "I think if I'm permitted to leave, I will convince my followers to leave as well and thereby prevent a lot of complications to this situation." It was Ethan's turn to blink in surprise. Reverend Banks stood and offered his hand in friendship, a gesture which Ethan ignored. Standing and glancing at Trevor and Quentin, who had remained silent up until now, Ethan nodded.

"Before you go, Reverend, I was wondering if you could clear something up for me," Quentin took a step forward as he spoke. Ethan and Trevor knew what was coming but apparently Reverend Banks did not.

"Yes, my friend, what can I do for you?" Reverend Banks' countenance showed he was supremely confident he had talked his way out of a difficult situation. Facing Quentin he waited for Quentin to say what was on his mind.

"Are you the Reverend Banks that was the head of that church in Toronto and brought up on charges of fraud and embezzlement a while back?" Quentin asked. The smile vanished off Reverend Banks' face. In fact, his entire face became blank.

"I paid my debt to society and that life is behind me. I will thank you to not bring it up again, Mr. . . "Banks tried to get Quentin's name but Quentin never answered him. Instead, Trevor stepped forward.

"Wait a minute, aren't you the same Reverend Banks who is the head of the Puritan group that blackmails its parishioners into doing what they want?" Reverend Banks' eyes became mere slits as he looked at Trevor.

"Don't I know you from somewhere?" he asked as he tried to jog his memory to place Trevor. "Have you been in Redwood long?" Banks asked as the memory was right at the edge of remembering.

"I'm just a visitor. And no, we haven't met," Trevor answered in a monotone. "I'm sure you'd remember if we did meet in person. The contempt Trevor felt towards Reverend Banks was evident in the tone of voice he directed at the Reverend. Feeling the wave of dislike coming at him from all three men, Banks knew it was time to leave.

"If you'll excuse me, I think it's time to leave, and I'll be taking my congregation with me." Reverend Banks turned back to Ethan. "I do hope my withdrawal from this situation means that there will be no repercussions against my parishioners?" Ethan nodded.

"Farewell then. Gentlemen, until we meet again." The superior attitude preceded the man as he took a step towards the door. Neither Trevor nor Quentin moved and they remained blocking Reverend Banks' departure. The silence in the office was ominous as a wave of resentment was felt by Reverend Banks.

"I'm sure the good Chief Barns would not want a larger problem on his hands at this point," Banks spoke out in his superior attitude. Trevor and Quentin looked at Ethan and Ethan cleared his throat.

"Reverend Banks, I want you to know that I am aware of your past, and just as you say, it is behind you. Do not let it color your future and determine your length of stay here in Redwood. I will not put up with your illegal actions here anymore than they did in Toronto," Ethan finished his little speech and Banks turned slowly to face Ethan once more.

"Is that a warning, Chief Barns? If it is I am highly insulted by your boorish attitude," Banks said with contempt.

"My boorish attitude is all that is keeping you safe right at this moment. I would think a man such as yourself would understand that. You will not break the law or trample on the freedom and reputation of the good people of Redwood while I'm still Police Chief," Ethan vowed. Nodding his acknowledgement, Banks turned to leave and walked right between Trevor and Quentin. Opening the door he turned back to Ethan and paused, nostrils flaring.

"Message received, Chief." Reverend Banks went out through the front door and into the crowd that was waiting impatiently for him without even closing the door. The three men saw him stand on the top step and raise his arms up in a gesture pleading for quiet. The crowd hushed as he exerted his influence and power upon his parishioners. Trevor, Ethan, and Quentin moved towards the open door so they could hear what the Reverend was saying.

"My parishioners, it has come to my attention that our little gathering here is on private property and we do not have a permit for it. I have decided to take you back to the church property and we can discuss our grievances in peaceful solitude there." The crowd cheered and booed at the same time. Reverend Banks looked good in the parishioner's eyes, and Ethan seemed to be the villain. "Let us disperse now." With a final wave at the three men in the window and a smile to show that he considered himself the victor of their little discussion in the office, Reverend Banks smirked and stepped down into the crowd to lead them away. Ethan watched them walk away in silence. Trevor and Quentin went back into the office and closed the door.

"I see they left without any egg-throwing at least." Temperance's voice came from behind Ethan and he turned.

"They're gone for now." Ethan commented.

"I sent Dorothy and the boys upstairs a few minutes ago to look through the new clothes we bought them. The boys deserved them. After all they've been through." Temperance shook her head at the thought of the pain and suffering those two young little bodies had gone through.

"Are they okay?" Ethan asked out of concern.

"Of course they are, they're with Dorothy," Temperance answered. "You have an awful lot on your plate these days. What with the attempted kidnapping, Elva's injuries and Ben Johnston passing away." Ethan nodded at his future mother-in-law.

"That's true. But it won't mean I can't spend time with Dorothy. I have my priorities," Ethan tried to assure Temperance.

"So does Dorothy. Once she makes up her mind to do something, it gets done. And she is in love with those boys. They're already a part of her family. If anyone should try to take them away from her, it would devastate her," Temperance explained. "Are you sure you can keep the boys here safe from those terrible people?"

"Yes I can. Trevor and Quentin have said they would be here to help if need be," Ethan said. Temperance surveyed the worried look on Ethan's face and saw the determination there as well.

"Perhaps it would be good if you concentrated on helping your fallen officer and taking care of the legal proceedings and charges in this fiasco. I will talk with Trevor and Quentin and we will take over the security of this family until such time as you can focus back on them once again." Ethan understood the message Temperance was sending him. Focus on one thing and she would make sure her daughter and the boys were well taken care of until Ethan could handle it himself.

"Are you sure?" Ethan asked.

"Ethan, how long have you known me?" Temperance asked with a hint of mischief in her voice.

"Longer than I've known Dorothy," Ethan replied.

"Then trust in me and have faith that I can do what I said I can do," Temperance turned and went into the office with a grace that made Ethan smile.

"Now I know where the term 'velvet and steel' came from," Ethan said out loud.

CHAPTER TWENTY SEVEN

Ida Johnston smiled as she checked her bank account on her computer. The insurance money had finally been placed in her account and she knew the time to leave Redwood was at hand before anyone knew what she had been up to. Turning to go back into the hallway, she knocked on the door to Anna's bedroom.

"Yes?" came a voice from the other side of the door.

"Anna? Are you and the two children ready to go?" Ida called out. She had waited for this moment for over twenty years when the idea had first entered into her head. All the careful planning, the years of abuse, and then finally being able to tell Anna about her plan had been a God-send. She really was looking forward to the 'holiday' that she and Anna had organized.

"Come on in, Mother," Anna's voice called out.

Ida entered the room as Anna was closing her suitcase. Ida only saw one suitcase and not one for the children. A puzzled look crossed her face as she looked at Anna.

"Where is the suitcase for the children?" Ida asked, not even thinking for one moment that she couldn't trust Anna.

"I didn't pack one, Mother," Anna stood demurely looking down at the floor with her hands by her side.

"Well why not?" Ida asked. "What are the children going to wear?"

"I changed my mind about them coming. I am going to miss them very much but I can always send for them when we get to the Caribbean." Anna looked so much like the innocent she was, Ida didn't want to break her heart. She had been through enough. But still, leaving the children behind didn't feel right to Ida.

"Sweetheart, the children have to come with us. We can't come back for them. We'll have to pick them up something after we land. We have to hurry and pick them up from the babysitters." Ida gripped

Anna by the shoulders and smiled. She really cared about this girl. She was different from the rest of the family. Ida had felt that from the start. They both had been through so much.

"Is the money there yet?" Anna asked in her innocence. "And are you sure you can access it from your lap-top? I wouldn't want the children and myself to be a burden on you, mother." Her plaintive little voice tore at Ida's heart and Ida knew she had made the right choice in telling Anna her plans shortly after she found out her son was beating her as well.

"All the money is there and the Cayman Islands account is up and running. We can get as much money as we need anytime we want," Ida assured the girl.

Ida felt the knife go deep into her abdomen but it didn't register until the pain hit her. The look of horror that passed over her face made Anna smile as Ida slowly sank to the floor.

"Why?" Ida gasped. "Why did you do this?"

"I decided I wanted all the money to myself," The girl stated flatly. "And I certainly don't want to share it with those two snivelling children." Anna's cruelty didn't seem to register in her own mind as she smiled again.

"When . . . ?" Ida gasped with her last breath.

"It doesn't matter now, but right after you first came to me with this idea of yours." The smile on Anna's face reflected her cruelty as she stood and turned to the door. Walking out on the woman who had helped her to plan both of their get-a-ways didn't bother Anna one bit. Neither did leaving her children behind. They would have been nothing but a nuisance to her. Anna closed the door to her bedroom and went to the bedroom where her children had been sleeping. Picking up the case with the lap-top in it, she turned and walked out the front door, locking the door behind her.

She started the car after placing the case in the backseat and buckled herself in. Smiling, she drove out the front drive and kept going all the way to the airport. She had started her new life and she knew she was going to enjoy it. Anna briefly thought of the children she had left behind at the babysitters. *"A couple of loose ends but nothing to worry about. What can they do to me when they won't even be able to find me?"* Anna chuckled to herself and parked the car. She was getting on the first flight bound for someplace warm and she didn't really care where it went.

CHAPTER TWENTY EIGHT

The Pablo brothers were in the back of an old abandoned barn not far from the outskirts of Redwood. They had been there since the night before when they had sent some of their men to take care of the officer who had found the two missing boys. The older one and more vile than his brother, grinned at the two men in front of him who were reporting on the results of their morning task at the precinct.

"They were so surprised, they never even knew what hit them." The smaller of the two men spoke in English and gestured with his hands. "We walked in and were almost out the door when the Chief showed up outside the precinct." Shaking his head his expression showed his fear of his employer's anger. A small growl came from the larger of the two.

"What is it Manuel?" Brother number two asked his lieutenant.

"That idiot, he botched it right from the beginning." Manuel looked at his shorter cohort.

"What do you mean? I did exactly what I was told to do when I was told to do it. I didn't see you helping very much," Shorty yelled at Manuel. Shorty's hair was black and greased back from his face, revealing a ferret-like countenance that had spent too many days inside. Small for his size, Shorty was very wiry. Many of his enemies had short-changed him because of his size and they had paid dearly for it with their lives. Shorty would have loved to make Manuel the next one who paid for that mistake.

"Enough!" The youngest of the Pablo brothers made a motion with his hand to cut off the conversation. "Tell me what happened next. You, Manuel, keep quiet until he's done!" Manuel did not take the rebuke too well. Shorty smiled and kept on talking.

"Manuel was in the lead and Roberto was behind him. Then I came out with the two brats we had found in the cells. No one even knew we were there until the Chief showed up. We could have made it out by shooting our way out, but Manuel here, he threw down his gun first and put his hands up like a little fairy!" The insult was cut short by a coughing sound coming from the older brother's handgun. It had a silencer on it and when brother number two looked over at him, he was smiling. Manuel just stood there in silence, afraid to speak.

"Is that true, Manuel? Did you just give up? Like a little fairy?" A trickle of sweat began to flow down Manuel's forehead and into his eyes. He dared not anger this man even more.

"No. I did not give up. That pig lying on the floor there told us to give up. And you, my Chief, told me to follow his directions, so I did. If I could have shot him where he stood, I would have. I was not afraid to die for you."

"And where is our other friend now?" Manuel seemed to growl again at the thought of the third man who wasn't even present.

"He took off from the precinct when they let us go. The lawyer you sent to us said he wouldn't even get in the car with us. We went out the front with pride and he slunk out the back like a coward." His contempt for the missing member of the trio was evident.

"Did he say anything to the cops?" came the question from brother number two.

"No. But he pissed himself in the holding cell when they came to take him in for questioning." Manuel shook his head in disgust. It was when he was looking down that he saw the straw he was standing on was hiding the fact that he was also standing on a sheet of plastic. He looked up and held out his hands in a pleading gesture.

"No, please. I didn't say anything. Please!" There was another cough from the gun and both the Pablo brothers smiled at each other. The two men from their cartel lay dead at their feet and they knew they now had a way to solve their legal problems.

"We must bury these two and then go after the two little ones," The older one said. The younger brother, who was by far the slowest, shook his head.

"No, we will not go after the two little ones. They are now in the possession of the girlfriend of the Chief of Police. My sources tell me they have so much security, we cannot simply just walk in the front door and start shooting. We have to be smart about this." They stared at each other and thought about it for a few minutes. Brother number two started to smile.

"What is it my brother?" Number one asked.

"We will ask our friend in the church to take care of it. We will also give the church a sizeable donation. We have used him before." Brother number one nodded his agreement to the plan.

"He did well that last time. He even went to jail instead of giving us up in Toronto."

"So it is agreed between us, that we call the Reverend again and remind him of who his friends are." Brother number one smiled and laughed with his younger brother.

"Then when we are done with him this time, we will send him on his way like we did our two close friends here." Both the brothers began to laugh at the same time while three of their men started to silently wrap the two failed assassins up in the plastic that had been beneath them.

CHAPTER TWENTY NINE

The officer assigned to the wellness check at the Johnston farm knocked on the front door of the farmhouse and waited. His sweat was beginning to run down the back of his neck making wearing a vest in this hot humid weather such a pain. He knocked a second time and waited. Finally he went to the window that seemed to show the living room area and the officer didn't see anyone. Alarmed, because he had been specifically told to watch out for anything out of the ordinary by Chief Barns, he circled around to the back of the farmhouse. He found a window up high enough in the wall he had to jump up to see inside, so he found an old milk crate lying by the corner of the building. Stepping up carefully, he was just barely able to see into a secondary bedroom. The bed was neatly made, but when the officer looked down to the area rug beside the bed, he took in a sharp breath. Leaping off the box, he ran to the back door and kicked it in while drawing his weapon. Crouching along the wall he slowly slid up to the bedroom door and glanced in. There was Ida, on the rug, with blood all around her and one hand clutching the wound in her abdomen.

The officer reached for the lapel mike and reported in to dispatch on his finding and quickly cleared the rest of the house. It was completely empty.

Kneeling back at Ida's side, he checked her pulse. There was none but Ida's skin felt warm to the touch. That meant to the officer that there was still a chance. Placing his hands on Ida's chest, he began compressions.

"Come on, Ida! Stick with me," the officer seemed to chant. Off in the distance, the officer could hear sirens. "Come one Ida! The EMTs are just about here. Don't leave me hanging, darling, breathe!" Suddenly there was a gasp as Ida took in a small breath. The officer smiled at Ida as her eyes opened.

"Atta girl, Ida. You're going to make it." The officer said with tears in his eyes. "You're going to make it!" Seconds later the EMTs entered the front door with a loud noise and were there beside Ida and her benefactor. Minutes later, with Ida stabilized and on her way to the hospital, the officer made a call on his cell phone to Detective Harmon.

CHAPTER THIRTY

Temperance was in the office with Trevor and Quentin and she looked pointedly at Trevor.

"You do security measures and work for people who need it in Toronto, am I correct?" she asked.

"Yes ma'am," Trevor answered immediately. Temperance's tone brooked no argument.

"And you, Quentin, you have a large security force of your own in Toronto, am I right?" Temperance asked Quentin.

"Yes I do. May I ask why?" Quentin and Trevor were curious as to why Temperance was asking.

"I want to know why they are still in Toronto when they are needed here in Redwood," Temperance asked. "You two should be ashamed for waiting until I had to tell you what to do." Temperance pointed out.

"Yes ma'am!" They both responded at the same time.

"Now let's get down to it. This place is going to have to be an impenetrable fortress and we will need at least a dozen men around the clock. Can you handle that?" The two men nodded again simultaneously. "Then get to it! You're wasting time!" Temperance began to get cross with the two businessmen.

"I already have one of my men here, and he is making a sweep of all the places where your family has been and we have found numerous listening devices from two different sources."

"Two? How do you know there are two different people trying to listen in?" Temperance demanded to know.

"We can assume that one type of listening is used by one company and we found two different types of listening devices." Quentin answered her. "So we got Thomas to go around and replace those listening devices with our own brand of device."

"And what have you learned so far?" Temperance asked.

"We found out that the manager of the newspaper here in the city is being blackmailed by the Puritans. They want him to muddy the waters by reporting hear-say and innuendoes. We have already talked to the man and we have remedied the situation by our own means," Trevor said as he glanced at Quentin.

"Well I don't want to know what those means are, but I hope you were gentle in dealing with the man. He is a friend of mine, you know." Temperance said.

"Of course, my dear," Quentin said. Temperance turned to him with annoyance.

"I don't want you constantly talking down to me Quentin. I have a little knowledge of security myself. Now tell me the rest." Quentin sat back, surprised at finding out Temperance had knowledge of security.

"May I ask where you acquired your knowledge?" Quentin asked.

"You may, but I won't tell you." Temperance met Quentin's direct stare with one of her own.

"Listen, you two. I've learned not to under-estimate the Adams family when the chips are all in," Trevor intoned. "Let's get this mess straightened out once and for all and let Dorothy and Ethan start their life together with those two boys without having to worry about looking over their shoulders all the time."

"Quite right, Trevor. Let's do it," Quentin agreed. Temperance nodded and began the conversation again, only this time, they all had a say in what to do next.

CHAPTER THIRTY ONE

Ethan sat behind his desk as quitting time drew near and knew he had to take something for the awful headache he had. With everything that was happening in his professional life and his personal life, he was having a hard time focusing on either one of late. The intercom buzzed him and he picked up the hand set.

"Yes? What do you need?" he barked into the phone.

"Sir, there is a gentleman here to see you. He says he is the lawyer for Reverend Banks and he has information that you may need," The receptionist answered.

"What was your name again?" Ethan asked. He didn't recognize the voice.

"Sir, it's Phyllis. Roxanne didn't show up for work this shift and we can't get in touch with her. I am covering right now." Ethan's mind digested this information and asked Phyllis to show the lawyer in. Getting up from his desk he sighed and reached for the door handle to let the lawyer in.

"Just put one foot in front of the other and take one moment at a time," he told himself. Opening the door he met face-to-face with a tall, well built, well-manicured man with blond hair, slicked back hair and one of those 'I can sell you anything' smiles. Ethan smiled and held out his hand in greeting.

"Welcome to my office, sir. What can I do for you?" Ethan ushered the man to the chairs in front of his desk and the lawyer sat in one while placing his briefcase in the other. Ethan then sat in his own chair and tried to keep the friendly smile on his face.

"I think there has been an error in communications, Chief Barns. I'm here to give you information that you may need in order to conduct your investigation into the incident that happened out at the Johnston Farm." The lawyer's supremely confident smirk was still on his face and

Ethan dearly wished he could wipe it off. Instead, Ethan maintained his smile and asked a question.

"What kind of information do you have?" Ethan queried. He leaned forward and crossed his fingers in front of him, tilting his head to the side.

"It has come to my attention by Reverend Banks that there has been an inquiry into his financial past and his criminal past in Toronto. He sent me here to give you the information I carry and to let you know he is not the man you think him to be." The lawyer smoothed his tie down the front of his shirt and he was still smiling his oily smile. It was starting to drive Ethan crazy. So much so that Ethan found himself staring at the man's lips, trying to see if they actually moved while he spoke.

"Well, first of all, I will need your name, and I will need to see some sort of identification telling me that you are who you say you are," Ethan held his hand out.

"Why certainly sir." The lawyer reached into his left breast pocket of his ridiculously expensive suit and handed Ethan a business card. Ethan read the card and sniffed.

"Well, Mr. Ronald Mack, Esquire. I am going to have to check with one of my lead detectives before we can discuss anything and see what he has to say about our investigation." Ethan reached for the intercom and buzzed Phyllis again.

"Certainly Chief Barns," The man spoke as if he was giving Ethan permission to call Detective Harmon. Ethan paused in his actions and his eyes squinted at Ronald Mack, Esquire, who, when he saw the glare, became quiet and he lost his oily smile.

"If you wouldn't mind, I'll just go and talk to Detective Harmon and I will be right back. Could I persuade you to step outside into the other room for now? It shouldn't take long," Ethan placed the phone down and stood up.

"Oh, certainly." The lawyer picked up his briefcase and followed Ethan into the reception area, and left instructions with Phyllis to keep an eye on him until he came back. In the back of Ethan's mind he was doing cartwheels.

I finally wiped the smile off his face. I don't think he likes being kept waiting. Ethan walked to the conference room for his meeting with Detective Harmon humming a little tune.

Phil looked up and saw Ethan enter the conference room with a little smile on his face.

"Are you humming?" Detective Harmon asked.

"Yep. It's not every day I get to make a lawyer unsure of himself like that. I have him waiting in the reception area while we hash out this Johnston Farm case. What do you have?" Ethan asked.

"Well, here is what we have chronologically." Harmon began. "Johnston went to blow a small hole in the damn early in the morning, like he always does once a year. Unfortunately for him, someone got there before he did and blew the damn while he was literally bending over the device used to do it."

"Really?" They waited until he got that close before they hit the button?" Ethan was astounded at the cruelty of the action. "That means this person must have had an awful big hate on for Johnston," Ethan's voice was now thoughtful.

"Right. The person was either someone who hated him or just wanted him out of the way," Phil explained.

"Phil, I tend to believe that if someone is watching and waited until he was standing right over top of the explosive device to push the button, they must have wanted to inflict major damage to that person. To obliterate Johnson." Phil nodded his agreement. "Therefore, the motive is hatred for the man," Ethan concluded.

"I think we may have two motives in this case," Phil stated. Opening a file folder to his right, he took a sheet of paper with some banking information on it. Handing it to Ethan, he waited until Ethan had finished reading it.

"This doesn't seem like enough of a motive for killing him. It's Ida's bank statement showing the life insurance payment she received. It doesn't mean she did it for his life insurance. There was no hatred or malice in her demeanor at the farmhouse when we were there," Ethan pondered.

"Then read the rest of the file." Phil handed over a fairly thick file and let Ethan read it through quickly.

"You mean to tell me, she actually sold the farm to Reverend Banks' Puritans for 1.5 million dollars?" Ethan sat with a thump, hardly able to believe his eyes and equate it to the Ida he knew and cared about. The Ida who was devastated by Ben's death.

"The title was signed over last night, and I have been unable to trace it to the actual purchaser. I am sure, once we talk to that lawyer of Reverend Banks who is sitting out there," Phil indicated the lobby, "we will be able to trace the title and find it has his name on it." Phil sat back, confident of his findings.

"But what would the motive be?" Ethan pondered it. "Phil, have you dug into the financial aspect of the rest of the Johnston family?" Phil passed Ethan yet another large file containing the information he requested.

"You might also want to read this file of abuse that I obtained from the hospital under a court order. I just wanted to dot all my I's and cross all my ts," Phil smiled in answer to Ethan's raised eyebrows.

"Can you sum this up for me in one short little sentence?" Ethan pleaded.

"Sure. From the record of hospital visits, and not only for Ida, I might add, I feel that the abuse in that family has gone on for more than two decades. Brad's wife has been hospitalized several times in the past as well. I thought at first that it was Brad who may have planted that device, but when I took a look at his wife's statement, something didn't ring true with the evidence at the scene. Plus, we found a witness that testified that Brad Johnston was in the bar until after midnight, and he was so drunk, his wife had to come and get him and drive him home." Ethan was surprised at that announcement.

"Then it wasn't Brad who planted it," Ethan said out loud to himself. "His wife Anna planted the idea that he was the one who did."

"Right," Phil agreed. "Now remember, we're just following the evidence here, Ethan." Phil warned Ethan he wouldn't like the rest of the evidence because of his friendship with Ida.

"I understand, Phil. "I'm a cop. We follow the evidence despite how we feel about the suspects," Ethan nodded.

"We traced several of the phone calls to the church here in town owned by the Puritans," Phil began again. "Some of them were made from a throwaway cell phone which was untraceable." Phil passed another sheet to Ethan so he could see it for himself.

"Okay, what about fingerprints, DNA, etc.?" Ethan asked.

"You mean from the crime scene?" Phil asked.

"Yeah, I want to get that pinned down first before we go off on another tangent," Ethan said.

"We found several plastic fragments from a trigger device that was set off by remote control. Someone had to actually be there to push the button at the right time," Ethan nodded.

"We are processing several partial prints, but so far we don't have a match. There is no useable DNA, but that would take another couple of weeks anyhow," Phil explained.

"Okay, good," Ethan nodded. "Now the motive. Was it financial or hatred?" Ethan asked.

"We have gone through a lot of financial information and found that Brad Johnston's farm is failing. He is an abusive tyrant who likes to drink a lot and blame his failings on others," Phil explained.

"I wonder where he got that." Ethan asked more for his own benefit than to get an explanation from Phil.

"Statistics say that he most likely learned from the environment and emotions around him. Someone in his family influenced him while he was growing up," Phil said. "I know that doesn't explain why he made the choices he did, but it does show the gradual evolvement of an abuser."

"Phil, we all make choices, good or bad. This man has not been held responsible for any of his choices until now. He could have decided to be a hardworking, energetic man with a love of life, but he chose to go the other way. That is *his* responsibility. *He* chose," Ethan pointed out.

"Yes, Ethan, but listen to the rest of this." Phil went on to explain how Brad's farm went into bankruptcy, and then the Provincial Government decided to propose a new route into the city so that it would lessen the wear and tear of traffic on the City of Redwood itself. Then came the surprise that Ethan didn't know about. The route of the new highway was planned to go through Ben Johnston's farm, effectively cutting it in half. That meant that the price of Ben's farm nearly tripled in value, but the only people who knew about it was the planning committee at the City Hall of Redwood. Factor in that Reverend Banks came to town shortly after the announcement in the Mayor's office, and Phil put two and two together.

"Right now, we are trying to connect those phone calls to Reverend Banks. We are unable to do that at this time. They have to be coming from someone in that congregation, as the pings from the cell phone towers locate that throwaway cell phone was in the church when they were placed," Phil pointed out.

"Okay, then we will try to place any person talking on a cell phone and who had to walk out of the service to do so," Ethan said.

"How so, Ethan?" Phil asked.

"Look at the times those calls were placed. Reverend Banks was preaching up a storm at the time those calls were made." Ethan pointed to the sheet with the phone records on it.

"You're right, Ethan. Banks couldn't have made those calls," Phil began to get excited.

"No, but he could have had someone do it for him to divert suspicion somewhere else," Ethan said. Both men looked at each other and pondered the situation.

"Do you think that maybe a lawyer could have done that?" Phil asked Ethan. Ethan smiled.

"I think it's time to go and talk to a lawyer. I'll go and get him settled in him my office then you join us as soon as you pack this up, okay?" Phil nodded and began to close the files as Ethan headed back out to the reception area.

"Lawyer Mack, if you don't mind, we can go back into my office now." Ethan smiled at the expression of the lawyer who showed his displeasure at having to wait so long for a meeting with the Chief of Police. *He looks positively frosted,* Ethan hummed to himself.

"It's about time, Chief. I was beginning to think you had changed your mind about me," Lawyer Mack complained.

"Not a chance of that, sir. I just needed the time to talk to my lead detective and find out where we are at with all of the evidence we have," Ethan explained to him with a smile. They seated themselves and then Detective Phil Harmon came into the room and closed the door.

"Oh, I'm sorry, I didn't know there was going to be someone else present," Lawyer Mack said with trepidation. "Perhaps we should put this off until such time as you can see me on your own." He started to rise from his chair as Detective Harmon sat beside him and opened his note book.

"Sit down, Mr. Mack," Ethan ordered in a voice tinged with anger. "You have evidence in a murder investigation and you will not leave here without telling us what it is. If you try, you will be arrested and charged with obstructing an investigation." Lawyer Mack slowly sat back into his chair and cleared his throat, while smoothing down his tie.

"Now, Mr. Mack, this is my lead detective, Phil Harmon. He will be taking notes and will verify that the information you give us is correct," Ethan explained and introduced Phil.

"I am not giving a statement at this time, sir. And I will thank you to remember that I have client privileges with Reverend Banks," The lawyer objected.

"Duly noted," Phil Harmon began scribbling in his notebook.

"What is he writing?" Lawyer Mack asked.

"Every word you say," Ethan explained. "Unless you want me to record you on this." Ethan took out a small digital recorder and placed it on the top of his desk. The lawyer eyed the machine with suspicion and swallowed. He could always refute what was written down on paper, but the spoken word could be used as evidence in court.

"I think we'll stick to his notes," The lawyer decided.

"Good, now we can begin." Ethan sat back and folded his hands in front of him and waited.

"Right, well, Reverend Banks contacted me several months back when he noted an undercurrent of suspicion forming between his parishioners over the possible chance to purchase some land on the edge of the city to build a new church. One of his parishioners was pushing for the church to buy it and move so we could accommodate our growing numbers. Unfortunately, the man who owned the farm kept saying no. The person pushing for the sale seemed unaccountably upset about it, so the good Reverend asked me to look into it and find out why." The lawyer pulled some papers out of his briefcase and placed them on the desk in front of Ethan. "These are some of the findings I obtained through a special investigation firm based in Toronto. Which is where I am from." Mr. Mack sat pensively straightening his tie and clearing his throat while Ethan went through the papers.

"Your papers are telling me, that you traced the grumblings of your church to a man named Burton Price?" Ethan said with surprise. Phil paused in his writing and looked up with surprise.

"He's our city manager, Ethan. He does go to that church, but I can't believe he would do something like this!" Ethan was nodding and then he looked at Ron Mack with a piercing stare.

"Do you verify that this information is true?" Ethan asked. Ron Mack nodded and stared right back.

"I will testify to that on the stand if you want," he answered.

"Phil, we have to follow the evidence to where it leads us," Ethan said. "I want you to verify this information and get back to me as soon as you can." Phil jumped up and reached out for the information the lawyer had provided them. In an instant he was gone and there were only Ethan and Ron Mack in the office.

"I am going to turn this tape on because I want a record of the answer to the next question," Ethan stated flatly. The lawyer nodded his agreement and then waited while Ethan stated the time, place, and who he was interviewing into the recording machine.

"Mr. Mack, can you state with absolute assurance that Reverend Banks is not involved with the investigation into the death of Ben Johnston?" Ethan asked.

"Reverend Banks is not guilty of involvement of any kind in this matter," Ron Mack stated as the sweat began to pour down his neck and forehead.

The office felt hot and stuffy as Ethan wound up to ask the next question and Ron Mack loosened his collar.

"Why did Reverend Banks send you to me with this statement? Why didn't he come to me himself?" Ethan asked the question that Ron Mack was dreading.

"Reverend Banks fears for his life if he brought you this information himself. The man Price has apparently been siphoning money out of the city's infrastructure fund for years, and recently started to pressure Reverend Banks to help him with some zany get-rich-quick scheme so he could replace the lost funds and get away scott free." Now that the words were out and on tape, Ethan was stunned by the immenseness of the plan that Burton Price had devised to steal more money from the people of Redwood.

It made sense to him, really. The appropriations committee would take funds ear- marked for fixing sidewalks and landscaping city parks, and nothing would be done. People had been complaining about the state of their municipal government for years. There seemed to be no money to do anything, even when the federal government sent funds after funds and grant after grant to the city. Staring at Ron Mack, he decided to wait for Phil to come back into the room before he let the lawyer go.

"You'll have to stay here in this building with me until we get this investigated." Ethan rose from his desk and walked towards the lawyer, dangling the cuffs in front of him.

"Now wait a minute! Am I under arrest?" Ron Mack jumped up with alarm.

"No sir, just placing you under a witness protection order." Ethan smiled as he cuffed Ron Mack and walked him out to the holding cells."

"Phyllis, can you please have one of my officers come here and take care of Mr. Ron Mack and keep him comfortable until we can verify the information we have?"

"Of course, Chief." Phyllis summoned one of the officers who came and booked the discontented lawyer into one of the holding cells. Ron Mack went down the hall yelling all the way. Ethan just smiled and dusted his hands then placed them on his hips as he watched the lawyer struggling to get away from the officer assigned to him.

"Are you having a good day, Chief?" Phyllis asked.

"At the moment, yes." Ethan answered. Turning he looked at Phyllis. "Still no word from Roxanne?"

"No sir. I'm beginning to get a little worried." Ethan's brow furled. "Keep trying. If you don't contact her by the end of the day, send a unit over to her house," He instructed.

"Yes, Chief." Phyllis turned back to the phone in front of her as it started to ring. Putting the person on hold, she looked at Ethan.

"It's a Miss Dorothy Adams, sir. She says she needs to speak to you as soon as possible." Ethan grinned and told Phyllis to put it through to his office, then he sprinted through the door and closed it as fast as he could. Phyllis, knowing exactly who Dorothy was, just smiled and put the call through.

CHAPTER THIRTY TWO

The Pablo brothers worked their way through the dense underbrush surrounding the abandoned barn they were currently inhabiting. Their friend, who had let their men into the main police precinct, had allowed them to stay there. Not because she was such a good person, but because they were blackmailing her into doing what they wanted. She had been on their payroll for several years and they were using that to squeeze information and favors out of her. The botched attempt to remove the two young boys that could point out who their captors were had angered the both of them with its absurdity. Their three leaders had intended to go in, pretend to be lawyers, and their friend Roxanne would let them in. Unfortunately, they did not think to plan a second way out in case they became trapped in there. Which is exactly what happened. Now the two brothers, who ran a fairly large cocaine and human trafficking ring were furious at having to find Roxanne and the third man who had botched the entire plan.

They had to find the third man and dispose of him because if caught, the man could be squeezed hard enough, he would spill his guts eventually. And Roxanne as well because she had outlived her usefulness. They had been on their way up the path to Roxanne's house when a squad car had pulled into the drive. Ramirez, the older brother, quickly pulled the younger brother into the dense brush and they squatted to hide and look through the branches to watch what was happening at the house.

Two officers got out of the unit and walked up to the door to knock. There was no answer, so one of the men circled around the back and the first one waited. The first officer knocked again with no answer. A sudden movement from behind brought the first officer to the edge of the front porch. He looked back to the yard and was summoned by the second officer. Disappearing from sight, Ramirez looked to his brother and growled his observation out to his brother.

"She's not home. And they've found something interesting in the back yard," Ramirez spat. Balthazar turned to look at the scene unfolding in the back yard of the small farmhouse. Named after a biblical man, Balthazar showed no inclination to be like his namesake was.

"We should have killed her when we had the chance." He growled back to his brother. Little ringlets of black, greasy hair were falling down upon his forehead and his clothes were made from a highly expensive linen fabric, which was stained by sweat and dirt. Ramirez admired his younger brother, except when he got that look in his eyes. He became a crazy man and lost all sense of logic.

"We will get her little brother. We need to be patient." He grabbed his brother around the back of his neck and embraced him, trying to calm the anger that threatened to take over in his brother. "For now, put away your gun. We need to be hidden for a little while longer. When these cops are gone, we will search for her and we will find her. If she has betrayed us, she will wish she had never been born." Balthazar's pearly white teeth showed up startingly white in the evil smile that formed on his face.

"I want to play with her first." Balthazar's smile scared even Ramirez. In order to keep him happy, Ramirez knew he would have to let Balthazar do what he wanted with the woman. At the moment, they had to find other shelter.

"You can do what you want, but first, we need to find more shelter. These police will find nothing and they will search the grounds. We will leave and go to our secret place that we use when we are in this area." Balthazar nodded his agreement and the two of them faded back into the dense brush.

At the house, the two officers had found a pile of papers in the back yard that had been burnt but some was still intact. The first officer looked up when he read part of a sentence which read "….paid by Pablo brothers …." And he dropped it like he was stung. Glancing around he motioned for the other officer to drop and take cover. They dove behind a large pile of chopped firewood and stayed under cover while they called on their cell phones for backup. The day was hot and the sun beat down on them mercilessly while they waited for what seemed like hours but was in fact, only minutes. Soon they heard sirens blaring in the distance. When the squad cars finally pulled in they numbered four. The mention of the Pablo brothers always brought concern to the uppermost of every cop in Redwood. Not knowing what they were dealing with made caution a strict rule.

The two officers hiding in the back yard came forward and explained what they had found and informed the Sergeant in charge that they had not cleared the house yet or the surrounding environment. The Sergeant, knowing that time was important, ordered everyone to suit up in tactical gear and then dispersed them around the property to look around while he and the two first responders went into the house to see if they could find anything of the missing Roxanne.

What they found in the kitchen was negligible. Just an ordinary small farmhouse kitchen with an eat-in dinette. The living room was sparsely furnished and one of the bedrooms, the Sergeant surmised was being used as the master bedroom. It was the washroom, and the second bedroom converted into an office that brought the Sergeant to a halt. The files in the office had all been spread out, and empty file folders were scattered everywhere.

"You said that you found some burnt files in the fire pit in the back yard?" the Sergeant asked the two junior officers.

"Yes, sir." The officer then went on to tell the Sergeant they found a fragment of one page held the words "paid by the Pablo brothers" and they all agreed, that the person who lived here was trying to hide evidence by burning their files. The computer monitor and keyboard were there but the tower was missing and the Sergeant suspected they would not find it intact.

"You two start bagging evidence in here and taking pictures. I want this scene all wrapped up tight before the Chief gets here. Roxanne is still a member of this force, and until further notice, we shall proceed with caution in the search for her. Understood?" The two men nodded and began to take pictures of everything before they bagged it, showing where each missing file folder and piece of paper was found.

The Sergeant went into the washroom and found several items that made him think someone had tried to alter the color of his or her hair. The remnants were just left lying on the counter next to the sink. Discarded as if the owner didn't care anymore.

A siren from far off could be heard by the Sergeant and he summoned another officer in from outside. "I need you to take pictures of this mess and then bag the items. Take an inventory of the medicine cabinet first. I need to go out and talk to the Chief." The officer nodded and complied with the Sergeant's instructions.

Outside in the yard, the Sergeant watched as Ethan pulled up in his truck and grimaced. He had heard the rumors that the Chief's proposal to Dorothy Adams was interrupted by a break-in at the Bed and Breakfast Dorothy owned. It had been nothing but non-stop action since that night and the Sergeant knew his boss wasn't going to be a very happy camper.

"Chief, I have everything under control," the Sergeant said as he greeted Ethan.

"Good to hear it Sergeant. Walk me through it anyhow." The Sergeant nodded and explained how he had arrived after being summoned by the first two responders when they failed to contact Roxanne and searched the back yard. The file fragment in the pile of ashes had alerted them to the possible presence of the Pablo brothers and they had immediately taken cover and called for help. A search of the house had produced some evidence but they weren't sure what it had to do with the missing Roxanne.

Ethan nodded while the Sergeant spoke in a terse and professional manner, just saying the necessary facts. Looking at the Sergeant, Ethan realized it was the same Sergeant that had showed up at the Bed and Breakfast the night Ethan had proposed to Dorothy.

"Thank you Sergeant. Now if you don't mind, I will go through the house and see what kind of mess it's in. When Phil Harmon gets here, please ask him to join me." Ethan pointed to the truck just pulling in to the yard. The Sergeant nodded and stepped down off the porch.

"Sergeant?" Ethan called.

"Yes sir?" he turned back to Ethan.

"Well done," Ethan said.

"Thank you sir. Just doing my job." The Sergeant went over to report to Phil Harmon and Ethan placed little blue throw away booties on his feet so he wouldn't track in evidence and contaminate what they already found.

After being joined by Phil the two of them went through the house, taking in the scene in each room and coming to the same conclusion. Someone had been in a hurry to hide evidence by burning it in the fire pit. They knew that a person had altered their appearance by changing their hair color, and packing in a huge hurry.

"Phil, I want you to go back into Roxanne's personal and work history and find out what you can about her. Obviously there was something we missed when interviewing her for her receptionist position." Phil nodded and took notes. Finishing in the house, Ethan went out into the back yard just as a shout went up at the front of the house. Running around the side of the house, Ethan came up to a very excited young officer who had difficulty stammering out the reason why he was so excited.

"Slow down, officer. You need to be absolutely clear in your words," Ethan said.

Taking a deep breath, the young officer pointed to the stand of dense bush in the front of the house that went all the way around to the back.

"We found tracks and a spot where at least two people had lain in wait for someone right in the middle of that thicket. Then they went around to the back and their trail just disappears," he gasped.

"Sergeant, I want another squad out here to find and take casts of the tracks, and I want those tracks matched to the database. Then I want the K-9 unit out here on the double," Ethan directed. "Quickly now. We have no time to lose."

And so the wheels were set in motion to follow the trail of the Pablo brothers with the canine unit. Ethan grimaced when he realized just how little time Roxanne may have had at that moment. It seemed she had some "not-so-nice" playmates. The wind began to blow gently caressing the sweat soaked back of Ethan's uniform. Letting out a deep breath he told himself out loud: "One more step, one more step."

CHAPTER THIRTY THREE

Thomas surveyed the grounds of the Bed and Breakfast and didn't like it. Something was wrong. He watched from the driver's seat of his truck as he waited for whatever it was that had alerted his sub-conscious thoughts to formulate in his mind. Taking a deep breath, he leaned forward. That was it. The window of the dining area had been opened, the screen pushed aside, and the curtains parted. He knew everyone inside the building had been told to leave all the doors and windows shut and locked. The curtains were to shut out the sight of anyone inside from the street and he knew something was **very** wrong.

Thomas pulled the phone out of his pocket and called Trevor's number. Trevor answered on the first ring.

"Trevor here," came the voice.

"Boss, are you in the Bed and Breakfast?" Thomas asked in a clipped voice.

Sensing the urgency of the question and knowing the situation, Trevor focused his attention on the call.

"What's wrong?" came his voice.

"A window is open and I can't see anyone around the building at all." Thomas was now running in an open crouch with his handgun pointed in front of him towards the front door.

"I'm on my way!" Trevor said and didn't even bother to end the call. He threw his phone onto the dash of the truck as he and Quentin buckled themselves in.

"What's up?" Quentin asked.

"Trevor just got back to the Bed and Breakfast and there was a dining room window open. He couldn't see anyone." Trevor slammed the vehicle into gear and they went flying into traffic with a terrifying speed.

"Darn!" Quentin smashed the dash of the truck with his open hand. "I thought they would be safe while we went out to do this one errand! Ethan was arriving as we left, what happened there?"

"How should I know?" Trevor roared as he blew a traffic light and almost creamed into a large white delivery van. Quentin almost screamed in fright as he grabbed for the security handle in the ceiling.

"Try and hold it steady while I do this." Quentin pulled a very large 9 millimeter handgun out of his suit jacket and placed a silencer on the end of the barrel.

Surprised, Trevor almost hit another vehicle.

"Quentin, you know those things are illegal, don't you? And since when did you learn how to shoot one of those?" Quentin smiled.

"There are many things about me you will never find out," Quentin said tersely as they rounded the corner and saw the Bed and Breakfast right in front of them. Ethan's truck was gone and Thomas's was there with the driver's door open and motor running.

Trevor stopped the truck with wheels screaming as he flew out the door, his weapon in his hand.

"Go around the back and make sure everything is okay," Trevor motioned to Quentin. Without saying a word, Quentin Tallas, multi-millionaire and real estate developer in a three piece suit, went around the corner of the building and blended in with the shadows. Trevor shook his head, unable to believe what he had just seen. He crouched beside the open front door and went in low, clearing each corner and doorway as he went. He was just going into the kitchen when Thomas came out in the same crouch. Trevor pointed to his eyes and looked at Thomas, silently asking if he had seen anything. Thomas shrugged, smiled, and shook his head no. Then Trevor pointed to himself and then to the stairs, while he motioned for Thomas do go towards the back of the building, wondering why Thomas was smiling so much for a critical situation like this.

Trevor was half-way up the stairs when he heard a small scream from the back yard. Backing down the stairs, he knew the scream was from a child. He knew Thomas would reach the door before he could so he turned and went back up the stairs, silently hoping Thomas was in time to help. The heat in the upper hallway was oppressive as Trevor noticed all but the room at the end of the hall had open doors. Advancing at the ready, Trevor reached silently for the door knob. A muffled sound from behind the closed door made him hesitate. It had come from somewhere in the center of the room and to the right.

Trevor smashed through the door going in low. The sound he had heard was the muffled cries of a man tied up and on the floor. There was a gag over his mouth and he was struggling to get free. Trevor knew he was someone who was not supposed to be there because of the black ski mask on the floor beside the trussed up man. There was no-one else in the room.

Trevor quickly surveyed the room to make sure it was clear, then turned and went back down the stairs, after giving the man on the floor a good sound kick in the butt. Down the stairs he went to the hallway which led to the back deck and the backyard. Crouching at the ready with his firearm, he leapt out onto the deck to surprise anyone there, and his eyes met with such an incredible sight.

Dorothy had a man hog-tied on the ground and was soundly kicking him in the butt, while the two boys scrambled out of the pool. Quentin was watching in fascination as Dorothy demonstrated to the two boys how to subdue someone who threatened them harm. The ski mask that the man had worn had been ripped off, apparently when Dorothy had flipped him over her head as he tried to harm the three of them while they were setting up their wading pool.

Just then, Maria came out of the back door, waving her newly dented frying pan and actually swearing in Spanish.

"Maria!" Dorothy glanced at the boys then back to Maria. "Watch your mouth. The boys don't need to hear that kind of language."

"Sorry, Dorothy, I forgot myself." Maria made the sign of the cross on her chest.

"Maria, you're not catholic so stop it." Dorothy smiled at her. All three men stood motionless in amazement as Temperance Rose came gliding through the door to stand beside Maria.

"Where did they come from?" Dorothy hissed through her teeth. Quentin shook his head.

"I don't know," Quentin answered. Dorothy turned to her mother, who, surprisingly, was very calm and collected.

"Are you okay, Mom?" Dorothy choked on the question. Dorothy turned to her with fear on her face. The boys did not need to see Dorothy break down at this most critical point in their lives. They needed her to be strong. Temperance smiled at all of them and surveyed the scene in front of her.

"I have decided that I do not want my family put in danger any longer. While I know that my daughter is an able protector, and my friend Maria is very handy with the frying pan, I will not let my two grandsons be placed in jeopardy any longer." With that announcement, Temperance turned and went back into the building and into the office.

"Mom? Mom!" Dorothy could not understand the statement her mother had made and became alarmed when, after she followed Temperance into the house, she could not open the door that Temperance had locked behind her.

"Dorothy! Your mother is fine!" Maria called out to her. Quentin, Trevor, and Thomas were still standing rooted to the spot, watching this drama play out.

"Unlike you, she will not 'freak out'." Maria shrugged and held the boys a little closer. "Now come here and let your boys know you are just as strong."

Dorothy didn't believe her ears. Maria had just told her to stop freaking out in front of the boys. Maria never spoke to her like that.

"Freaking out? I am not freaking out, Maria. I am getting mad." Dorothy went over and stood beside Maria as she held the boys. "I am madder than hell and I am not going to stand for anyone hurting my family, no matter what." She reached for Sam and he came to her willingly.

"No matter what!" the little boy's voice parroted Dorothy's words loud enough for Maria to hear them as well. She stared at him with awe.

"Dorothy, did you hear that? He spoke!" Maria squealed. Dorothy held Sam out at arm's length. With joy she repeated her own words, as if unable to believe the little boy had spoken at all.

"No matter what!" Dorothy called out.

"No matter what!" Sam repeated with laughter. Everyone on the deck was amazed at Sam's resiliency. What they had all been through and the seriousness of the situation paled at the sound of those three words uttered with such happiness.

"Sam, you did it!" Juan cried out. He threw his arms up in victory. Sam did the same.

"I hate to interrupt this English lesson, but we need to get you and the boys out of here. They know you're here." Quentin said in an icy calm voice.

Thomas came down the stairs at that point and agreed with Quentin. Trevor went outside, to wait for back up to arrive in the form of police cars.

"Do you have anywhere we can take the boys and keep a closer watch on them?" Quentin's question angered Dorothy. His barbed comment went deep, and Dorothy didn't feel as if she deserved it.

"Quentin," Dorothy began.

"We could go to the Manor," Maria announced. She had recognized the spark of anger that flashed Quentin's way.

"Maria, we can't go to the Manor. They would still get to us there." Dorothy shook her head.

"Well, we can't stay here," Maria said with concern.

"The Manor may be our best bet," Quentin announced like it was his decision and only his decision that mattered.

"Quentin, I am going to tell you this only once. You do not tell me what to do." Dorothy's anger flared at him again. Just then the door to the office opened and Temperance flowed smoothly into the middle of the lobby, beckoning to all of them.

"Mom, are you . . ?" Dorothy began.

"I'm fine, Dorothy. I just had a talk with a friend of mine and told him of the situation here. He is going to send some of his security detail to help us out until this mess can be straightened out. He is also going to call Ethan and offer his assistance so that Ethan can do what he does best. Investigate instead of go around putting out little fires," Temperance said all this in a matter of fact voice. Now she reached out for her grandsons and took them by their hands.

"Come children. We are going to go to a big house where I live and we call it the Manor. Would you like to go there and see if you would like to live there?" both the boys nodded up happily to their new grandmother as the tears dried on their faces. Dorothy and Maria glanced at each other and then back at the sight of Temperance leading the boys up the stairs to pack some belongings to take with them.

"That is quite the mother you have, Dorothy," Quentin said in his cultured voice. "She's all fire and ice, but she knows how to get things going." Dorothy looked at Quentin in surprise.

"I'm sorry I spoke so hastily, Dorothy." Quentin tried to straighten his tie and his jacket.

"Quentin?" He looked at Dorothy. "I didn't know you carried a weapon."

"It seemed like a good thing to do, considering the situation," Quentin answered.

"Do you think we could stay friends and not get mad at each other?" Dorothy offered a truce.

"Of course. Sometimes I forget myself without meaning to," Quentin nodded in acceptance.

"Okay, let's go upstairs and get some things for the boys. We are going to have to hurry." Maria clapped her hands and flew up the stairs to help Temperance and the boys. Dorothy went to follow Maria when Quentin stopped her with a hand on her arm. When Maria was out of ear shot, he pulled a second weapon out of his dual holster and placed it in Dorothy's hands.

"I assume you are ready to use that if need be?" Quentin asked. Dorothy nodded and put it in the back of her waist band.

"Let's go. Mother will be getting impatient." Dorothy walked up the stairs.

Quentin and Thomas let her go. They had decided to make sure the man on the ground by the wading pool was trussed up tight. They also knew someone had to call Ethan and let him know what was happening. The wounded needed tending to and they had to gather the three assailants together. Trevor heard the two men discussing what to do when he suddenly heard there were three men.

"Where is the third man?" Trevor asked in surprise. Thomas started to grin again and crooked his finger at both Quentin and Trevor.

"Follow me." Thomas led the other two men into the kitchen where they found a third assailant lying prostrate on the floor with his hands and feet tied. His ski mask had been removed and all three men could see the giant sized lump forming on the front of the man's forehead. His nose was bloody and they realized it was broken.

"I came in to search and clear the room just after Maria had hit this guy over the head with that frying pan she was carrying. She must have hit him in the nose with an upward thrust, like one of us would do to incapacitate him. That woman is phenomenal." Thomas smiled at the other two men.

"Those three women are all phenomenal." Trevor shook his head then smiled at Quentin. "And what about this phone call Temperance made?" Thomas shrugged at Trevor. "Who does she know that has that much pull and influence?" Quentin smiled and walked out to the front porch without saying a word. Thomas looked at Trevor and smiled.

"We didn't ask. But nothing would surprise me about this family." Thomas walked out the front door behind Quentin.

CHAPTER THIRTY FOUR

Ethan was in his SUV travelling back from the scene at the farm house when he received a call. The number ID was blocked but he pulled over and answered anyhow. He thought it might have been Dorothy. He had stopped and was going to have dinner with Dorothy and the boys when the call had come from the farm house. Now his thoughts went back to Dorothy and their boys.

"Barns here." The voice on the other end of the line was cultured, and very familiar to Ethan as he sat in shock.

"Ethan Barns?"

"Yes sir," his reply was all automatic.

"I need you to do me a favor. Temperance just called me on my private line and I heard you are having a bit of trouble out there. Would you like some extra hands?"

"Ahh, yes sir. I could use all the spare hands you could send me," Ethan answered. I just can't afford to pay them, sir." Ethan's voice sounded breathless.

"This would be on my dime, Chief. Do you have an idea who is responsible for the situation you find yourself in?"

"Yes I do. I have a couple of missing people, but the facts keep pouring in. The cases are all but solving themselves," Ethan almost stammered into the phone.

"Good. I am sending you some help immediately but you are in charge and they will answer only to you, do you understand?"

"Yes I do, sir."

"I want no mention of my name in any of this."

"I understand, sir."

"Good. Then I will leave it in your hands. The men will arrive shortly." The phone went dead in Ethan's hands and he finally remembered to breathe. The phone rang again almost immediately.

"Barns here," Ethan's voice was strong and confident. It was Trevor telling Ethan what had occurred at the Bed and Breakfast and that they were going to move the family to the Manor. Trevor assured Ethan about Temperance's phone call as well. When he ended the call, Ethan sat for a long moment and shook his head.

"I had no idea Temperance knew him!" Ethan began to slowly smile.

Starting his SUV, Ethan put it into gear and proceeded down the road. His job had just gotten a little easier. He had meant what he said when he said the facts just kept rolling in. Putting it all together was not going to be all that hard to do. He just needed the manpower to do the searches, seizures, and security. His force was taxed to the limits with all this running around. It was time to fight fire with fire. And Temperance Adams had surprised him with her phone call to Ethan's new benefactor.

Ethan pulled into the parking lot of the precinct and as darkness fell on the City of Redwood, Ethan was weary and tired. Opening the door of his vehicle, he barely managed to crawl out and up to the door of the precinct. A vehicle pulled in blocking Ethan's truck and he whirled and drew his weapon at the same time. It was a news van and Ethan's fear was replaced with anger. The driver of the van saw Ethan standing there with his weapon drawn and his mouth fell open. Holstering his weapon, Ethan went over to the window of the news van.

"I want you to move this van out of here and don't come back." The look on Ethan's face and his demeanor, told the driver that no one was going to get a statement from Chief Barns this evening.

CHAPTER THIRTY FIVE

Roxanne had known from the minute the kidnapping attempt went bust that she was living on borrowed time. It wouldn't take long before her boss, Chief Barns, would figure out who let the three bogus officials into the cells. They were smart enough to try to look the part, but stupid enough to put ski masks on when they tried to leave the building. She was working with amateurs. Very dangerous amateurs.

She finished packing what few belongings she wanted to take with her and looked in the mirror. Her hair color went from blond to auburn in just 45 minutes. It completely changed her looks. The right clothing, the right eye makeup, and she looked ten years younger than she really was. Roxanne new she had to leave and go to a place where she would be safe for the rest of her life, but somehow she knew she would never find that now. Still, she had been a con-artist most of her life, and her father had taught her well. She didn't really like what she had become, but there was no one else she could turn to. The Pablo brothers had paid her well to keep an eye on the investigation, and when the two boys had been brought into the cell section of the precinct, she knew immediately who they were.

Roxanne turned away from her reflection in the mirror as if she couldn't stand the site of herself and picked up her bag and headed for the door. It was a long way to the airport and she had to travel it on the moped she kept hidden in the shed behind the house. Checking the pile of ashes smouldering in the fire pit, she put on her helmet and stored the bag in the little trunk seat. If anyone saw her in this outfit and on this moped, she would be considered an older teenager going to town for a little fun and relaxation. No one would recognize her at all once she put the goggles on.

Starting the engine, Roxanne slowly let herself glide out of the gate and onto the main highway. Her false driver's license and passport, her wallet and a toothbrush were all she was taking with her. Life might not be easy for a while, but at least she would be alive.

It took her just over forty five minutes for her to make it to the airport, going her top speed. The day was beautiful and Roxanne enjoyed the ride on the moped. Parking it in its own little timed spot, she walked into the terminal and up to the receptionist's desk.

"Hello, thank you for choosing Trans Canada Airlines. How may I help you?" the young lady smiled at what she thought was a younger traveller.

"I'm on the 9:10 flight and I hope I'm early enough." Roxanne smiled like a lost teenager.

"You sure are, just give me your name, and I'll find you your tickets." Roxanne gave the girl her alias, Carol Martin, and showed her the ID she had saved from her last little project. "Your flight is number 1261 at gate five. It is just starting to board." The flight registry clerk smiled and looked around. "Do you have any baggage?" she asked.

"I'm carrying it right here." Roxanne, alias Carol, held up her back pack.

"They'll want to check it before you go on board, but if they know you're on the next flight, they'll put you at the head of the line."

"Even carry-on luggage?" Carol asked as if it was the first flight she had ever been on.

"Yes. They're very strict about what you can carry onto the plane," The clerk said.

"Oh, okay." Carol looked over to where the luggage was to be inspected. There was only one person in the lineup. With any luck, she would make her flight.

"Thanks, bye!" With a youthful wave of her hand, Carol scampered over to stand in line. When it was Carol's turn to have her luggage inspected, she didn't stop smiling. They looked through nothing but underwear, socks, her iPad, and a couple of bras.

"Not much in here for a trip abroad," The security guard mumbled, more to himself than to Carol.

"I'm meeting family at the other end of my trip, and they have the rest of my things." Carol twirled the end of her hair in her fingers and snapped the gum in her mouth to emphasize her flightiness. "Can I go?" The security guard nodded and Carol grabbed the bag and almost sprinted to the boarding gate.

She handed her ticket to the clerk and waited for him to inspect it. He handed it back to her and Carol found her seat number at the rear of the plane and sat down. There were a few more passengers to board and Carol spent that time pretending to read a magazine. She looked up as a tiny little woman with a large carry-on bag went past and jostled her as she went by. Carol's eyes opened in surprise as the woman sat down across from her after stowing her carry-on luggage in the overhead compartment. Snapping her gum, Carol pretended to look away and caught the woman's reflection in the window. She looked absolutely ticked at someone. And Carol was right. It was that woman who had her husband charged with domestic violence. Carol had been the one to help her fill out the forms. If she didn't recognize Carol, Carol knew she would be okay. She just had to stay away from the woman.

The stewardess at the front of the cabin started into her security routine and Carol sank into her seat. There was no way she was going to get tripped up by that witchy little woman who was as mean as a wasp.

Carol suddenly had an idea that could make up for all the hurt she had caused lately. She surveyed the woman as she settled herself into her seat and watched carefully so she herself wouldn't be noticed. Deciding that the lady had no idea who she was, Carol excused herself and went to the washroom, taking her purse with her.

"I'm sorry, ma'am. You will have to return to your seat until take off. It's the rules." The flight attendant motioned for Carol to return to her seat. Carol nodded and did so. There was time for her to go to the washroom after the flight had left the airport. She could leave her secret message on the mirror then. Hopefully the message wouldn't be discovered until everyone had disembarked, giving Carol a chance to get away free and clear.

Carol intended to leave a message for one of the flight attendants and tell them about the woman named Anna. That way Anna would be detained and she would possibly get away. Carol herself could start a new life. She wouldn't have much, but Carol figured she owed it to the Redwood Police Chief. She had lived on less before and Carol knew she would have no problem starting over. Anna, however, stood to lose so much more.

CHAPTER THIRTY SIX

The Pablo brothers had searched for the woman named Roxanne for most of the day. She wasn't at any of her usual haunts and they finally decided to go back to the cave. It wasn't really a cave, but a second basement or bunker built into the dirt of the hill not too far from the barn they had just left. Tired and dirty, and very thirsty, they entered the bunker and both of them were angry. Sure, they had avoided the cops, but they still didn't have their situation taken care of.

Ramirez looked at Balthazar and shook his head in resignation as Balthazar angrily kicked the chair legs out from under one of their very loyal soldiers. Then Balthazar started beating the man about the head and shoulders with the heel of his gun.

"Balthazar, stop!" Ramirez hollered. "Let the man alone! He isn't the reason why we are in this mess." Balthazar stopped his beating and glared at his brother.

"And who do you blame for this mess we are in?" Balthazar screamed. Ramirez calmly leaned against the wall of the bunker and crossed his arms.

"We are. We're not thinking, brother."

"Don't you mean I'm not thinking clearly?" Balthazar advanced towards Ramirez with murder in his eyes. The other man he had been beating slowly slipped to the floor unconscious.

"No, Balthazar, I mean *us*." Ramirez went to the bare table and sat on the side opposite of Balthazar and waited for his brother to join him. Balthazar, whose mood had slipped into just slightly crazed, sat with him.

"So what do we do?" he asked his older brother. "We can't stay here forever."

Ramirez stared at the table top and tried to think. After a few moments, he looked up and started to smile.

"We cut our losses." Balthazar started and jumped up from the table.

"Are you crazy? Do you know what those two kids can do to us if they testify?" Balthazar asked.

"Yes, I do. But only if we're here when it happens." The smile spread across his entire face. "We create a diversion. An explosion at the farm house. No one will know if it is us or not, and by the time they figure it out, we will be back home and starting over in our new identities." Balthazar started to smile as well. "Well, do you like the plan?" Balthazar sat back down and looked at his brother. The crazy light had dimmed from his eyes and Ramirez knew that now he was thinking.

"All right. We'll do it." The three soldiers they had left were quietly listening in the back ground but had gotten a little closer so they could hear the plan. "But where do we get the explosives?" Balthazar asked.

"We will use the fuel in the tank at the farm. It will burn so fast they will not know we set the fire before we are gone." Balthazar nodded his agreement.

Both brothers got up from the table and smiled at each other. Looking at their three remaining men standing so staunchly loyal beside them, they knew it was time to leave. The dim light provided by the one and only bulb made the entire room seem so dark and murky. Ramirez longed to be back in his own bed at home, where they had Egyptian cotton sheets, soft dove-white comforters, and many beautiful women to please him.

"Balthazar, you go first. You have the better eyesight. When you have decided it is safe for us to come out, we will follow you. With you leading us, I know we will not get caught." Ramirez knew the only way to get his brother to do what he, Ramirez wanted him to do, was to praise him for his courage and knowledge. It was a ploy he used often. Balthazar nodded his head and his chest swelled with pride.

"Okay!" Balthazar moved towards the trap door in the ceiling at the one end of the bunker. It was the way they came and went in this pitiful bunker. "You three men, follow me and we will go now!" The men nodded eagerly and took a firm grip on their rifles. Everyone fell into line to go out, including Ramirez. He knew that Balthazar was actually the best man for the lead.

Opening the heavy steel trap door, Balthazar raised himself up the ladder so that he could see in a 360 degree view from the top rung of the ladder. The trees and the bush were so dense back here, he knew it would be safe to just sit there for a moment. There were no sounds of the forest, no birds, no crickets, and no bees. This didn't register on Balthazar's eagerness to lead his men and his beloved brother out of the bunker and go back home to where they belonged. He glanced down to his three men and his brother and gave them the okay signal. Balthazar moved to the trunk of a large leafy tree at the side of the trail that would lead them out of the woods. Still nothing. His three men were now at his side, surveying the area around them. Ramirez was now approaching to stand beside them with a smile on his face. The sunlight on this gloriously hot day fell down upon his eyes for a moment and Balthazar's surprise was replaced by his anger. They were suddenly surrounded on every side by Canadian police officers with guns pointed right at them. Dogs were winning and barking and confusion was rampant for the Pablo brothers and their men until finally the dogs were silent. One man walked up to them, he had a vest on, helmet, and fatigues in blue. His rifle was pointed right at Balthazar's chest.

"Balthazar and Ramirez Pablo, you are under arrest," Detective Phil Harmon's voice broke through Ramirez's stunned thoughts.

"Hey, it was him. It was my brother who ordered this. I will testify against him. You have to keep me away from him!" Ramirez screamed in his terror. He knew what would happen if Balthazar would catch him alone in a cell.

Balthazar immediately lunged at his brother with his hands cuffed behind his back. Shouting from officers and dogs barking sounded like beautiful music to Phil Harmon's ears.

"Take these prisoners to the precinct and their holding cells. We have a lot of work ahead of us," Phil directed his men.

Detective Harmon knew it was not only good police work, but a great idea for Ethan to have ordered the K-9 unit to search for the body of Roxanne. They had followed their invisible trail to the bunker under the hill, and when they realized what they had, Phil knew exactly what to do. Lying in wait for the Pablo brothers to come out was the only solution. It didn't take long to implement their plan and see the results. The Redwood Police had been instrumental in rounding up one of the most notorious drug cartel kingpins and human trafficking rings ever seen in Canada. It would be a feather in Ethan's cap, and quite possibly earn him, Phil Harmon, another promotion.

The officers were carting away the prisoners and silencing their loud protests by placing some restraints over their mouths when Phil pulled his phone out of his pocket and smiled. This phone call was going to be sweet. Even Elva would love to hear this.

CHAPTER THIRTY SEVEN

Ethan arrived at the Bed and Breakfast bursting with news to find the only people who were there, was a unit of his own men. Ambulances and cruisers were strewn around the parking lot along with a wagon from the medical examiner. Jumping out of the truck with its lights still flashing and the sirens still blaring, Ethan bounded up the steps with speed and ran into the medical examiner as he was coming out.

"What in the hell is going on here?" He yelled as he tried to untangle himself from the medical examiner. One of the officers on duty tried to help pull Ethan off the doctor.

"Chief, we arrived here just as your family was leaving. They went over to the Manor, and they took three men with them. Apparently, they will only give their statements to you, and seeing as we need all the help we can get right now, I let them go. I assume you would have done the same thing." The officer finished his explanation by trying to brush the dirt off Ethan's uniform. Slapping the officer's hands away, Ethan helped the medical examiner up from the floor.

"Sorry, doc. Didn't mean to bull-doze into you like that." Ethan explained.

"It's quite all right, Ethan. This old body has been through worse." The doctor brushed dirt off his lab coat and looked up at Ethan sharply. "By the way, I will not charge you for this house call. It isn't often I get to work on live bodies." Ethan gave a huge sigh of relief.

The two men went back inside as the doctor took Ethan through the crime scene. The doctor did it quickly because he was sure Ethan would want to get back to his family as quickly as possible. "The three weapons we have logged into evidence are highly unusual in this case. There is no cause of death because there are no dead people. I did send them to the hospital, three of them, to be checked. One complained of a broken nose, one said he has a broken tailbone, and the other still wasn't awake," The doctor finished his explanation and looked at Ethan.

"Well, that's good. Good." Ethan tried to look like he really cared about the investigation at this crime scene, but all he could think about was getting over to the Manor and making sure his family was okay. Hitching up his belt in a completely futile gesture, he saw the first officer watching with caution. Ethan was acting a little funny.

"Officer, ah, come here please," Ethan motioned the officer over. "Come on, come on, I'm not going to hurt you." Still the officer moved cautiously. "How long have you been with the force?"

"A year, sir," the officer answered nervously.

"That long eh?" Ethan patted the man on the back and smiled a little lop sided at him. The officer nodded. "How do you think you would do as the lead investigator at this scene?"

"Me?" The officer almost swallowed his tongue. "I don't have the experience, sir," He protested.

"Well suck it up officer. We're shorthanded what with all the problems we have had lately. Get your men going and clear this scene as soon as possible. Report to me first thing in the morning."Ethan slapped the man soundly on the back and the officer began to puff up with pride.

"I gotta go!" Ethan turned and ran for his vehicle and almost ran over one of the ambulance attendants on his way out of the driveway.

"Why don't you get yourself a real license!" the angry man said to the disappearing vehicle after he picked himself up off the ground.

Pulling into the gated driveway of the Manor, Ethan stopped long enough to push the intercom buzzer at the gate. Without even asking who it was the gate began to open. Ethan drove right through as soon as there was enough room for his vehicle. He stopped in front of the door with gravel flying and bounded up the steps. The door opened and Dorothy met him on the door step. They wrapped their arms around each other and held on for dear life.

"Come in and close the door so we can reset the alarm," Trevor's voice was quiet. Ethan turned to Trevor and almost decked him.

"You said you would keep them safe!" Ethan yelled at him.

"Ethan!" Dorothy raised her voice so it would penetrate Ethan's anger. "It wasn't his fault." Dorothy tried to hold Ethan back. Just the presence of Dorothy seemed to have a soothing effect on him. Ethan calmed down and wrapped his arms around Dorothy again. He stepped back and looked into Dorothy's eyes with an apology.

"I'm so sorry I wasn't there to protect you and the boys," Ethan's hand rubbed up and down Dorothy's arms in a warm caress.

"Don't worry about their protection, my friend. She is quite capable of taking care of those boys quite well. Her whole family is capable," Trevor's voice had pride in it. Ethan turned to face Trevor.

"Just what do you mean?" Ethan held onto Dorothy's hand.

"Shall we go into the office and discuss this?" Trevor motioned towards the office. "Our two counterparts are there discussing what to do next." Ethan's grin split his entire face at the mention of what to do next.

"Ethan?" Dorothy asked in a puzzled voice when Ethan turned to her.

"Wait until you hear what happened to me today." Still holding Dorothy's hand, he led the way into the office.

CHAPTER THIRTY EIGHT

The next morning, with the boys and Dorothy safe at the Manor, Ethan drove into the office and watched with a smile as several news reporters tried to get into the front entrance to ask for information. There were men in green fatigues, berets, and sunglasses, all clean shaven, and armed with tactical vests and fire power, standing guard at the front door. Knowing that he, himself, would never get in the back door until the men stationed there knew who he was, Ethan had parked in the front parking lot and was watching the difficulty of the news vans parked in a no-parking zone.

"What a beautiful day," Ethan said out loud to himself as he walked up to the front door. He pulled his cell phone out of his pocket and called a tow truck to come and tow the vans out of the lot. That done, he turned back to the two men in fatigues standing fast and not allowing three reporters to get past them.

"Morning boys!" Ethan pulled his ID out and flashed it at the two men who immediately pushed the reporters aside in a very professional manner and allowed Ethan to get past them.

"Chief Barns! Could we have a word with you?" Ethan stopped inside the front security door and cupped his hand to his ear then shrugged. "Chief that is not fair!" Ethan heard as he slipped in through the security door and laughed all the way to the front reception desk. There he stopped short. Elva was sitting there with her uniform on and a smile on her face. The only sign that she had been through a very harrowing experience was the gauzed bandage wound around the wound on her head and barely peeking out from under her hat. Her crutches were hidden under her desk.

"Elva! Thank goodness you're back!" Ethan would have given her a huge hug but Elva held her out her hand to ward him off.

"Chief, I don't want any special favors or hugs. I was just doing my job, you know that," She said.

"Uh, yes, I do," Ethan assured her. "But you were hurt in the line of duty. And to top it off, the doctor didn't tell me you were fit for duty yet." Ethan stood with his hands on his hips.

"I may not be fit for duty out there on the street, but I know I can give you a hand in here. It doesn't take much to answer the phone and direct calls, do paperwork, or make coffee," Elva said as she looked down and shuffled the papers around. "Besides, I can't just sit around at home when there is this much exciting stuff happening!" She smiled at Ethan.

"All right. Seeing as we don't have a receptionist right now, I would be pleased if you would maintain your old station until we can find someone else to do it. That way I can keep an eye on you." Ethan smiled at her and placed his hand comfortably on her shoulder. "I'm proud of you, officer." Ethan gave her a little pat then walked down the hallway to his office.

"You're going to give her something for what happened to her, aren't you?" Tony joined Ethan and walked with Ethan to his office.

"Of course I am, Tony. As soon as she isn't looking, I want you to call the local flower shop and send over the biggest bouquet of flowers they have. Spare no expense." Ethan tapped Tony's chest and Tony nodded. Turning to go into his office, he was startled when two men in fatigue uniforms jumped to attention and saluted. One of the men had several stars on his collar.

"At ease, gentlemen," Ethan returned the salute.

"Chief Barns, I'm Major Stewart. Pleasure to be working with you, sir."

"Major Stewart, my department thanks you," Ethan grinned at this preferential treatment. "Have a seat Major. We have lots to discuss." For the next hour, Ethan and Major Stewart discussed what extra security was needed and where to place the men under Stewart's command.

"Whatever you need sir. My boss told me we are dealing with the Pablo brothers, and seeing as there are still some of his men at large, until we have them in custody, my men are your men," Stewart explained.

"Thank you Major. If you can have some of your men over to the Manor as soon as possible, it would be greatly appreciated." With those words being said, the meeting was over. Major Stewart collected his aide and they left the office in precise military fashion.

Ethan admired the men as they left. Now he wouldn't have to worry about Dorothy anymore. Sitting back in his chair he put his feet up on his desk and gave a big sigh. Suddenly, Tony was skidding to a stop in front of the desk with an excited light in his eyes.

"Chief!" Tony's hands that were holding the sheet of paper in front of him, were shaking. "Chief, have I got something to tell you." Actually, Tony's whole body seemed to be shaking.

"Yes Tony?" Ethan sat up straight.

"I just got a message from the RCMP in Fredericton. It seems they picked up Anna as she was trying to board a flight out of the country. Someone had phoned in a tip about where she was and the RCMP picked her up."

"Why Fredericton?" Ethan looked confused.

"She has relatives there," Tony almost laughed. "But the person who phoned in the tip said her name was Roxanne." Ethan smiled again and sat back.

"Well now, that's wonderful." Ethan smiled. "Has anyone checked on the condition of Ida at the hospital?"

Tony nodded and pulled a second sheet of paper from the bottom of the other one and smiled. "I did some work on Ida's background and found out she was the one who put the Reverend Banks up to taking his people over to the Bed and Breakfast."

"Okay, Tony, why don't you find Phil Harmon, wherever he is, and tell him I would like to have a meeting in the conference room in an hour and then we'll go over all the facts?" Tony nodded and went racing out of the office.

"Well, like I said, the facts are now just pouring into the office and the cases are literally solving themselves," Ethan grinned again. Ethan only blinked and a second later, Elva came wobbling in with a large cup of fresh coffee and a couple of donuts. Ethan froze.

"What did I do this time?" Ethan wondered out loud.

"There is a very angry mayor outside. He was searched and patted down before he was let into the front office. Would you like to speak to him, or should I have our junior G-men out there frisk him again?" Ethan burst out laughing at the dead-pan way Elva explained what was going on.

"What would you do?" Ethan asked.

"I would have him frisked a couple more times. It's about time he realizes how hard it is to work in this town without enough officers," Elva said in a loud voice, hoping it carried to the frustrated man in the front office.

"Bring him in, Elva, let's see if he can put a light on some of this mess." Elva grimaced in disappointment then left the office. She then ushered the mayor in and closed the door behind him.

"Chief Barns, did you know you have some strange men in uniform performing search and seizure tactics on my person when I tried to get in here to see what in the heck is going on around here?" Seeing the steaming hot coffee on the desk and the two donuts, the mayor reached out for a donut and the coffee. "Don't mind if I do," He said. Ethan quickly moved the plate of donuts and coffee out of the mayor's reach without saying anything. The mayor began to sulk and then sat in his own chair.

"Ethan, did you hear what I said?" the mayor whined.

"I did, Mr. Mayor. I did indeed. Those men out front are courtesy of a friend of Temperance Adams. She was tired of having to defend herself and her family from the dregs of the drug underworld when a few more police officers would have helped out nicely." Ethan took a huge bite out of the first donut and chewed, then swallowed before he spoke again. "So those men are just doing their job."

"We can't afford to pay those men, Chief Barns." The mayor said in a deep nasal voice.

"This is not being billed to the City, Mr. Mayor. Not at all." Ethan took a sip of coffee and then another bite of his donut.

"Ethan, we are trying to have a meeting here and you seem more concerned about those donuts and that coffee. Is that all you do around here?" The mayor almost screeched.

"I think you should apologize to the Chief." Phil Harmon walked into the office with an armload of file folders and Tony in tow behind him.

The mayor's chin began to jut out like a little boy who had been chastised.

"I do not think you have the authority to force me to do that. After all, I am the mayor."

"Not for long," Detective Harmon said with a steely gaze.

"What do you mean, Phil?" Ethan quizzed Phil.

"Ethan, I was wondering if you would allow us to have our meeting while we ask the mayor to sit in the conference room for now," Phil's voice was hard and cold when he asked that question. Tony went and stood behind the mayor's chair while the mayor's mouth fell open.

"How dare you even try to do that? I am a powerful man in this city and you have just lost your job." The mayor tried to stand up but Tony pushed down on his shoulders. Ethan stared at the mayor and knew he wasn't going to like what Phil was going to say.

"Tony, please escort the mayor to the conference room and have an officer supervise his stay in that room. I do not want him left alone under any circumstances," The anger in Ethan's voice had finally gotten through to the mayor's brain and he knew he was in trouble.

"If you would please come with me, Mr. Mayor, I'll escort you to the conference room." Tony motioned for the mayor to walk in front of him, and kept a hand on his elbow the whole way.

"Come in and sit down, Phil. Apparently, we have a lot of things to discuss, including that thing of a new mayor we have," Ethan's voice had a tinge of contempt to it as he invited Phil to sit.

"Ethan, we have uncovered an entirely unprecedented problem with the new mayor." Phil set the stack of files on the desk in front of him and waited for Tony to come in and close the door before he continued.

"What did he do?" Ethan asked.

"Remember when we thought there was something wrong with the municipal election? And we had the votes recounted?" Ethan nodded.

"We had that large firm do the recount, the new one that opened up just last year," Phil continued. "The owner of the firm happens to be a cousin of our new mayor. Something which totally slipped past the city manager. But then, the city manager has been doing a little finagling of his own as well." Phil went on to tell Ethan of a city clerk named Ryan who had come in to give a statement about being blackmailed into losing all the permits for Dorothy's Bed and Breakfast. Ryan had no reason for the blackmail, until he heard of Ben Johnston's death. The Province had decided to put a new highway through to Redwood, which would bypass the city and would appropriate the land along a section of the city for the highway. Word had gone out to the mayor before it was announced to the rest of the province. The mayor, Burton Price the city manager, and his cousin, the lawyer, were all members of the Puritans. Phil had followed the trail from man to man and almost cringed when he saw how much the forensic auditor had said was appropriated to the personal bank accounts of those three men. A good sum was offered to Ben Johnston for his land and when Ben refused, they contacted Ida. Ida agreed to sell the land to the men once Ben was out of the way. Ida wanted to get a new life but Ben was adamant in refusing the asking price. He did not want to leave his beloved farm.

Ida then came up with a plan and brought Anna in on it, whereby they would leave the city for parts unknown when the money was finally transferred. Unfortunately, Anna's dreams were stronger than Ida realized when Anna stabbed her with the knife. Ethan knew the rest and finished the conversation and told the two men what to do with the mayor.

"What do you want done with the Pablo brothers?" Phil and Tony asked at the same time.

"I want this station in lock down until the RCMP from Toronto arrive here to transport the Pablo brothers and their three men back to Toronto," Ethan explained. The two men smiled and nodded, liking the decision.

"The sooner those idiots are gone, the better," Tony said with relish.

"What do we do with the mayor, his cousin, and Burton Price?" Phil asked.

"We charge them, of course. They can sit in a cell beside the Pablo brothers until they are brought up in front of the judge." The other two men nodded again.

"And finally, what about Roxanne?" Phil asked. "She did help us capture Anna, but then, from what the Pablo brothers are saying, she helped them get their men into the station in the first place."

"Do they have any hard evidence to back that up?" Ethan asked Phil with a look that made Phil smile.

"I don't believe so."

"Then we will let Roxanne be until we know anything different. We will still look for her as a person of interest, but no warrants. Not yet." Phil and Tony were both laughing as they left the office and went to their desks. They started filling out arrest warrants for Burton Price, the mayor, and the mayor's cousin. Ethan picked up the phone and called his friend, the former mayor, and asked his wife if he was home.

"Ethan? It's me. What's up?" The mayor said into the phone. "You caught me while I was digging in the flower bed." Ethan could hear the smile coming from the former mayor.

"Say Mr. Mayor, I'm going to need your help with something." Ethan said into the phone.

"Now Ethan, you know I'm not the mayor anymore. Would you please not call me Mr. Mayor? And what is it that you need from me today?" When Ethan had finished his explanation of what had just gone on in his office, the former mayor of Redwood lost all feeling in his knees and he sank into the plush chair that was sitting beside the end table where the phone was. He seemed out of breath and speechless. This caused his wife some concern. She rushed over to his side and took the phone that was slipping out of his grip.

"My love," the mayor gasped. "I'm afraid I'm not going to be able to do any more weeding for a while." Ethan hung up his end of the phone and was grinning. He loved a good ending to the story.

CHAPTER THIRTY NINE

Dorothy smiled into the mirror as her mother placed the veil on her head and pushed the hairpins to hold it into place.

"There you go. All done," Temperance announced as she stepped back to survey what she had done. Her breath caught as she saw how beautiful her daughter was on this day.

"Mom, don't cry. Please don't cry." Dorothy stood and turned to hug her mother. "If you cry, I will and then a whole hour of makeup and the expense is going to go down the drain," Dorothy pleaded with her mother. "Maria, make her stop crying!" Dorothy appealed to Maria, who was hovering in the doorway. Maria nodded and went to hug Temperance.

"It's okay, my friend. You are not losing a daughter, you are gaining a son-in-law, two grandchildren, and some new friends." Maria began to pat Temperance on her shoulder.

In the three and a half months since the Puritans had announced they were disbanding their association, Dorothy's Bed and Breakfast had opened, Reverend Banks had stayed on as the Pastor of the church, and Dorothy and Ethan had applied to adopt the two boys, Juan and Samuel. The Federal District Attorney had okayed it seeing as they didn't need the boys or their testimony any longer. That was when Maria had stepped up and announced she was retiring as the family cook, and was going to plan Dorothy's wedding for her and Ethan. Temperance convinced her to let Dorothy help just a little bit, seeing as it was her wedding, anyhow. Maria relented, and was continually over at the Bed and Breakfast day and night until the big day.

Ethan didn't mind not being let in on the plans. He had so much paperwork to do, and charges were laid against Ida, Anna, and the three gentlemen who had tried to bilk the city out of much needed funding to run the city. The former mayor had stepped up with a promise that if the City wanted another election, they could have one when they had everything straightened out. The city was polled and not one person argued the point when they found out, from the honest reporters, that Ethan and the mayor would work hand in hand. To the city of Redwood, Ethan was their hero.

Elva decided to stay on as receptionist and only take on the odd assignment, as she realized that is what she loved best about the job. She was the real power in charge when she was behind the desk and she let Ethan know it in subtle ways. Like when that big beautiful bouquet was delivered to her desk, Elva sent it back because of the cost. She was pink with embarrassment and secretly she loved the attention, but with all the missing money from the city coffers still not found, she said she really didn't have a choice. Ethan just grinned and secretly gave a sigh of relief when she told him to quit interviewing candidates to take over her job. She just wasn't ready to give it up.

Phil Harmon and Tony were still searching for the elusive Roxanne. Just when they thought they were closing in, she would disappear into the woodwork. They knew she was still in Canada somewhere, but they weren't too concerned. They were so busy considering where the missing millions were from the city hall fiasco, that when a telegram came in one morning, they were totally unprepared for the information it contained.

Phil read the telegram out loud to Tony and both men sat down open-mouthed across from each other in the conference room. Running to Ethan's office, they both tried to get in at once.

"Boys! Boys!" Ethan remonstrated. "This is my wedding day. What is so important?" Phil just handed Ethan the telegram and let him read it himself.

Found what you were looking for. Stop. Here are the numbers for the bank accounts. Stop. Have a great wedding day. Stop.

The telegram did not say who was sending it but Ethan knew. Roxanne had done it again.

"Phil, put this in the evidence room and you can begin working on it first thing in the morning. We have a wedding to get to. You know what Temperance is capable of, so let's not keep her daughter waiting," Ethan said by way of an answer to Phil's silent question. "When we're gone on our honeymoon, I want the both of you to take care of my kids and make sure they're okay."

"On it Chief." Phil Harmon smiled as he went to the evidence room to enter the telegram into evidence.

Half an hour later, as he waited for Dorothy to walk up the aisle on the arm of her brother Matt, Ethan almost came to tears. Knowing it wouldn't be good to let his second in command see him crying, he turned to look at Reverend Banks. Reverend Banks smiled and handed him a handkerchief.

Phil Harmon smiled and punched Ethan in the shoulder as Dorothy took her first step up the aisle. Ethan turned to look up the aisle and lost his breath. Dorothy was so beautiful in her dress he couldn't take his eyes off her.

"*I love that woman so much,*" he said to himself. "*Between her and those two boys of ours, I have the perfect life.*" Ethan smiled at Dorothy as she slowly glided up the aisle and Matt put her hand in Ethan's.

"*I have never loved anyone as I love this man,*" Dorothy smiled back at Ethan with tears starting to flow. "*I wonder when the perfect time would be to tell Ethan I would love to adopt a little girl.*"

Maria was getting all misty-eyed as Dorothy went up the aisle. "*I couldn't have picked a better man for her.*" She thought to herself. "*Quentin Tallas better not show up at the reception or I'll use my new frying pan on him.*"

Trevor watched the touching scene at the front of the church and then slipped out the door to leave on another assignment. Quentin Tallas was right behind him. Getting into the SUV, they left the little church in Redwood behind as they headed out to the airport.

"Cheer up, my friend. We'll be back some day," Quentin told Trevor with a smile.

"And how do you know that?" Trevor smiled back.

"Did you see that young thing near the back on the other side of the church?" Quentin smiled.

"Yeah?" Trevor wondered if he had caught the same vibe Quentin did from her. She was beautiful.

"The one with the red hair, right?" Trevor asked as he checked his side view mirror.

"That's the one." Quentin smiled as if he knew something Trevor didn't.

"Okay, what about her?" Trevor asked.

"I think she likes you," Quentin said.

"And how do you know that?" Trevor asked.

"I got you her number." Quentin laughed and handed the number over.

When they had finished laughing they reviewed the whole situation in Redwood and how it had started.

"You know, the papers started the problem by not reporting accurately," Trevor said. Quentin shook his head no.

"Wrong. It was the rumors spread by those petty little tyrants who were trying to take off with all that money," Quentin answered with a tight-lipped smile. "The case could still have gone the wrong way, if the rumors weren't stopped." Quentin answered.

"When you talk about your neighbors and your fellow workers, you have to be careful what you say. Anything negative can take on a life of its own. Rumors run rampant, can destroy people in the blink of an eye. Take Dorothy's past for instance, if the newspaper had not come out with the truth, that they had been blackmailed by the men from the city into printing those lies, Dorothy would have been destroyed. No one would come to her Bed and Breakfast," Quentin cleared his throat and continued. "Just one wrong word, heard by one wrong person, can create a crisis that sneaks up on you like a silent enemy, with a life of its own, destroying everything and everyone in its path." Trevor drove on in silence for a few minutes, digesting what Quentin had said.

"A silent enemy, huh?" Trevor asked. Quentin nodded. "Okay, you're right. Now let's talk about that pretty little thing whose number you gave me." Trevor smiled as he turned into the airport.

"You should give her a call. She likes men who are mysterious." Quentin smiled back.

THE END

Edwards Brothers Malloy
Thorofare, NJ USA
October 22, 2014